FREAKY PLACES
A MYSTIC CARAVAN MYSTERY BOOK FIVE

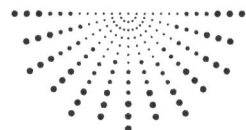

AMANDA M. LEE

WINCHESTERSHAW PUBLICATIONS

Copyright © 2018 by Amanda M. Lee

All rights reserved.

No part of this book may be reproduced in any form or by any electronic or mechanical means, including information storage and retrieval systems, without written permission from the author, except for the use of brief quotations in a book review.

※ Created with Vellum

PROLOGUE

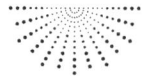

TWENTY YEARS AGO

"Hello, Poet. How is life, my favorite niece?"

My Uncle Sidney sat on the front step next to me, ignoring the chilly bite of the air as he offered up a huge smile.

I'd never liked him. It wasn't that I was uncomfortable with him as much as I found him boring and fake. He always tried to go out of his way to talk to me, to listen to what I had to say, but there was never any real interest sparking behind his eyes. It was all for show … and we both knew it.

Instead, it was more that he wanted to be able to say "I'm Poet's favorite uncle" rather than "Poet is my favorite niece." It was a weird differential, but one I picked up on all the same.

"I'm fine, Uncle Sidney." I watched him with careful eyes. He had a package in his hand, long and rectangular, and I was fairly certain it was a gift for me. As part of his desperate desire to be my favorite uncle, he often brought me gifts when he visited. He thought bribing me was the way to go. I liked many of those gifts, so I didn't dissuade the practice.

"You're turning into a pretty girl." He patted my dark head. "You look like your mother."

He was my father's brother, so I didn't know what to make of that. "Thank you." It seemed the thing to say.

"So, I brought you something." He flashed a keen smile as he handed the package to me. I returned the smile, but there was something in his eyes when our gazes snagged that caused me to pause. I wasn't sure what it was, but for a second I thought he was afraid of me. But that couldn't be right. What did he have to fear from me? Sure, I'd started to manifest some rather interesting abilities of late – including being able to read minds every once in a while – and I knew my mother was worried that people would find out, but I would never purposely hurt a family member. Uncle Sidney had to know that.

"What is it?" I tried to keep my voice light and airy as I accepted the package.

"You have to look to find out."

That was all the prodding I needed. I ripped into the wrapping paper and removed the box, widening my eyes when I saw what looked to be a huge coffin-shaped container. "I don't … what is it?" I shifted nervously on my seat. I wasn't exactly worldly and knowledgeable – at least not yet, even though I pictured myself ending up that way – but I knew that giving someone a box shaped like a coffin was odd by almost everyone's standards.

"You'll have to open it to find out," Sidney prodded. "That's how gifts work."

"Right."

I carefully balanced the box on my knees and lifted the top, widening my eyes to what must have been comedic proportions when I saw the miniature me in the box. It seemed my uncle had gone all out with this gift, visiting a ceramic doll maker and having a doll designed to look exactly like me.

From the long black hair, to the big blue eyes, to the mischievous smirk, to the long skirt and simple shoes, the doll was me. It was freaky.

"Wow." I didn't know what else to say. I wasn't much of a doll fan. I thought my uncle should know that. There were no dolls in the house because they'd never been my thing. Stuffed animals were a different story, but dolls ... I didn't like dolls. Just because he had this one designed to look like me didn't mean I was going to change my stance.

"Isn't she lovely?" Uncle Sidney beamed as he reached into the box and carefully pulled back the tissue paper to unveil the doll in all her glory. "I think she's going to make a good friend for you. You're an only child, but she can be a sister of sorts."

That sounded like a terrible idea. Still, she looked expensive. I didn't want to hurt my uncle's feelings, so I forced a smile for his benefit. "She's ... awesome."

"She is, isn't she?" Uncle Sidney smiled so wide the rest of his face was obliterated by the blinding grin. "When I found the doll maker, I knew you had to have her."

Too bad he couldn't have found a stuffed animal maker ... or action figure maker ... or even a board game maker. I was a big fan of board games. I especially liked Risk.

"I love her," I lied, hoping my smile came off as genuine instead of deranged. "I really, really love her."

"Good." Uncle Sidney kissed the top of my head and left me on the front porch with the doll. I could hear him boasting how much I loved the little beast as he walked inside before requesting a glass of wine. He seemed ridiculously proud of himself.

I stared at the doll for what felt like forever. The longer I stared, the more I got the feeling that she was staring back. I didn't like it one bit.

"Is anyone home?"

I had no idea what made me ask the question. It seemed like a stupid query. I asked it all the same.

"Can you hear me?"

The doll didn't answer, but she seemed to watch me with the same wary curiosity I reserved for her.

"I don't like you," I said, opting to be honest. "I don't like how you look like me. I don't like that you look like you have tiny little glass fingernails that can scratch out my eyes. Yeah, I heard that story from the girls at school. I know about the china doll that attacks and scratches your eyes out when you're not looking. I won't let that happen to me."

The doll didn't answer. Instead it stared. I heard eerie laughter in my head. I convinced myself it was an echo from the doll's head, and managed – with shaky fingers – to return the fragile plaything to the box before standing on wobbly knees.

I stared at the doll and she stared back.

She didn't move, so I didn't move.

We shared the same space, yet it wasn't exactly what I would call a comfortable visit.

Finally, I heaved a sigh and stood, descending the porch steps so I could grab the basketball from the garage and shoot some hoops rather than stare at the creepy doll. I was halfway down the walkway when I felt a prickle between my shoulder blades. I told myself I was imagining things – that there was no way the doll was really watching – but I couldn't stop myself from looking back.

What I saw when I glanced over my shoulder almost floored me. There, in the middle of the pretty purple tissue paper, the doll sat, watching me walk away. It didn't speak (thankfully) but it was very obvious that it was watching.

My heart caught in my throat as I struggled to draw in oxygen. I could hear the pounding of my heart as I stared, and for a moment I thought I might pass out – which was a bad idea because I was convinced the doll would claw out my eyes if I didn't stay alert – but somehow I remained on my feet.

I watched the doll, a mixture of fear and trepidation threatening to overwhelm me.

The doll watched back, something akin to mirth flitting across its face.

We stared each other down for what felt like forever. When I finally spoke, it was with a bravado that I didn't legitimately feel.

"I don't know what you are, but I'll smash your face in as soon as my uncle is gone," I warned. "I'm not afraid of you."

The doll didn't speak, but I heard it all the same.

You should be.

My heart skipped a beat. "You listen here … ." I moved to stride back, perhaps to shake the doll and end things immediately. I didn't get the chance, because my mother slipped through the front door and fixed me with a pointed look when she saw the determination on my face.

"What are you doing, Poet?"

I regained my senses, although only marginally. "I was just talking to my new friend," I lied, faking a sweet smile. "Did you see Uncle Sidney made her look exactly like me?"

"I did." Mom pursed her lips as she glanced at the doll. "I know you don't like dolls … ."

Like them? I hate them. It turns out I felt that way for good reason. This doll was clearly possessed by the spirit of something evil, and it wanted nothing but to scratch out my eyes as I slept. "I don't dislike her. I just … like other toys better."

"Uh-huh." Mom wasn't convinced. "Once your uncle leaves, we'll put her in the closet and only drag her out when he comes to visit. How does that sound?"

If she thought I was sleeping under the same roof with that doll – even if the doll was locked in a closet – she was sadly mistaken. Still, I didn't think she'd take it well if I admitted my plans, so I merely shrugged. "That's fine. I don't care either way about her."

"It's obvious you're disappointed in her." Mom lifted the doll, causing me to internally scream out a warning even though the doll didn't move. "She's quite lovely. She looks so much like you it's a bit fascinating."

I found my voice. "And you don't find that creepy?"

"She's just a doll." Mom smiled. "You don't have to play with her. I know you fancy yourself too old for dolls. This one isn't really meant for playing anyway. She's more of a fancy doll. Maybe we'll get a nice stand for her and put her on the dresser so you can always look at her but not risk breaking her. How does that sound?"

That sounded like pure torture. "I don't think that … ."

Mom didn't give me a chance to finish. "It's a doll, Poet. Your uncle went through a lot of trouble to have her made. You should be thankful."

I would've been thankful for a new Yahtzee or Monopoly game. That doll – that face – were not things to be thankful for. "I thanked him." I was almost positive that was true. "I don't know what more you want from me."

"You could at least fake some excitement," Mom suggested.

I stared at the doll. "I thanked him," I repeated. "I'm never going to like her." In fact, I was going to destroy her the first opportunity that arose ... no matter what Mom wanted.

"You don't have to like her," Mom said. "You like your uncle, though, and he went out of his way to have her made. You have to be nice to him, gracious. You need to be polite."

That sounded like the exact opposite of what I wanted to do. Still, I forced a thin-lipped smile. "I was polite."

Mom searched my face for a long moment and then smiled. "Good." She returned the doll to the box and stood. "We're having cake in a little bit. Why don't you come inside?"

"I'm going to shoot a few baskets," I countered. "I'll come inside when I'm finished."

"Okay." Mom nodded. "Keep the ball away from the doll."

"Oh, I will." I watched my mother disappear into the house before letting my eyes track back to the doll. She seemed to be watching me from a slightly elevated position, although like before, I hadn't seen her move. "Keep it up, freak," I murmured when I thought I heard the laughter again. "The second I can manage it, you're toast."

The doll didn't look worried.

Sadly, that only caused my stomach to revolt even more.

"I'll make you wish you'd never come to this house," I warned, lowering my voice. "I'll end you right here ... and nothing will save you. This is my world, and there's no way I'll let you live in it.

"You're a doll," I continued. "I'm bigger, stronger and smarter. This is my world and I'm not going to let you stay in it."

I meant it ... but I didn't get the feeling the doll felt the same way.

1
ONE

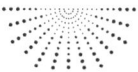

PRESENT DAY

"I'm glad to get out of here."

My best friend Luke Bishop hefted a box of outdoor equipment into the back of his truck, grunting as he flexed his muscles and settled the box toward the back of the truck.

"I would have thought you liked it here," I countered, wiping the back of my hand across my brow. We were in the middle of summer, which meant that places like Great Falls, Montana, were almost suffocating with heat and humidity. "This is wolf country, after all."

"Ugh. I knew you were going to bring that up." Luke scowled. "I'll have you know, the only good wolf shifter is … well, me … and I think the rest of my kind are a bunch of furry fiends with nothing on their minds but sex, drinking and more sex."

Those tended to be Luke's favorite topics, so I wondered how he could differentiate himself from his wolf brethren – who had been constant visitors at the Mystic Caravan Circus during our weeklong stop in their territory – with a straight face. I knew Luke well enough to know that I'd have to watch what I said if I didn't want to deal with a meltdown, though.

"Yes, it was definitely a different experience for us, huh?" I tried to keep my smile placid rather than letting it go feral. "I can't remember the last time I saw you do a keg stand before this."

Luke, his blond hair wet and slicked back with sweat, shot me a withering look. "I didn't do a keg stand!"

That wasn't how I remembered it. "I'm pretty sure you did. I distinctly remember you rolling up and drinking straight from the communal tap. I believe you did some sort of dance afterward, too."

"You're remembering it wrong."

I had a few magical abilities that ensured I had almost perfect recall when I wanted it, so we both knew that wasn't the case. Yes, I'm Romani by birth and magical by proxy, which means I, Poet Parker, am not someone who can be easily swayed by simple denials and lies. Luke knew that, yet he persisted with his story.

"You were too drunk to remember anything that happened," Luke pressed. "You imagined things. I would never do a keg stand. In fact, keg stands are for college kids. I'm an adult." He puffed out his bare chest, which he shaved diligently every day so he could look good without a shirt, and practically dared me to call him out.

"Huh." I licked my lips. "I guess I must be remembering things wrong."

"I guess you must." Luke pinned me with a hard look. I could practically hear the mental admonishments even though his lips didn't move. They were cold and full of warning. He wanted to put the keg stand incident behind him as soon as possible. I would allow it – for now – but I planned to remind him when we got to our next stop. What? It's a best friend's job to torture her platonic soulmate. I was merely holding up my end of the bargain.

"Well, I apologize for getting confused." I turned back to the packing and surveyed the remaining work. "I think we only have furniture left."

"You do, and you're behind."

I shifted my gaze over my shoulder at the new voice, a smile flitting unbidden across my lips when I caught sight of Kade Denton. He, too, was shirtless. Unlike Luke, though, he boasted dark hair that was shorn close to his scalp and he had a smile that made me go weak in the knees.

No, seriously. It's a little embarrassing to admit it, but Kade can turn my stomach to Jell-O and my knees to marshmallow with a simple look. I tried to tell myself it was okay to feel this way because we're dating, but I remained a bit embarrassed all the same.

As if reading my mind, Kade shot me a hot look as he gestured for Luke to get in the back of the truck so he could start handing him furniture. "Hello, darling."

I pressed my lips together to keep from saying something stupid. Kade and I had only been dating a few weeks, so I convinced myself we were still in that heady "new relationship" space. I wasn't being a complete ninny when I allowed my emotions to overtake me. That argument only worked fifty percent of the time.

"Hi." I felt stupid at my wide-eyed response, but that didn't stop me from staring at him. What? He looks really good without a shirt, and once we start driving I won't get a chance to see the phenomenon again until we land in Washington and start unpacking. That's hours of driving that I'll have to suffer through. I deserve a few minutes of hormonal overload.

"Oh, you guys make me want to puke." Luke rolled his eyes as he accepted the metal bistro table Kade handed him. "I don't know why I put up with this ridiculous high school display every time we pack and unpack at venues. I'm thinking of banning you two from seeing each other until all the work is done."

Kade merely lifted an eyebrow. "Are you still hungover after your keg stand the other night? Is that why you're in such a foul mood?"

Luke scowled. "How many times do I have to tell you people that I don't do keg stands?"

"I guess until we believe it," Kade shot back. "You seem to forget that we were there and saw everything ... including that little dance you did in your underwear after the fact."

Luke's mouth dropped open. "Poet!" His voice was unnaturally high and screechy, and caused me to cringe. "Did you hear what he just said to me?"

"I did."

"Make him stop."

That seemed like a bad idea. "I've decided, from here on out, I'm not getting involved when you guys argue," I countered. "I don't like being the 'mommy' in this threesome when the arguing starts, so I'm removing myself entirely from the situation."

Luke looked affronted by the announcement, but Kade let loose with a lazy smile as he watched me shuffle to a spot a few feet away to collect the bistro chairs.

"Oh, well, are you happy?" Luke scorched Kade with a hateful glare. "You've turned Poet into Switzerland. She's neutral. How do you think that's going to go?"

Kade shrugged as he accepted the chairs from me. "I think it will be fine. I don't think it's fair to put her in the center of things all the time. She shouldn't have to choose."

Luke rolled his eyes to the sky. "Did you hear that? He doesn't think she has to choose."

"Who are you talking to when you do that?" Kade asked, interested.

"The great wolf in the sky," I answered for him.

"Is that what all those wolves were talking about while Luke was doing his keg stand?" Kade asked. "They said they were dancing for the great wolf."

"I had trouble keeping up with everything that was going on," I admitted, sheepish. "I had a little too much to drink, too."

Kade's grin lit up his already handsome face. "Yes, but you were cute ... and you didn't do a keg stand."

"I didn't do a keg stand!" Luke stomped his foot and caused the truck to shake. "Stop saying that."

Kade held up his hands in mock surrender. "Fine. You didn't do a keg stand. I'm clearly mistaken. It must have been some other blond wolf wearing flamingo boxer shorts I'm thinking of. Sorry for any confusion."

Kade delivered the apology with such dry precision that I had to bite the inside of my cheek to keep from laughing.

"That's better." Luke heaved a sigh. "That's everything but the grill."

"Which I'm grabbing now." Kade slid me a sidelong look before grabbing the huge metal contraption in question. "Are you riding with Luke or me this time?"

That was a loaded question. I'd been trying to split my time between the two most important men in my life the past few weeks – mostly because Luke was feeling left out and I didn't like that – although I couldn't remember exactly where I was in the rotation. Ultimately it didn't matter, because there was no way I would risk riding with Luke when he remained so adamant he wasn't the keg stand type.

"You." I smiled. "In fact, I'm going to check the trailers and then get in your truck."

"Sounds like a plan." Kade smacked a kiss against the corner of my mouth and then turned his attention to the grill. "Are you ready for this?"

Luke made a face, but nodded. "I'm ready." He flexed his muscles as he readied to accept the grill from Kade. "I didn't do a keg stand. You need to stop spreading that rumor. It makes me look bad."

"I agree it makes you look bad," Kade gritted out, his muscles straining as he hoisted the grill. "You know we have photos, right?"

Luke's face drained of color as he struggled to lift the grill. "You're lying."

"We have video, too."

Luke managed to flick me an annoyed look as he lifted. "You're in big trouble."

I could do nothing but smile. "Why do you think I'm riding with Kade?"

KADE STOPPED AT MCDONALD'S once we were on the road and ordered snacks and sodas. The drive to Washington would take hours, and even though we'd have a full meal when we stopped, we were both starving and didn't want to wait.

Plus, well, it meant we fell out of the group driving formation and were on our own. It wasn't a big deal, because we would arrive at the next site within thirty minutes of the rest of our group, but it was sometimes the closest we came to having time alone on moving days. We often purposely scoped out detours to carve time out for ourselves during busy days.

"Are you really going to show Luke the photos we took of him?" I asked as I munched on my fries. "He'll melt down if you do."

"Why do you think I'm going to do it?" Kade grinned as he bit into his double cheeseburger.

"I know you like messing with Luke – I do, too, because it's easy and often amusing – but he's pretty adamant about this keg stand business," I said. "He doesn't want anyone to think he did it."

"Yeah, I find that weird. I mean ... he kind of acted like an ass that night. Everyone was drunk. No one cares."

I shrugged. I wasn't sure how much of Luke's private business I should share with Kade. Ultimately, I figured Kade should know some of it so he wouldn't accidentally say the wrong thing. Kade enjoyed messing with Luke, but he didn't want to purposely hurt him.

"Luke is kind of an outsider when it comes to wolf shifters," I supplied.

Kade slid me a sidelong look as he swallowed. He was new to the magical world we lived in – even though his biological father was a mage – but he was doing his best to absorb everything because he was genuinely interested. "What do you mean?"

"He's gay."

"I know. That's the reason I don't have a problem when he climbs into bed with you to gossip."

I shot him a wry look. "Most wolf shifters aren't gay. It's a big deal to be able to populate the species in wolf shifter circles. Luke is basically an outsider because he has no interest in finding a nice female to mate with."

"That's kind of sad." Kade rolled his neck as he considered the statement. "So you think he got out of control with the other wolves because he wanted to fit in for a change."

"Montana is big wolf country. He's always nervous when we go there. These guys accepted him with open arms and he had fun."

"He did have fun." Kade was thoughtful. "Does that mean you don't want me teasing him about the keg stand? I won't if you think it will hurt him."

I snorted. "Oh, we're definitely teasing him about the keg stand. It was ridiculous. He's almost thirty and was acting like a teenager."

Kade's shoulders drooped, relief washing over him. "Good. I've got some really great photos."

"It will be fine." I rested my hand on Kade's knee for a moment, happy simply to touch him. "Luke will eventually get over it and won't even remember why he was so embarrassed."

"I think he's going to remember."

"Yeah, but eventually he won't care." I popped another fry into my mouth. "It will be fun to torture him for a few days."

Kade's smile was wide. "I'm always excited when those opportunities arise."

"You and me both, honey."

We lapsed into amiable silence as we finished our meals. As soon as we were done, and I'd balled up the wrappers and put the bag of trash by my feet, Kade changed the subject.

"So, tell me what I should expect in Washington," he prodded.

I was confused. "What do you mean?"

"Is this another shifter stronghold? I mean … I would think it would be because of the landscape. Plus, well, isn't that where *Twilight* was supposed to be set?"

I pressed my lips together while debating how to answer. Finally I went with the obvious question first. "How do you know about *Twilight*?"

Kade made a disgusted face. "Oh, I knew you'd latch onto that part."

"Yes, and I'm going to tease you mercilessly for it," I said. "For now, though, I'm more interested in how you know about it."

Kade balked. "I know things. I keep up on pop culture."

"You asked Luke if he was a New Kids on the Block fan while he was drunk the other night."

"So? He strikes me as a boy band type."

"That's kind of stereotypical, but we'll forget that for a moment," I said. "New Kids on the Block were popular twenty-five years ago. You kind of dated yourself with the reference."

"That doesn't mean I don't know things," Kade challenged. "I'm better with movies and books than bands."

"Fair enough." I patted his hand, which rested on the seat between us, in a consoling manner. "I can give you a music tutorial later if you feel that you're being lapped in the knowledge department."

"Ha, ha." Kade shot me a warning look. "I was merely trying to learn about our next destination."

"I know." I decided to take pity on him. "Washington used to have a few wolf shifter strongholds, but *Twilight* essentially forced them out of the state. They've relocated to Idaho and Montana for the most part."

Kade quirked an eyebrow. "I don't understand."

"When all that *Twilight* mania hit, people everywhere started visiting the state," I explained. "That means that tourists were actually heading into the woods to pay some sort of homage to Bella, Edward and Jason."

"Jacob," Kade automatically corrected.

I pursed my lips to keep from laughing. That had been a test – something he realized after the fact – and now I was certain he knew a lot more about *Twilight* than he should. "Jacob. Of course."

"Oh, geez." Kade kept his eyes focused on the road in front of us. "You're going to turn this into a thing, aren't you?"

"Of course not."

"Yes, you are."

"I think it would be cruel to turn this into a thing." I adopted a pragmatic tone. "I don't want to be cruel."

"Oh, baby, you idle at cruel when you get going with that mouth of yours," Kade argued. "I'm not going to let you turn this into a thing, though. It's not important. What is important is the new area where heading to. I don't know a lot about it, and since I'm head of security I thought you could fill me in."

He was deflecting with duty. I made a mental note for later to challenge him on it. For now, I let it go. "We're on the Elliott Bay side of the city. We set up camp in a waterfront park. It's actually a really pretty location. It's a new spot, but not all that far from where we usually land. I guess we're part of some big festival or something. I'm not exactly sure."

Kade was clearly glad about the teasing reprieve because he nodded and relaxed his grip on the steering wheel. "And what kind of paranormals are we dealing with?"

"There's not any one big faction taking over the area in Seattle."

"Really?" Kade was surprised. "I would think that's a coveted area. I can't believe there are no paranormals there."

"Oh, I didn't say there were no paranormals. I just said there wasn't one big faction there."

"What does that mean?"

"It means there're a lot of little factions. Some shifters, some mages, a lot of witches. It's an interesting and bohemian area."

"What does that mean for us?"

I shrugged. "It changes every year. That's why I like it."

"Huh." Kade was stymied. "So you're basically saying we won't know what we're dealing with until we get there."

"Exactly."

"Well, I guess that's that." Kade didn't look happy. "I was hoping to get a heads-up before we arrived and not get thrown straight into the fire, but it doesn't appear that's going to be possible."

"No. It's okay, though." I focused my eyes on the passenger side window so I could appear nonchalant. "That gives us plenty of time to discuss why it is you know so much about *Twilight*."

"Oh, geez." Kade slapped his hand to his forehead. "I just knew you weren't going to let that go."

"Sorry, honey. That's not how I roll."

2
TWO

By the time we landed, Kade was over my *Twilight* teasing – er, well, at least mostly – and he was in a good mood as we started unpacking. Unlike some of our previous locations, we were close to the water, and the park we settled in had a relaxed ambiance. We weren't out in the open, although that created another set of problems.

"Did you know it was going to be like this?"

Raven Marko, our resident lamia, sidled up to me and crossed her arms over her chest as she looked out at the busy boardwalk stretching to both sides.

I shook my head. "I knew we weren't going to be in the same location as years past, but I didn't realize we'd be on top of everyone else."

Raven scanned the grounds, trying to give the impression that we were having a normal conversation and weren't particularly bothered by the new set-up. "How are we going to erect the dreamcatcher?"

That was a very good question. We created the dreamcatcher, the magical net we used to draw in evil paranormal creatures … and the occasional human sociopath, by combining my magic with Raven's, along with our two resident pixies Nixie and Naida. We usually erected it on the night we arrived, but because we were in such close quarters, we would have to figure a way to do it without drawing attention.

"I don't know how we're going to do it." I opted for honesty as I turned to my left and forced a smile for the people setting up shop at the crafts show area. They watched us with unveiled interest and it made me uncomfortable. They weren't exactly right on top of us, but there was very little room to navigate.

I rolled my neck as I turned back to our parcel. It was plenty big, but it wasn't a square. We usually put our trailers on three sides – segregating into various groups – and then erected the midway and tents in the same configuration each go around. We had a wedge-shaped plot this time. We were going to have to come up with something different.

"I think we should have a meeting before we set anything up," I said after a beat. "This is going to take some planning."

Raven nodded. Our relationship wasn't always easy, but we'd made strides of late to keep our working relationship amiable, even when we still tended to snark at one another on a personal front. "I think that's a good idea. I'll spread the word."

I left Raven to her task and headed toward Luke's truck. He was parked in the lot behind our parcel, and he looked to be having a row with Kade.

"I think you're a complete and total jerk sometimes," Luke complained. "Why do you have to be this way?"

"I think you're being overly sensitive," Kade shot back. His back was to me so he didn't see me approaching. "I think you should suck it up and act like a grownup instead of a child."

"Ugh. It's as if you don't even know me."

At first I worried they were fighting over something massive – it wouldn't be the first time, after all – but when I realized Kade had his phone in his hand and was displaying photos of Luke doing a keg stand, I instantly relaxed.

"I see you two are doing your usual flirting," I drawled, drawing their attention to me. "Should I be worried that you have so much sexual chemistry?"

"Ha, ha," Luke wrinkled his nose. Before Kade came along, we spent most of our time together. I still spent a lot of time with him, more than most boyfriends would be comfortable with, but Luke and Kade's relationship was a work in progress. They both cared about me, so they tried to get along – or at least not kill each other – but they were hardly best friends.

"What are you guys doing?"

Kade shrugged as he switched off his phone and slid it into his pocket. He was trying to act smooth, but I knew better. "We're discussing unloading the truck. It's not a big deal."

"You're a terrible liar."

Kade frowned. "I wasn't lying."

I internally cringed. Lying was a sore spot between us. I lied when he first joined the circus as security chief because I was trying to protect the big paranormal secret and my friends in the process. He understood that. It was the second lie, the one about Mystic Caravan owner Max Anderson being his father, that didn't go over well. We got into a big fight, he pulled away so he could pout and glare, and I was miserable. Eventually we worked things out, but the lie still hung over us at odd times.

"I didn't mean ... ."

Kade held up his hand to silence me. "It's okay. I know you didn't mean it that way."

"Ugh, do we have to bring up that again?" Luke rolled his eyes. "It's over and done with. Why is it still a thing?"

"It's not a thing." Kade kept his voice even. "It's simply a memory that occasionally trips us up. It's not a thing, though."

I pressed my lips together and remained silent.

"It's really not." Kade grabbed my hand and gave it a squeeze. "Everything is okay."

I nodded in thanks at his giving nature and then returned to the problem at hand. "I'm still staying out of it when you guys fight. I happen to know you were torturing Luke with photos, so that's what I was talking about."

Kade's expression filled with faux innocence. "I think that's a terrible thing to say about your boyfriend. I think I might cry over it later."

"Your take on sarcasm isn't always good either," I offered. "As for the rest … um … we're going to have a meeting over there and discuss the setup."

Kade's face reflected surprise at the conversational shift. "What do you mean?"

"I mean that we have a problem. This site isn't like our normal sites."

Kade craned his neck as he glanced around, reality finally settling on his broad shoulders. "Oh, I see what you mean."

Luke turned serious. "Yeah, this is going to be interesting."

"We need to come up with a plan before we do anything else," I supplied. "We only want to do the work once, so we need to make some tough decisions."

"Let's do that." Kade grabbed my hand as I moved to turn, linking his fingers with mine as he fell into step with me. "We're really okay."

"I still shouldn't have said it. What a stupid thing to say."

Kade was congenial. "I *was* lying, though. I didn't want you to know I was torturing Luke."

"Torturing Luke is essentially the official Mystic Caravan hobby. You don't need to lie about it. I'm not going to get involved."

"I heard that," Luke growled from in front of us. "You'll have to get involved if he won't stop being a douche. I won't stand for anything less."

Sadly, I thought that was probably true. "You guys are on your own."

"You won't say that if I wrestle him to the ground and make him eat mud," Luke warned.

"Maybe not, but I look forward to seeing that. If you guys could be shirtless when you're doing it that would make it even better."

Luke and Kade offered up twin expressions of disgust.

"You are a total pervert," Luke complained.

"You don't have a problem when you're the pervert."

"That's because I'm funny."

"That's not exactly how I see it."

Luke held up his hand to silence me. "I can't even look at you right now. Our friendship is tarnished and you're in the doghouse."

Kade snorted. "That's kind of funny because you're a wolf when you want to be, which makes you the dog."

Luke's expression was withering. "Ugh. You two really found each other, didn't you? It's so disgusting."

Kade cast me a sidelong look. "I don't think we're disgusting."

I smiled. "Me either. I think we're totally adorable."

"I'm totally going to puke," Luke complained. "It's not going to be a small amount of vomit either. It's going to be a huge pile of it. Then I'm going to rub your noses in it to teach you that you're disgusting. That's right, I'm going to start treating you like puppies. In fact … someone get me a rolled-up newspaper. You two clearly need a spanking."

Kade snickered as he tightened his grip on my hand, legitimately amused. "And all is right with the world."

"WHAT ARE WE going to do?"

Nelson "Nellie" Adler wasn't one to waste time standing around when there was work to be done. In addition to being our bearded lady – he's a dwarf, but the real kind from a parallel plane of existence – he also fancied himself in charge when the mood struck. Today he wore a flowery summer dress that blew up a bit when the breeze decided to kick in. I could only hope he was wearing underwear with so many people watching us. What? It's not always a given.

Kade shot Nellie a quelling look to silence him before he got up a full head of steam. "That's what we're here to discuss." He glanced over his shoulder, making eye contact with one of the craft show artisans and raising his hand in what I'm sure he thought was a friendly greeting. It looked anything but. All he was missing was a clown costume and razor-sharp teeth to make it appear we were in a horror movie.

"Yeah, that wasn't creepy at all," Nellie drawled. "Seriously, man, what are we going to do? We can't erect the dreamcatcher with this many people watching, and our usual setup won't work on this site."

"The dreamcatcher is the least of our worries to start," I offered. I was second in command at Mystic Caravan, behind only Max when it came to making decisions. Kade could overrule me on security issues, but he usually left the day-to-day circus operations to me. "We need to come up with a plan that allows us to box ourselves in and keep people out when necessary."

"Why would we want to do that?" Melissa asked. She was the newest member of our happy circus contingent. She was also the youngest. That meant she was often eager and enthusiastic without understanding why she felt any of those things. She was still catching up when it came to procedure.

"Because we don't want anyone prying into our business," Raven replied. "We have certain things to cover up."

"Not the least of which is the fact that we don't really have animals," Nellie said. "We have to put that tent specifically at the back corner over there so anyone who tries to get close stands out."

I followed his finger with my gaze. "That's a good idea." I nodded in agreement. "For this go around, I think we should put our line of trailers back there with the animal tent. That way we'll be on top of things if we have any looky-loos."

Mark Lane, the greasy conman who ran the midway, immediately balked. "We're usually at the back."

"And that's generally fine, because we have woods backing up to us in your location." I fought to keep my voice even. Mark always knew the right buttons to push when he wanted to set me off. I didn't think this would turn into an example of that, but I wouldn't put it past him. "We don't have that this time, so we have to be open to change."

Mark made a face. "I don't like change."

"Yes, well, if I cared what you thought I might try to fix your feigned outrage," I shot back. "You can't always get what you want, Mark. The real world doesn't work that way."

Mark dramatically rolled his eyes. "Like we live in the real world."

I ignored his tone and focused on the rest of the group. "We'll put our trailers at the back and buffer the animal tent between them. Someone would have to be crazy to try to enter."

"I don't understand what the big deal is," Melissa prodded. "There aren't any animals in there, so it's not as if some random kid is going to be eaten."

"No, but the fact that we don't really have animals is the problem," Kade said calmly. "We don't want people to know we have shifters rather than real animals."

Realization dawned on Melissa's face. "Oh. I get it."

"And in record time, too," Raven drawled, cocking a challenging eyebrow when I pinned a dark look on her. "What? She's slow. It's not my fault you added a slow person to the mix. That's on you."

So much for Raven playing nice when it came to business. I shook my head to keep from snapping at her and instead held up my hands to calm everyone. "I had no idea that we were going to be in the middle of a city-wide festival when they changed our location."

"What did they tell you?" Kade asked.

"They mentioned a carnival and crafts fair. I thought we could deal with that. This is so much more than I was picturing, though."

"I'll say it is," Nellie said. "They've got a classic car show going down at the end there. A huge carnival. I mean, this is double the size of any carnival I've seen in recent years. They've got the crafts show. They've got a flea market on the other side. Then, over there, they've got one of those food truck rallies. There are, like, fifty food trucks."

"It's not just that we're surrounded on two sides," Kade added. "We're in the middle of a huge festival. Right smack dab in the window. At least if we were on the end we'd be afforded some privacy."

"So what do we do?" Nixie asked, her aquamarine hair gleaming under the sun. "How are we supposed to fight whatever comes for us

– and something always comes for us – when everyone is watching us as if we're the main act?"

We were definitely in a pickle. "I don't know," I said after a beat. "We can only take it one step at a time. For starters, we're putting the animal tents and our trailers at the back. I want the midway trailers put to the east side and the clown trailers to the west."

Kade kept his eyes on me so he wouldn't have to inadvertently look at a clown. He was terrified of them, which I found funny most days, but there was a method to my madness today. That method played right into his fears. "Why do you want the clowns over there?"

"Because people are afraid of them," Luke answered. "You're not the only one afraid of clowns."

Kade balked. "I'm not afraid of clowns. I simply find them unnatural."

"I totally believe you." I patted his arm as a form of solace. "Much like you, though, most people are uncomfortable around clowns. If we put them in the spot right over there, that will keep people from trying to cut behind them in an effort to visit the animal tents."

"That will also keep them away from us," Raven noted. "That's smart. We'll move the main tents to the front and build our hideaway in the back. It's the only thing we can do."

"I still don't like it," Mark complained. "That puts my people on the front line."

"Yes, and your people don't exactly engender friendliness in others," I pointed out. "That's what we want. It's not like other locations. We've got carnies, crafters and flea market folk on our doorstep. They're going to be spending nights out here, too."

"Oh." Mark cracked his knuckles. "I didn't even think about that. You're right."

"I am. We're all going to be on our best behavior. We have no other choice."

Nellie raised his hand. "Does that include me?"

"That especially includes you."

Nellie scowled. "I can already tell I'm going to hate this place."

I wasn't sure I agreed. The location intrigued me. That didn't mean

I wasn't concerned. "Let's get unpacked. The sooner we do that, the sooner we won't be the center of attention."

"I don't know," Kade grumbled, his gaze focused on the people watching us from across the way. They didn't even bother to hide their interest. "I have a feeling we're going to be the center of attention no matter what."

Unfortunately, I had a very strong feeling that he was right.

3
THREE

The change in our layout wasn't so drastic that more than a few people should have been agitated. We're creatures of habit, though, so everyone was thrown for a loop.

That included me.

"Luke's trailer is on the wrong side." I scratched at the back of my head to straighten the scarf I wore over my hair – I'm a fortune teller, so my clothing choices can be best described as bohemian chic with a dash of gypsy melodrama thrown in. On moving days I opt for cargo pants and sneakers. On circus days I wear ankle-length skirts with bells and scarves. It was hot and I was distracted today, so I opted for the scarf ... and I was starting to regret it.

"What are you doing?" Kade followed me out of my trailer and grabbed my hand before I could dislodge the scarf.

"What are you doing?" I challenged, my agitation firing.

Kade cocked an eyebrow. "I'm trying to keep you from turning your hair into a messy bird's nest."

"Well, if you don't like my hair ... ."

Kade held up a finger to quiet me. "I like your hair however you do it. I simply know that you will melt down if you mess up your hair. I want to head that off before it happens."

"Oh." I pursed my lips. I wanted to be annoyed that he thought he knew me so well, but I kind of liked it. "This is weird, right? This whole set up is weird. I'm not sure we can leave it like this."

Kade moved his hand to my back, rubbing soothing circles as he surveyed the row of trailers. "I think it's okay. It looks professional and cuts off wanderers from the animal tent should they make it that far in."

"But ... Luke's trailer is supposed to be on the other side." I pointed for emphasis. "Now he'll be on my right when I'm sitting in the living room rather than my left. It's all wrong."

When Kade didn't immediately speak, I risked a glance in his direction and found him smirking. I slapped his arm, annoyed.

"It's not funny!"

"I didn't realize how OCD you were before this." Kade refused to hide his smile. "It's kind of cute. It's kind of weird, but it's kind of cute."

"I'm not OCD," I grumbled, crossing my arms over my chest. "This is weird. I don't like weird. I like things in their proper place."

"Which is OCD."

"Oh, I can't even talk to you." I moved to walk away, but Kade snagged me around the waist before I could escape. "Knock it off!" I smacked at his hands.

Kade refused to let go, instead drawing me back so I was pressed against his chest and he could rest his chin on my shoulder. "I said I thought it was cute."

"Yes, but you didn't mean it."

"Don't tell me what I mean." Kade's voice was low, even a bit playful, but I sensed an edge I wasn't aware of seconds before. "I mean what I say. I also like to mess around and tease you. It's okay to enjoy both. It's okay to be annoyed by both. There's no reason to get worked up about it."

It took me a moment to realize he was referring to our minor kerfuffle from the afternoon. "I didn't mean ... ."

Kade cut me off with a shake of his head. "I know. You don't have to be afraid to say what you're feeling to me."

"That's not what I was doing."

"I saw the look on your face. You were afraid for a few seconds. You thought maybe I'd take it the wrong way. The thing is, I want you to feel free to say what you want without worrying that's going to somehow derail us."

I ran my tongue over my lips as I debated how to respond. "I guess I didn't realize I was doing it," I hedged. "It's not that I'm afraid of you, it's just ... things are going so well."

"And you feel as if the bottom is going to drop out," Kade surmised. "It's okay, Poet. Things are going well and we're both happy about that. I'm not going anywhere." He rubbed his cheek against mine, and I couldn't stop myself from giggling thanks to his scratchy stubble. "I understand why you did what you did. We're in a different place. I want you to let it go."

"I thought I had let it go," I admitted. "I didn't realize I hadn't until that moment of panic."

"Well, hopefully there will be fewer moments of panic going forward." Kade swayed, keeping me pressed tightly against him. "I'm happy, too. Don't be afraid ... and don't hold anything back. It's okay. It's going to stay okay. I promise."

I sighed. He had a calming effect that I couldn't put a name to. It was interesting and terrifying all the same. "Thanks."

"You're welcome."

"I still think Luke needs to move his trailer," I added, knowing it would lighten the mood.

Kade chuckled. "Why don't you bring it up with him over dinner? Something tells me you're not getting your way on this one."

Something told me he was right. Still, I wasn't about to give up the fight without a good browbeating. "Do you want to place a wager on it?"

Kade, intrigued, linked his fingers with mine as we fell into step together. "What did you have in mind?"

"I was thinking we could bet massages."

Kade chuckled. "I think you can persuade me to play. What are the terms?"

"I win, you massage me. You win, I massage you. I think it's pretty simple."

"And what do we need to happen to force us to massage each other?"

I bit the inside of my cheek as the skin on the back of my neck flushed hot. "I think we can work something out on that front regardless."

"That's what I was hoping you'd say."

DUE TO THE CHANGE IN layout, the food preparation area had been moved to the opposite end of our row. Usually it was in front of my trailer, which made things convenient for me. Because we had to switch things up this go around, the kitchen area was now in front of Nellie's trailer, and he seemed to think that made him head of the circus if his demeanor was any indication.

"Good evening, Poet." He beamed as he leaned back in his chair, his dress crawling up his hairy thighs and threatening to give me a gander of something I didn't want to see.

"Keep the mouse in its house," I warned, tugging his skirt down. "The crafters over there have kids in their camping area. We don't want them getting an eyeful."

"That's true," Nellie said. "They'd be traumatized for life if they saw the king outside of his castle."

"You're sick."

"You say that like it's a bad thing."

I turned my attention to Nixie, Naida and Raven as they toiled in the kitchen area, releasing Kade's hand so I could help. "I'll be back in a little bit. See if you can get Luke to agree to move his trailer."

Kade balked. "What makes you think I'm going to do that?"

"Because even though you want to win the massage you're debating about whether or not it's going to be worth it to put up with my whining over the next few days."

"You're not much of a whiner," Kade countered.

"No, but what I lack in quantity I make up for in quality when I put my mind to it."

"Good to know." Kade pressed a quick kiss to the corner of my mouth before peeling off to join the men around the bonfire. That left me to question the women without anyone looking over my shoulder.

I opted not to beat around the bush. "What do you think of this setup?"

Raven quirked an eyebrow as she worked on a cucumber, onion and tomato salad. "I think we did the best we could do," she said after a beat. "Why? What are you worried about?"

"Well, for starters, I'm worried about the dreamcatcher." I moved to the grill so I could help Naida with the hot dogs and hamburgers. "I don't think we can risk camping here without erecting it. This place is thick with paranormals, and because there's going to be so many people in this area for the festival we'll be open to attack if we don't do something to protect ourselves."

"So what do you think we should do?" Naida asked. "I guess we could drop a veil so everyone doesn't see us, but that comes with its own set of risks. It works on the people underneath the veil, but if more people move to join us ... ."

She had a point. "What if we employ the veil and combine it with a lullaby?" I suggested. "We can design the lullaby to lull the people underneath the veil and turn away any late joiners."

Raven's eyes sparked with interest as she tucked a strand of silver hair behind her ear. "Now that right there is an interesting suggestion."

"Do you think it will work?"

Raven licked her lips as she surveyed the area, slowly nodding as the plan took form. "I do. I've seen the interest from the other groups. They're going to come check us out before long. We're the newest element. They'll want to get to know us."

"Then we'll let them get to know us. I think we should provide drinks for those who come, drop the lullaby first when people are comfortable, and then Naida can add the veil once we're sure the lullaby is working. After that, we need to move quickly."

"I'll eat dinner with everyone and then disappear to mark the lines for the dreamcatcher," Raven offered. "You keep the people who join us distracted. When I come back, you'll know the lines are drawn. We can move forward with the rest of it from there."

I nodded, pleased with the plan. "Okay. Let's do this."

BARNEY TOLLIVER WAS a local historian and stained-glass artist who liked to tell tall tales. He was the first to approach us, and then he proceeded to make himself at home around our fire as we plied him with drinks and snacks. He seemed to be enjoying himself, and once he made nice with us it was only a matter of time before the others approached.

I stood at the edge of the fire and watched the artisans converse with our group, sparing a glance over my shoulder to study the bonfire on the other side of our site. The midway folks and clowns set up shop on that side, so I wasn't exactly surprised to see the carnies congregate there. Carnies and midway workers were unique breeds ... and they seemed to like each other.

As for the clowns, no one liked them. They were tolerated by the other misfits, so they stayed with the midway workers and carnies, content to be tolerated. Well, except for Percival Prentiss, our newest clown. He spoke with a fake British accent and sparked a romance with Raven that defied all logic. They seemed an odd couple, but I opted not to put too much thought into it because Percival's presence kept Raven's focus off Kade. I considered that a win.

"What are you thinking?" Kade moved to my side and watched as my eyes shifted back to Barney. He was a natural storyteller and I couldn't help but like him. His daughter, Paige, was another story. Barely out of her teens with a surly attitude, all she seemed to do was roll her eyes when she thought her father wasn't looking and bend her head together with Melissa to giggle and snicker. In fact, as the crowd grew, the girls increased the distance from the gathering, not stopping until they were closer to the crafts fair and almost completely hidden from view when they wanted to duck behind a tree. For some reason, the two of them pairing up made me nervous.

"It won't be long," I replied. "Once Raven gets back we'll know the lines are drawn. We've already started with the lullaby." I inclined my chin in Naida's direction. She stood behind the crowd, tapping her fingers on her arms as she weaved a soft song into people's heads. She was so good at it no one seemed to notice. Except for Paige. The young woman kept shifting her eyes and looking around, as if she heard a whisper she couldn't identify. I was starting to think it was because she heard the lullaby ... even if she didn't recognize what it was.

"And is this lullaby working on me?" Kade asked.

"I honestly don't know." I dragged my eyes from Paige and focused on him. "Do you have the urge to leave the area?"

"You're here. I don't want to go anywhere."

I bit the inside of my cheek to keep from laughing. "That was smooth."

"Thanks. As for your question, I don't feel the urge to leave. I don't feel the need to stay, either. I'm sure I could leave if I wanted to."

"You're aware of what's going on, though," I pointed out. "You could force yourself to leave because of that. The lullaby isn't a control spell. It's merely meant to inspire. In this case, we want to inspire the guests already in the veil to stay. We also want to inspire those outside to stay outside ... at least until we draw the dream-catcher."

"How long will that take you?"

"About twenty minutes. Raven is handling the boundaries. We should be okay."

"I'll wander up front while you're doing it, just to be on the safe side. When you're done, come and get me. I'll be ready for bed ... and my massage ... after that."

The warmth I'd been feeling only moments before dissipated. Luke had refused to move his trailer, saying it was too much work and I could simply suffer through my obsessive compulsive issues on my own. He and Kade seemed to get along during dinner, so I couldn't help but wonder if my boyfriend bribed my best friend to get his way. It was a concern I filed away for later, when it came time to start talking to the locals.

"And then – I swear this woman was the size of a bear – she grabbed the front of my shirt, lifted me off the ground and said, 'Do you want your kiss now or later?' I said I wanted it later ... like thirty years in the future ... and she said she would be back to give it to me then." Barney wrapped his story with a flourish, causing everyone sitting around the fire to roar with laughter. We'd acquired quite the eclectic bunch during the course of the evening and they seemed to be having a good time.

I flicked my eyes to Paige, who seemed to be one of the only people in earshot not laughing. She made a face at the end of the story, and turned back to Melissa to whisper something. They were away from the fire – hidden in the shadows of some nearby trees – and I couldn't help believing that was on purpose. They were outside of the dreamcatcher boundary, but not so far that I felt Melissa was in danger.

"Paige and Melissa seem to be getting along," Kade said, following my gaze. "I think it's good for Melissa to have someone close to her age to hang around with for a bit."

"Hmm." I made a noncommittal sound as I watched them, knitting my eyebrows when Paige cocked her head as if she was listening to something only she could hear. "I think Paige has some witch in her."

Kade straightened, surprised. "What makes you say that?"

"I'm almost positive she can hear the lullaby."

"Is she dangerous?"

I slid my eyes to him, genuinely amused. "Witches aren't good or evil. They're like people. They choose their destiny. I'm sure Paige is fine."

"Yeah, but you don't look convinced of that." Kade took his role of protector very seriously. "Maybe I should collect Melissa."

"I wouldn't worry about Melissa," I said. "She's fine. I'm not even sure Paige realizes she's a witch. She was probably born into it and part of her recognizes the magic. I'm going to guess she has no idea what she's hearing. She's merely confused."

"You don't know that, though," Kade hedged. "If Melissa is in danger ... ."

"I don't believe Melissa is in danger," I soothed. "I didn't say that. I simply said I catch a whiff of witch when I get near Paige. It's okay."

Kade didn't look convinced. "Fine. I'll watch them while you're gone."

"You do that." I bit back a smile as I caught Raven's gaze over the bonfire. She was back and ready for action. "I shouldn't be gone long."

Kade nodded before giving me a quick kiss. "Be safe."

"I've done this hundreds of times."

"And I still want you to be safe."

"It will be fine." I cast one more look at Paige and found her laughing hysterically with Melissa. They looked like two young girls having a good time. "You don't have anything to worry about. We have everything under control. This is going to work and absolutely no one will notice. Have faith."

"I have faith in you. That's enough."

4
FOUR

We knew our jobs, so erecting the dreamcatcher wasn't an issue. We simply put our heads down and did it, stretching ourselves to the corners of the site and weaving the necessary magic to set the trap.

In truth, Naida, Nixie and Raven supplied the bulk of the magic. I oversaw anchoring the power threads, reforming it and then designing the dreamcatcher so it was tight in the center and grew wider as it expanded outward.

It took us twenty minutes, about what I expected, and I rolled my neck when the task was complete, planting my hands on my hips as the dreamcatcher sparkled and settled. Only magically-inclined beings could see the dreamcatcher, and then only if they were specifically looking for it. Anyone else watching, even from a distance, would've seen nothing but us separating and talking to ourselves if they were paying attention.

I was about to head back to my trailer, thoughts of a quiet night with Kade dancing through my head, when a sound in the trees behind me caught my attention. I swiveled quickly, narrowing my eyes, and focused on the darkness.

I didn't see anything. The noise didn't repeat. It was as if I could *almost* see something and *almost* hear something. I never really managed either. That didn't stop me from wondering if someone – or some thing – was in the dense foliage watching me. The hair on the back of my neck stood as I stared. I licked my lips as I debated stepping away from the relative safety of the dreamcatcher to investigate.

Ultimately the choice was taken out of my hands because Kade appeared from behind the House of Mirrors, his eyes keen as they scanned the darkness, his face lighting when he caught sight of me.

"Done?"

I forced a smile and nodded. "Yup. Ready for bed?"

Kade didn't fall for my fake bravado. "What's wrong?"

"Nothing." It wasn't exactly a lie. It wasn't exactly the truth either.

"Poet, I can tell something is wrong."

I pressed the heel of my hand to my forehead. "I don't want you to think I'm an alarmist."

"I've seen you in action. I would never think that."

"Okay. Well, I thought I heard something in the woods. I was debating going over to check when you showed up." I risked a look in Kade's direction after a few seconds of silence and found him looking grim. "And now you know why I didn't want to mention it."

"I'm not upset about you hearing a noise, and I certainly don't think you're an alarmist."

"So what's the problem?"

"Why would you even consider going over there alone?" Kade's eyes flashed. "I mean … are you trying to drive me crazy?"

Of course. I should've realized that would set him off. "You know I'm capable of taking care of myself, right?"

"That doesn't mean you should do something stupid like take off into the woods in a strange location to check out an odd noise. You should've called me."

"I was considering it."

Kade's expression was dubious. "I think you're lying."

This time I didn't flinch at the word. "I guess we'll never know."

"I guess we won't." Kade grabbed my hand. "Come on. We're going to check near the trees."

"Are you sure?"

"Yup." I followed him toward the area, doing my best to relax my senses so I could pick up any anomalies. I knew right away that whatever I sensed there – if I indeed truly sensed anything – was gone.

We searched for ten minutes and came up empty. Kade wasn't agitated that I wasted his time. In fact, he was relieved when we didn't stumble across an evil magical being, and he pointed me toward my trailer when we emerged.

"I'm sorry. I swear I thought I heard something."

"I'm fine with it. I'm glad we looked. Now you can focus on your big task for the evening."

"And what's that?"

"My massage."

I groaned. "Geez. You're a pain in the butt when you win."

Kade snorted and lowered his mouth so it barely skimmed my ear. "Don't worry. I'll make sure you win, too."

I had faith he meant it.

BECAUSE WE'D SPENT SO MUCH time organizing the previous day, we had very little to do when we finished breakfast the next morning. While some of our brethren had things to finish – mostly in the midway area and the sales booth row – Kade, Luke and I were largely without chores. We decided to look around the festival.

We started at the far end, where the car show was located, and even though all the vehicles weren't yet present there was still plenty to wander about.

"I don't get the appeal of old cars," Luke said, staring with vacant eyes at a vintage purple Corvette. "The entire phenomenon is odd to me."

"Old cars are great," Kade argued. "I've always wanted one. In fact, if I ever get up enough money, I know the truck I'd buy."

This was news to me. "I never knew you had an old car fetish."

Kade wrinkled his nose. "You don't have to say it like that. It's not really a fetish."

It sounded like one to me. "What truck do you want?"

"It's a 1953 Chevrolet 3600. I want it to be green."

I had no idea what that meant – or what the truck looked like, for that matter – but I made a mental note to research it later. It wasn't exactly as if I could purchase the truck for him, but because I had control over magic and could make minds see things that weren't there, I thought it might be fun to set up a mutual fantasy we could both enjoy.

"Did you work on trucks with your dad when you were a kid or something?" Luke asked, his attention on the Corvette. "That's the only reason I could see for having an old car fetish."

Luke was oblivious to what he'd said, his attention fully trained elsewhere. I took the opportunity to scan Kade's face, readying myself to perhaps step in and remind Luke that Kade wasn't raised by his father, but I saw neither anger nor bitterness on Kade's face, so I opted to watch it play out.

"One of my high school friends worked on vehicles with his father," Kade offered. "I never had that opportunity. It's a nice idea for when I have kids of my own one day, though."

Luke jerked up his head, realizing too late what he'd said. "I'm sorry. That was a stupid thing to say."

Kade waved off the apology. "It's fine."

"Still, it was a dumb thing to say." Luke's eyes tracked to me. "The good news is, Poet, Kade is open to having kids ... and probably with you since you mentioned it in front of her." Luke shot me an enthusiastic thumbs-up. "Score!"

Now it was my turn to be embarrassed. "Thank you so much for pointing that out, Luke."

Kade chuckled as he slipped his arm around my waist and directed me away from the classic car show. "I love spending time with you guys. Sometimes it's as if I never left high school."

I scowled. "I didn't finish high school, so I wouldn't know."

"You didn't miss much. It's just like this."

Our next stop was the crafts fair, and I was instantly happier with the shift in offered items. Cars weren't my thing, but crafts were another matter entirely.

"Look at all of this stuff." I was beyond excited, so much so I ignored the looks of mirth that Kade and Luke shared when they thought I wasn't looking. Instead I focused my attention on each individual booth. "Oh, I love this."

I held up a dreamcatcher so Kade could see it, grinning at the taut lines. They'd been treated with some sort of substance that sparkled, which gave the item an ethereal quality that I found appealing.

"What is that?" Kade knit his eyebrows.

"It's a dreamcatcher, dummy," Luke replied. "It's what Poet uses as a basis for what we do whenever we land in a new location."

"Oh." Kade's expression was thoughtful as he took the dreamcatcher from my hand and studied it. "And what is a dreamcatcher supposed to do again? I think you told me, but I forgot in all the hoopla of learning the truth about the circus."

"You're supposed to place it above or near your bed," I replied. "While you sleep, it collects nightmares before they descend and traps them in the web. Then, when the sun rises, it hits the trapped nightmares and causes them to dissipate.

"They were created by the Ojibwa, and then other tribes slowly started embracing them," I continued. "I guess it depends on your belief system when it comes to having faith in them."

"What do you believe?"

I shrugged. "I believe nightmares can decimate you if you're not careful."

Kade didn't immediately respond, so I looked to him, expecting to find him laughing or sharing an exaggerated eye roll with Luke. Instead he handed the dreamcatcher to the woman behind the counter.

"We'll take it," Kade said, digging into his pocket for his wallet.

"You don't have to do that," I protested. "I don't need it."

"Maybe I want you to have it." Kade was calm as he handed the woman the appropriate amount of money. "Besides, we sleep together every night so I think it will be good for both of us. No nightmares. Only good dreams."

"Oh, geez." Luke made a face. "I don't want to hear this. You're grossing me out."

"I don't care." Kade accepted the wrapped dreamcatcher from the girl and handed it to me. "Only good dreams ahead, right?"

I offered up a sheepish smile as I accepted it. "Right. Thanks. It's really pretty."

"So are you."

"Oh, I so want to gag," Luke complained. "I thought things would finally get better when you started boning. Now I always want to vomit when I'm around you."

Kade cocked a challenging eyebrow. "Boning?"

"Hey, you said you liked hanging with us because it reminded you of high school. You can't change your mind now."

"I guess not."

"Knock it off," I warned, drifting toward the next booth. This one featured pottery, which I liked, but was impractical given how often we moved. Still, there were a few cute bottles with stoppers that caught my eye. They featured a variety of pagan symbols – the triple moon, a pentacle, the Eye of Horus, Hecate's Wheel – and I knew that Nixie and Naida would love them.

I purchased a set of three for each of them, made sure they were packed well, and then led Kade and Luke to the next booth. They seemed content to let me pick the direction, mostly because they were busy verbally sparring with one another over cars, kids, who had the better washboard abs and my general happiness. I tuned them out, happy to shop while they bonded – or whatever it was they were doing – and I was lost in thought when I came to a booth featuring some of the most godawful dolls I'd ever seen.

One of them happened to be at eye level – a particularly nasty one with red hair and a clown costume – and I reared back to avoid accidentally touching the arm that jutted from the table. In the process, I smacked into Kade, and he had to catch me to keep me from falling.

"Poet?" Kade was concerned.

It took me several seconds to collect my breath.

"Poet." Kade was insistent. "What's wrong? What happened?" He kept a firm grip on me even as my heart pounded and I glared at the doll.

"What's wrong with her, Luke?" Kade almost sounded desperate.

"I'm not sure." Luke was nonchalant when he circled in front of me and hunkered down so we were eye to eye. "What's up, Poet? Are you swooning from Kade's overbearing testosterone? Or is it that cologne he insists on wearing even though it smells like a used jockstrap?"

"My cologne does not smell like a used jockstrap," Kade argued.

Luke made a tsking sound with his tongue. "Now is not the time to argue about cologne," he chided. "Geez. Poet is clearly sick or something and all you can talk about is yourself. It's a little sad."

Kade growled. "You're a piece of work, man."

"Yeah, yeah." Luke waved off the dig and focused on me. "You're white as a sheet, hon. What's wrong?"

"Nothing." I collected myself quickly. The reaction was ridiculous. I knew it, and yet I couldn't stop the bolt of panic shooting through me. That panic stemmed from my childhood, an incident I'd long since thought past. Apparently I was wrong. "I just tripped over something, caught my toe on a rock. It's nothing."

Kade peered around my shoulder so he could stare at my face. "That didn't seem like nothing to me."

How could I explain my doll phobia without looking like an idiot? "Um ... ."

"Oh, I know what it is." Luke focused on the doll, realization washing over his features.

I focused all my mental energy on Luke, pushing forth instructions that I hoped would keep him from sharing my doll issues with Kade. Luke, as usual, didn't listen to anything other than his instincts.

"She's afraid of dolls," he volunteered, smirking. "She told me about it when we were drunk one time a few years ago. There was even some doll she had an incident with as a kid – one that apparently looked like her – and she took it out with bloody force to make sure it would stop looking at her."

"That's not what happened," I challenged, fury rising. "And I'm not afraid of dolls."

Kade licked his lips as he regarded me. "Hmm."

I ignored his tone. "I'm not afraid of dolls. I simply don't like them."

"She's afraid of them," Luke repeated. "I once won a doll in one of those claw machines at a grocery store and gave it to her as a present. She burned it in the bonfire when she thought no one was looking."

I ran my tongue over my teeth, a dozen horrible paybacks for Luke's loose tongue rolling through my head.

"Is that true, Poet?" Kade didn't bother to hide his amusement. "Are you afraid of dolls?"

"I'm not afraid of them," I gritted out, glaring at the clown doll that caught me off guard and caused this entire unnecessary conversation. "I just don't see the purpose of them."

Kade moved from behind me and plucked the doll from the counter, lifting it so he could study it up close. It didn't move – or laugh in my head – yet I was unbearably nervous having it that close to Kade's face. Out of instinct, I reached out and snatched it away.

Kade cocked an eyebrow. "Were you worried it was going to attack me or something?"

"Of course not." I managed to keep my voice even, but just barely. I moved the doll back to its previous spot, making sure to tuck in its arms and legs so they didn't hang over the side. "I just think it's creepy. It looks like a clown, for crying out loud. You're the one afraid of clowns."

Kade made a face. "I'm not afraid of them. They're unnatural."

"That's how I feel about dolls."

"But ... dolls are inanimate objects," Kade argued. "Clowns are real ... and completely ridiculous."

"He's right," Luke said.

It took everything I had to keep from snapping at Luke. He caused this entire kerfuffle, after all. "Not all dolls are inanimate."

"Excuse me?" Kade's eyebrows rose. "Are you saying dolls can come to life and hurt us?"

I shrugged as I led him away from the doll, thankful to increase the distance between us and the booth. "I'm merely saying that dolls aren't always helpless ... or inanimate."

"Well, that sounds like a story in the making," Kade teased. "I guess it's good that we're heading to the grocery store next, huh? You'll have plenty of time to tell me the story."

He would think that. "I'm not telling you that story."

"Oh, you're going to tell me." Kade was so sure of himself I could do nothing but cast a derisive look over my shoulder. When I did, my eyes landed on the doll. We were a decent distance away now, yet I couldn't mistake the fact that its leg was hanging over the edge again. I knew I arranged it so that wasn't the case, and yet ... it had changed position.

"Poet!" Kade snapped his fingers in my face to get my attention, only stopping when I pinned him with an irritated look. "You're totally going to tell me that doll story. I think I need to hear it."

"You'll have to bribe me with something really good to get that story," I shot back. "The dreamcatcher is nice, but I'm not spilling for that."

Kade's eyes lit with mirth as he shot me a look that warmed me to the very tips of my toes. "I love a challenge. Prepare yourself to be wowed."

"I'm looking forward to it."

5
FIVE

"So, were you stalked by a doll or haunted by one?" Kade refused to let go of the doll tidbit Luke dropped, so even when we hit the grocery store an hour later he was still harping on (and on and on and on) about it.

"I think we should get some peanut butter," I said, focusing on the display in front of me. "Just for us, I mean. We have plenty of communal peanut butter, but nothing in our trailer."

Kade tilted his head to the side, surprise flitting across his face. "Our trailer?"

"That's what I said."

"I know, but ... I didn't realize we'd moved in together."

"Oh. Um ... I didn't mean that." My cheeks burned with embarrassment. It was a different sort than I felt when he questioned me about the evil doll. "I just meant we usually eat in my trailer because we tend to spend the night there and ... stop looking at me that way."

Kade's smile was mischievous when he snagged the jar from my hand. "This is smooth peanut butter. If you expect me to move in, we'll need crunchy, too. That's my negotiating demand."

I stilled, dumbfounded. He was so calm I didn't know what to make of it. "You want to move in with me?"

"I believe you just insinuated that we already live together."

"I know, but … it's a big step."

"Is it?" Kade's demeanor was calm, as if he expected me to freak out so he had to be the mature one. It was a distinction that wasn't lost on me, yet I couldn't seem to stop my heart from racing all the same.

"Well, I think it's a big step." I tried to match his tone, make him believe I wasn't about to have some sort of meltdown. "We've been together only a few months now."

"I'm well aware of that. But we spend every night together."

"Yes, but we haven't had a big fight yet," I pointed out. "What happens if we have a big fight and you want to storm off? Are you going to sleep on the couch in my trailer? It's not very big. We'll be on top of each other during and after the fight."

"That's a very good point." Kade transferred the peanut butter to the cart, never moving his eyes from my face. "Or perhaps we won't have a big fight."

He was sincere, earnest. It tugged at my heartstrings. "I think it's sweet that you think that's a possibility." I lowered my voice. "I don't believe it, though. People fight. We're still in that heady 'new relationship' phase when all we want to do is jump each other."

Kade snorted, easing the tension. "I don't believe we'll never fight. I simply believe we won't have a fight big enough to matter."

I swallowed hard. "We already had one big fight that managed to matter a great deal."

"We did. And got through it. Are you keeping any other big secrets from me? Are you hiding an uncle or sister I don't know about?"

It was such a ridiculous question I couldn't stop from laughing. "No."

"So what are you really afraid of?"

"Honestly?"

Kade nodded.

"The trailer is small. There's only one bedroom. It's fun now when we want to be on top of each other all the time – get your mind out of the gutter – but what happens when we occasionally want some quiet time?"

Kade's smile was so wide it threatened to swallow his entire face. "Well, I'll try not to take it personally that you think you'll need time away from me."

"That's not what I meant and you know it."

Kade rested his hands on my shoulders and gave them a squeeze. "You're so uptight sometimes. You need to learn to take a breath and a step back."

That was rich coming from him. "Oh, really?"

Kade nodded. "Really. As for needing quiet time, I think you're probably right. We'll need a place to escape from each other if we expect to make it over the long haul ... and I am interested in making it the duration, in case you're interested.

"Perhaps we can ask Max to secure us a bigger trailer," he continued. "A three-bedroom trailer would give each of us a room to use as an office and one room for us to share as a bedroom. Also, it would be our trailer from the start rather than your trailer or my trailer."

It made sense, yet there was a minor stumbling block. "Do you think Max is simply going to buy us an expensive new trailer?"

Kade nodded without hesitation.

"You do?"

"Of course." Kade's smile was back. "If there was ever a time to play the 'You abandoned me when I was a kid and lied to me my whole life' card, it's now. He'll do what we want simply to make nice."

My mouth dropped open. "That's manipulative."

"So what? I plan to manipulate him right to his face."

"What, you're going to walk up to him, say, 'I want a fancy new trailer so I can shack up with my girlfriend and you're going to give it to me because you want me to like you' and call it a day?"

"Pretty much."

"Huh." I didn't know what to say. The manipulation didn't seem so bad when he phrased it the way he did. "Do you think he'll really do it?"

Kade nodded. "I think he's unlikely to say no given what he's put us through."

"Well, okay then." I took us both by surprise when I bobbed my head. "Let's move in together."

"Just like that?"

"Just like that. I'm looking forward to it." I reached for a jar of crunchy peanut butter and tossed it into the cart. "What other weird foods do you like? It will probably take Max a few weeks to get our new trailer – and we'll have to look online when we get back so we can pick out exactly what we want – but there's no reason we can't get a head start on the cohabitating."

Kade snickered. "I love that you're always willing to just go for it. It's one of the things I like best about you."

"It's one of the things I like best about myself, too. I was serious about the food, though."

"Okay." I could tell Kade was racking his brain for something to gross me out. I wanted to keep him from going back to his doll questions, so I was happy to focus on the food. "How about pickled okra?"

I smirked. "I happen to love pickled okra. It's especially good when you dip it in tomato juice."

"You're weird, and I like it." Kade grinned as he leaned over to rest his forehead on mine. "Are you sure you don't want to freak out about this? I was prepared for you to freak out for a bit so I'd have to talk you down later."

"I don't want to freak out. I'm too excited to freak out."

"Well, then we'll be excited together." Kade pressed a quick kiss to my forehead. "We'll also celebrate later. For now, we have to finish our shopping."

"Good point." I felt light, almost as if I was floating, as I pushed the cart along the aisle. Then something occurred to me. "Where did Luke go?"

"He found the coffee shop. He's buying, like, thirty pounds of stuff to bring back with us. He says we can't spend time in Seattle without having a caffeine buzz party with their superior coffee blends."

"He's not wrong."

"I tend to believe he's always wrong."

"That's because you believe you're in competition with him for my attention. Just wait until he finds out we're moving in together."

"And he's not getting a key," Kade muttered under his breath.

I had news for him: If Luke didn't have a key to wherever it was I rested my head at night he'd make both of us pay. I had a few weeks to ease Kade into that scenario, though.

"Also, I'm not in competition with him," Kade added. "We're not interested in you for the same reasons."

"I can't tell you what a relief that is," I teased. "I can barely keep up with you. If I had to satisfy Luke, too, things would be all kinds of exhausting."

"Ha, ha." Kade tapped the end of my nose. "You're feeling pretty good about yourself, aren't you?"

I shrugged. "I'm feeling happy. If that results in a little teasing, you'll simply have to deal with it."

"It's funny, but I was just thinking the same thing." Kade's expression told me I was about to be unhappy because he was going to change the subject. "So, about this doll you don't want to talk about, was it haunted by the soul of a dearly departed psychopath or was it evil all on its own?"

"Ugh." I slapped my hand to my forehead as Luke rounded the corner, his arms full of bags of coffee. "I thought you were going to let that go."

"I never said that. We simply got distracted."

Crap. We could either discuss our decision to move in together in front of Luke, thus risking a meltdown in public, or talk about the doll. That stupid, creepy, possessed doll.

I heaved a sigh. "Fine. What do you want to know?"

"I want to know why you're afraid of dolls," Kade replied without hesitation.

"Why?"

"Because I find it funny. Most girls covet their dolls."

"I'm not most girls."

"Oh, I know that. I still want to know."

"Geez." I rubbed my hand over my stomach before looking to Luke for help. He was so interested in reading the coffee bags he barely spared any attention for us. "Okay. You win." I threw up my hands in defeat. "When I was a kid, my uncle got me a doll. He had it made to look like me. It had dark hair and blue eyes, and it wore a dress that was exactly like a dress I wore back then."

Kade struggled to understand. "So the doll creeped you out?"

"From the moment I saw her."

"So what happened?" Luke asked, lifting his head. "I vaguely remember this story, but I was so drunk that night all I remember is when you tried to sing karaoke."

"You sing karaoke?" Kade was amused. "You're just full of surprises today."

Great. Now I would have to explain that, too. "I was drunk. It seemed a good idea at the time."

"We've all been there." Kade's grin was charming. "Go back to the doll. What happened with her?"

"It's hard to explain."

"Try me."

"She ... looked at me," I forced out. "She watched what I did, where I moved, and listened to what I said. She laughed in my head. I could hear her."

Kade furrowed his brow. Whatever he was expecting, that wasn't it. "So ... what? She was possessed?"

"I don't know. I was a kid. I didn't understand what was happening. I mean ... I knew I could do things at that point, but I didn't understand what was happening with the doll."

"Okay." Kade stroked his hand up and down my arm. "I didn't realize this was a serious story. I thought it was some crazy thing you did as a kid that would make us all laugh. You don't have to talk about it."

"It's a little late for that." I rolled my neck until it cracked. I wasn't angry, but I was frustrated. "I wanted to destroy the doll that night. She was one of those china dolls with a ceramic face. My uncle spent a great deal of money on her. He was always trying to spoil me; I think because I didn't really like him. I always sensed he was up to no good."

"He didn't, like, do something creepy to you, did he?" Kade's expression bordered on angry.

"No. He was always trying to get in good with my father. My father had more money and he was always begging for funds for whatever get-rich-quick scheme he had going. He wanted me to like him so my father would be more willing to give him money."

"Okay, but that still doesn't explain about the doll."

"I know. The doll story doesn't get better or more exciting. My mother caught me trying to destroy the doll, so she put it on a shelf in my room. She told me that I was to ignore it and not play with it. She thought I was being ridiculous."

"I can see that."

"I couldn't ignore the doll, though," I said. "I thought it was watching me in my sleep. I thought it was going to scratch my eyes out, because that was the story some girl at school told a few weeks before the doll arrived. So I started locking the doll up because I was seriously sleep deprived.

"I put the doll in the hamper ... in closets ... and in the basement. But it kept returning to my room," I continued. "My mother claimed she wasn't moving it, so I became paranoid. One day, I couldn't take it any longer. I waited for my parents to be distracted in the backyard. I carried the doll to the front driveway ... and beat its face in on the pavement."

Kade and Luke snorted in unison.

"I guess you showed her, huh?" Luke chortled. "What did your mother say?"

"I tried to explain, but they hated hearing about my abilities. They said I was acting crazy. It was an early lesson on who I should share certain things with."

"Oh, honey, I'm sorry." Kade pulled me in for a hug. "I thought the story was going to be a lot funnier."

"If it's any consolation, I looked deranged when I was killing the doll. I'm sure you would've laughed if you'd seen me."

"I honestly don't think that's true." Kade kissed my cheek. "Come on. Let's get the rest of the stuff on the list and then get back to the circus grounds. I need to talk to Max, and you've clearly had a tiresome day after the doll talk and everything else."

I rolled my eyes, but walked ahead of him, the excitement over the potential move eradicating the bad memories of the doll pretty quickly. I left Luke and Kade to check out with the groceries, including bagging everything, and surveyed a bulletin board located near the exit. I hadn't seen it when we entered, but now that I could focus on it the photographs sent a chill down my spine.

The bulletin board was completely covered with missing persons' fliers. There had to be at least fifty of them, and they all featured young women. None of them were for children – a mild relief – but some of them were very clearly teenagers and young adults. Nobody on the board looked over the age of twenty-one.

I read through some of the details. One of the girls, Robin McCullough, disappeared six months ago and hadn't been heard from since. Another girl, Katie Pace, had been missing for three weeks. Her parents were offering a large reward for information that led to her discovery ... dead or alive.

"What are you looking at?" Kade stole my breath when he walked up behind me.

"Look. These are all missing girls."

Kade's eyebrows rose as he scanned the fliers. "That's a lot of missing people for one small area."

"Look at them," I prodded. "They're all girls ... and young girls. There are no boys ... or older women ... or even younger children. It's all girls of a certain age."

Kade scratched his cheek. "What do you think that means?"

That was a very good question. "I don't know. It can't be normal, though, right?"

"It does seem odd. But it's not as if this has anything to do with us."

He was right. "I know." I forced a smile. "It simply caught me off guard."

"It's sad, but it's not our problem." Kade extended his hand. "Now, come on. I thought we'd spend the rest of the afternoon looking at trailers on the internet and then I'll hit up Max for the big gift at dinner tonight."

"Are you sure he's eating with us?" Max was hit or miss with dinners.

"I texted him to make sure."

"I'm not sure he'll like that his invitation is part of our manipulation."

Kade merely shrugged. "He'll live."

6
SIX

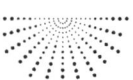

"Okay, apparently I was wrong." Kade stretched his arms over his head as he stared at my laptop screen at one of our communal picnic tables while I shucked corn and watched him with curious eyes.

"Wrong about what?"

"So many things," Kade teased, wrinkling his nose. "For one, I feel wrong about pressuring you to tell the doll story. I can tell you're still agitated by it."

"I'm not agitated." I said the words, but averted my eyes. We'd spent the last two hours looking at trailers online because Kade wanted something to show Max when he arrived for dinner. Because I had a lot of nervous energy, I decided to do something with my hands – hence the corn shucking – while waiting for everyone else to join us for our evening meal. It was only a matter of time before our privacy vanished and we were inundated with curious co-workers.

"You're agitated, and I'm sorry." Kade was sincere. "I'll make it up to you later. In fact, I'll make it so you don't even remember the doll story."

"How do you plan to do that?" It wasn't that I didn't believe him, I was simply legitimately interested because I was convinced I would dream about that doll again – and there were a few key details I left out of the story because I didn't want to be laughed at.

"I have my ways." Kade wiggled his eyebrows, smiled, and then gestured for me to leave the corn and join him. "We only have a few minutes before the rabid crowd joins us, and I know you don't want our plan getting out before I talk to Max."

Kade seemed completely at ease as he patted the bench, so I joined him, leaning close as he pointed at the screen. "I can't find any recreational vehicles that have three bedrooms. I honestly thought it had to be a thing, but apparently I was wrong."

I knew it was hard for him to admit he was wrong – he was a man, after all – but I decided to let a prime teasing opportunity slide. "I wondered if that was the case. I've never seen one like that before. I think three bedrooms would make the trailer too big to haul."

"I think you're right." Kade wasn't the type to panic, or give up on an idea, so he pointed toward the screen. "I like this one."

The recreational vehicle Kade pointed to was big and luxurious. My eyebrows practically flew off my forehead when I saw it. "The Durango Gold? That's like a hundred-thousand-dollar RV."

"So what?" Kade didn't appear bothered by the prospect of requesting the vehicle.

"Do you honestly think Max is going to just go out and buy that for us?"

"Yup. Don't worry about that." He patted my arm. "I want to make sure you like it first. It has some really nice features. Look through the online brochure and tell me what you think … and be honest. If you don't like it, we'll find something we both like."

I was dumbfounded, but did as he asked, widening my eyes as they darted between fancy cabinets to what looked to be a very nice laminate that mimicked rustic hardwood floors. It was absolutely beautiful. It was also wildly expensive.

"Kade … ."

"Don't look at the price tag," Kade ordered. "Look at the RV. Can you see us being happy in there?"

I nodded without hesitation. "The thing is, I can see us being happy no matter what we're in."

Kade's lips curved. "That was a very good answer. I like this one, though. As for offices, I've been giving it some thought. We clearly can't do that with one trailer, but if we turned one of the trailers we already have into an office, we could share that space.

"For example, if you're angry with me and need some air you can go to the office trailer," he continued. "I figured we could share that, too, but make an agreement that if anyone is agitated we'll cede it to the aggrieved party."

"Aggrieved party? Have you been watching *Matlock* when I wasn't looking?"

Kade snickered. "I think it's a good plan," he said. "We can store all our office stuff in the second trailer and spread out and make the new trailer homey."

It was a good plan. In fact, it was a great plan. Still ... . "I don't think Max will agree to do this."

"He will."

"He won't."

"Why not?"

"Because as much as he loves you – and I do believe he loves you – he can't buy you this trailer because everyone else will complain," I pointed out. "I can guarantee Luke will be a whining mess if Max buys this thing for you."

"For us," Kade corrected. "If he buys it, it will be for us. That was the whole point of this little exercise. Remember?"

I remembered every moment of it. "That RV is beautiful," I admitted. "I don't want to get my hopes up for that, though. We can still do the thing with living together in one trailer and turning the other into a mutual office. I think it's safer to focus on that."

"You, my little love bucket, are afraid to dream," Kade chided. "I'm going to prove to you that dreaming is perfectly fine ... and sometimes it even works out." He kissed the tip of my nose. "Now, go back to cooking. I'll handle the trailer."

I stared at him for a long moment. "You're going to handle the trailer ... just like that?"

Kade nodded. "I've got everything under control. Trust me."

I KEPT ONE EYE on Kade later as he schmoozed Max on the far side of the dining area and the other on food preparations as Nixie, Naida and Raven joined me to help with grilling duties.

"Have you ever noticed that it's always us cooking dinner while everyone else is lazy and eats the food but doesn't help prepare it?" Raven complained as she seasoned a steak. "I'm starting to get sick of it."

"Meh. I'm fine with it." Naida shrugged. "You guys wash your hands before handling the food, which means we don't get salmonella on a weekly basis. What's not to like about that?" She inclined her chin in Nellie's direction. The stalwart dwarf leaned back in a lawn chair, his legs spread so the person across from him could get a gander at his goods thanks to the dress. He dug in his nose with his index finger as if he expected to strike gold. "See what I mean?"

"You have a point," Raven conceded, making a face. "I stand corrected."

I smirked as I wrapped potatoes in foil and handed them to Nixie so she could punch holes in them. "What do you guys think about the groups surrounding us?" I asked. I was doing my best to keep from focusing all my attention on Kade – mostly because I didn't want to explain why I was more interested in him than dinner preparations. That would open us to a bevy of questions I wasn't in the mood to answer – and I thought a discussion about the people we would share space with the next few days was in order.

"I think most of them are harmless," Raven replied. "I was hanging around the crafts fair. There are a few weirdos, including a total pervert who asked me if I wanted to reenact the scene with the pottery wheel from *Ghost*."

I pressed my lips together to keep from laughing.

"That's ... I don't even know what to say."

"Yeah, he was fat and sweaty. He seemed to think I'd jump at the chance."

"Well, it takes all kinds." I rolled my neck. "Anyone make it down to the food trucks? We were going to go, but then we got distracted and had to hurry to the store if we expected to get back before dinner."

"We did," Nixie answered. "They have a lot of offerings, and I want to try a few things. We didn't talk to anyone, but I didn't get any bad vibes from them. If there are dangerous paranormals running around over there, they hide it well."

I told them about the fliers I saw on the bulletin board at the grocery store.

"Hmm. That can't be good, right?" Naida wrinkled her forehead.

"I wouldn't think so." Raven looked troubled. "You're sure they were all young women of a certain age?"

I nodded. "If I had to guess, I'd say they were all between the ages of sixteen and twenty-one," I explained. "They didn't all look alike. They weren't all blonds or anything like that. They were a mixture of hair colors, heights and the like."

"What about body types?" Nixie asked.

"What do you mean?"

"Were they all thin and willowy? Were some of them bigger boned? It helps narrow down a type if we know that," Raven answered for the pixie.

"Oh." I searched my memory. "They were all thin. I mean … they weren't waifs or anything, but they were thin. I guess that's another clue there, huh?"

Raven shrugged. "I think it depends on whether or not they were taken for the same reason. Girls that age run away. In fact, that's the predominant age for runaways."

"But all of them in such a small area?"

"I agree that's weird." Raven licked her lips. "You said they'd mostly been going missing for the past six months, right?"

I nodded.

"Then maybe we should find out what happened six months ago," Raven suggested. "That seems to be the obvious next step."

I was surprised by her reaction. "Kade said it wasn't our problem."

"He's right. It's not." Raven met my gaze without blinking. "It could become our problem if girls start going missing at this festival. Even though they've been disappearing for months, they're likely to focus on us ... or the carnies."

"Let's hope they blame it on the carnies," Nellie interjected, proving he'd been listening the entire time as he shifted his head to stare at us. "They're weirder than the clowns, by the way."

I wasn't sure that was possible. "You've been hanging around the carnies? Why?"

Nellie shot me a knowing look. "I love a good freak show."

"Ha, ha." I shifted my shoulders. "Why really?"

"They brought a lot of beer with them, and it's not that fancy-schmancy micro-brew stuff that makes me want to check to see if I've really become a woman when no one was looking."

"Ah, well ... ." I ran my tongue over my teeth. "I don't know what to do. We don't even know that anything is technically going on here. All we have are a bunch of fliers at the grocery store. We don't even have a theory."

"So we'll find a theory." Raven was calm. "All we have to do is keep our eyes and ears open. If something nefarious is happening – and if it's something we're meant to fight – we'll figure that out relatively quickly."

"I don't see what else we can do," I agreed, shifting my gaze to Kade as he moved in my direction. His body language was hard to read. He didn't look jubilant, but he didn't look unhappy either. He didn't stop until he was by my side. He reached for a potato to wrap rather than volunteer information, so I was genuinely irritated within ten seconds of his return. "Well?"

Kade slid me a sidelong look. "Well, what?"

"You know what."

"I'm not sure I do." Kade played coy. "You might need to remind me."

I flicked a gaze to Raven and found her watching us with overt curiosity. It didn't seem like a good idea to interrogate Kade in front of an audience, so even though I was dying to know how Max reacted now wasn't the time. "I guess we can talk later." I couldn't stop myself from being a bit deflated.

"Geez. You're no fun at all." Kade twisted his lips. "He said yes. I told you he would."

I stilled, dumbfounded. "I ... he said yes?" Even though I was hopeful, I didn't think that was a real possibility. "Wow!"

"Wow what?" Raven leaned closer, her gaze keen as she looked between us. "What did Max say yes about?"

"We're moving in together," Kade answered without hesitation, catching me off guard. "Max is buying us a new trailer and we're turning one of our other trailers into a shared office space."

Raven's mouth dropped open. "That doesn't seem fair."

"Well, get used to it." Kade was blasé. "Poet and I are moving in together. It's official."

"You're what?" I recognized the shriek, and I briefly pressed my eyes shut before turning. When I did, I found Luke's accusatory eyes burning a hole into me. All I could do was heave a resigned sigh. "Oh, well, this is the end of the world! I can't believe you did this to me!"

With those words, Luke turned on his heel and stalked away.

I pursed my lips as I lifted my chin and focused on Kade. "Could you have found a better way to announce it?"

Kade cringed. "I maintain this isn't my fault."

"That doesn't matter now. We're both going to have to fix it."

Kade didn't look happy with the prospect. "Yeah. I figured that out myself."

LUKE POUTED THROUGH DINNER, refusing to as much as glance in my direction. Even though I was excited at the prospect of getting a new trailer for Kade and me to share, my enthusiasm was tempered by Luke's rather apoplectic reaction.

Given everything going on around me, I didn't have time to baby

Luke. He would have to come around on his own eventually. Or, and it was far more likely to go down this way, he would wear me down until I exploded and gave him whatever he wanted in an effort to garner forgiveness. I'd have to wait and see which outcome it would be.

After dinner, everyone congregated around the bonfire. I wasn't surprised to see Barney back. He was a talkative sort, and from what I could tell he'd never met a story he wasn't keen to repeat for an audience. Of course, his stories grew bigger and bolder each go around. Thankfully he was a good storyteller, because otherwise he'd be almost unbearable to be around.

"We're going to walk the boardwalk," Melissa announced, catching me off guard when she popped up on my left.

I jolted as I swiveled, pressing my hand to the spot above my heart. "You scared the crap out of me," I complained. "Make a noise next time."

"Sorry. I thought you heard me coming."

"No." I shifted my eyes to Paige, who stood on the other side of the parcel, close to the trees, studying me with unveiled interest. There was definitely something off about the girl, and up close when I moved past her near the crafts fair I very clearly scented witch. Whether she realized she was a witch was another thing entirely. "Where did you say you were going?"

"The boardwalk," Melissa repeated. "Paige has been here a few days longer than us and she knows the cool places to hang out."

"And where is that?"

"It's a boardwalk." Paige's tone, dry and sarcastic, carried from across the way. She'd clearly been listening even though she did her best to pretend otherwise. That was something I would normally find intriguing, but coming from her it was beyond annoying. "There's only so much to do. It's better than hanging around here and listening to my dad tell the same stories for the hundredth time."

"Yeah, that's probably not nearly as much fun for you, huh?" I licked my lips as I raised my head. It was getting foggy out, something that made me uneasy. "Be careful and watch your surroundings while you're out."

"I think I have it under control," Melissa noted. "I am an adult, after all."

She seemed irritated by my mother hen routine. I couldn't blame her. At her age I would've chafed at the suggestion that anyone knew better than me, too. "You are an adult. I still think you should be careful." I gestured toward the fog, which seemed to be thickening. "Don't get lost, and keep aware of your surroundings."

"I will." Melissa offered a half wave as she bounded after Paige. They were excited, their chatter nonstop. Before they stepped out of earshot, I heard one final statement.

"Your mother is a trip," Paige complained. "How old does she think you are?"

Mother? I didn't look old enough to be Melissa's mother. In fact, I was only eight years older than her. I could barely qualify as a big sister. Mother? That was just ... ridiculous.

Ugh. Now I knew why teenagers were often the victim of violent attacks.

SEVEN

Luke was waiting for me in front of my trailer. I knew Kade wouldn't be far behind, but he was in the middle of listening to a hilarious Nellie tale that I'd heard several times, so I told him to follow when he was finished. I hadn't seen Luke in hours and wasn't surprised to find him lurking in the dark and waiting to pounce.

"You are the worst friend ever!"

I kept my face placid as I regarded him. "I'm sorry to hear that. I'm considering putting a complaint box on my front porch, so if you want to write down what you're feeling I'd be more than happy to read it tomorrow morning."

"Oh, don't take that tone with me." Luke wrinkled his nose. "How could you agree to move in with Kade without talking to me about it?"

That was an interesting question, although not for the reasons he envisioned. "It was a spur-of-the-moment thing."

"Which means it's probably a mistake."

"It's not a mistake." I kept my voice low so it wouldn't travel and alert people that we were arguing. Raven was the type to jump on a potential fissure between us and attempt to widen it despite the fact that we were in the middle of a truce as of late. "It's a natural fit."

"How do you figure that?"

"We spend every night together as it is."

"Then you shouldn't need to move in together."

"But we want to." Most days I found Luke amusing. Today I was weary from spending too much time with him. "Why is this such a big deal for you? It's not going to change our relationship at all."

"Our relationship has already been changed," Luke argued. "We don't spend nearly as much time together as we used to."

Was that true? "So you think I've been neglecting you?"

He bobbed his head in affirmation. "Absolutely."

"Okay. I'll carve out more of my day to spend time with you. In fact, I was going to get up early tomorrow morning and head down to the water to meditate, maybe do a little yoga, so I'll wake you up as soon as I'm ready and we'll go together."

Whatever he was expecting, that wasn't it. Luke's mouth dropped open as he considered what I offered. "That's not exactly what I had in mind."

"Oh, no. You think I'm neglecting you, so we're going to fix that." I folded my arms over my chest, keeping my eyes on Luke even as Kade hurried through the growing fog to join me. He pulled up short when he saw who I was with.

"Do you want me to leave you alone?" Kade asked after a beat. He looked worried.

"That won't be necessary. Luke and I were just talking about the fact that he feels neglected. We're going to get up before dawn tomorrow and do beach yoga together. I think it's going to be a terrific way for us to bond."

"That sounds fun." Kade's demeanor was unnaturally bright. "Is everything else okay?"

"I don't know," I replied. "Is it, Luke?"

Luke hated being put on the spot. He especially hated it because I could tell he was in the mood to bully me before Kade showed up. "Not really," he answered after a moment's contemplation. "I don't think that you and Poet moving in together so soon after you started dating is a good idea."

Kade was calm. "And why is that?"

"Because you barely know each other."

"We know each other quite well, and we're learning new things every day," Kade argued. "Just today, for example, I learned she hates dolls and wants to move in with me. I'm thrilled with those discoveries."

While I found Kade's expression charming – I've always been a fan of snark, after all – Luke clearly didn't agree.

"Listen, you muscled pain in the ass, she was my friend first," Luke barked, narrowing his eyes to dangerous slits. "You can't just steal her."

Finally, tempers were on full display and neither man in my life was pulling any punches.

"I am not stealing her from you." Kade's voice was low and full of warning. "It's not because you hate the idea of it happening, though. It's because of her. She loves you and would be miserable without you."

"That doesn't mean you're not trying to steal her," Luke sniffed.

"That's exactly what it means," Kade shot back. "I don't want her unhappy. On the contrary, I want her happy more than anything else. You're necessary to making that happen, so I have no intention of boxing you out.

"On the other hand, I also don't intend to let you run roughshod over her," he continued, his eyes flashing. "You and I are going to have to learn to play nice with one another for her. I'm willing to try. That means the ball is in your court."

"Oh, well, that's just typical." Luke was haughty as he rolled his eyes to the sky. "I don't understand why you have to move in together."

"Because we want to, and it's a growing exercise for us," Kade replied. "We want to live together. It's not the end of the world. I think it' will be good for everyone involved ... including you."

Luke didn't look convinced. "What happens if you break up? You've only been together a few months. It could happen. Once you're living together, that's going to make a breakup that much more difficult."

"You're not hoping for a breakup, right?" I asked, my stomach twisting.

Luke made an exaggerated face. "Of course not. I want you to be happy. He – however annoying – seems to make you happy. I'm the pragmatist in this threesome, so I feel as if I'm the one who has to be logical."

"Uh-huh." Wow. If he thought he was the pragmatist in our little group, he was even more deluded than I originally thought.

"We're not going to break up," Kade argued, holding up his hand to cut off Luke before he got up a full head of steam and mounted a bitter comeback. "We're not," he repeated. "If that should happen, we'll deal with it. It's not that hard to separate into two trailers again. We're technically going to have two trailers now – one for our living quarters and one for an office – so we'll be able to make it work."

Luke made protesting sounds as he clucked his tongue. "But ... it's too soon."

"Well, that's our concern," Kade said. "We don't believe that. If you're right and we're wrong, though, we'll both offer up apologies after the fact."

Wait ... what? "I'm not apologizing to him. He's being mean to me."

Kade ignored my petulant tone. "It's going to be okay, Luke. I promise." He rested his hand on Luke's shoulder. "We'll make this work for everyone."

Although mildly placated, Luke remained somber. "I don't want to get up and do waterside yoga tomorrow morning. Don't let her make me."

Kade's smile was indulgent. "I'll take care of it. We'll see you at breakfast."

Luke mustered a smile, although it wasn't one of his full-wattage wonders. "I really do love and want the best for her."

"I know you do. That's why I haven't killed you." Kade pressed his hand to the small of my back to prod me up the trailer steps. "We'll all have breakfast in the morning. We'll talk further about things then."

"Whatever." Luke scuffed his feet against the ground as he slumped his way back to the bonfire.

Kade waited until he was sure Luke was out of earshot to speak again. "Were you really going to do pre-dawn yoga by the water?"

I made a derisive sound in the back of my throat. "Of course not. I just wanted to shut him up."

"That's what I thought."

I HAD TERRIBLE NIGHTMARES.

I should have expected them. All the talk of dolls – that one doll in particular – was bound to leak into my subconscious. The dream I had was terrifying even for me, though, and I've seen some downright frightening things.

I was isolated in the dream, stranded on a foggy expanse. The only light came from the moon, allowing me to see the drifting fog but anything more than ten feet out was a murky mess. That didn't stop me from seeing *them*. I felt them moving in my direction even before I saw them ... or heard them.

Then they opened their eyes in unison, fake doll eyes glowing red as I turned in a circle to look for escape. They didn't speak as their feet shuffled across the ground. They were bigger than normal dolls – which made them all the more frightening, of course – and when I steeled myself to stare the nearest one in its evil blinking eyes, the laughing started.

I remembered the sound from when I was a kid. I was older now, so it shouldn't have been terrifying, but my heart shuddered all the same. At first it was only one doll, but then the rest joined in. Suddenly it was a hundred dolls, which meant there were a lot more ceramic faces waiting for me in the darkness.

They laughed ... and laughed ... and laughed.

When I couldn't take it any longer, I woke screaming.

"Poet!" Kade thrashed to a sitting position next to me, his hands clenched into fists and his eyes wide with terror as he searched the room for an enemy to fight.

I gasped for breath, working overtime to calm myself as the dream faded away thanks to the early morning sunlight filtering through the shades. My heart pounded so hard I thought I might pass out, but the minute Kade pressed his hand against my back the chill began fading ... as did the fear.

"Honey, what was that?" Kade slipped a strong arm behind my back, his hand shaking.

"I'm sorry." I gritted out the words. "I just ... I'm sorry."

"That's not why I asked. I don't need an apology." Kade's eyes filled with concern as he leaned over my shoulder. "What was that?"

"Um ... a nightmare. It was just a nightmare."

"I figured that out myself. You've had nightmares before – and some pretty vivid ones at that – but I don't ever remember you screaming like that. Do you want to tell me what it was about?"

I remembered the dolls in the dream and vehemently shook my head. "Not really."

"I don't think I can just let that be, Poet. I mean ... you weren't dreaming about moving in with me, were you?"

It took me a moment to realize what he was referencing, and when I did, couldn't stop myself from letting go a hoarse chuckle. "No, I definitely wasn't dreaming about you."

"Then what?"

"I ... it's not important."

"I don't believe that."

He wasn't going to stop pushing until he got a satisfactory answer. Still, I didn't want to admit to the dream. It made me feel weak for some reason, the same way I did as a kid when the first doll took over my life for a brief time.

"It was dark. I couldn't see beyond the fog. I was surrounded by dolls. That's it."

"Dolls?" Kade's eyes filled with sympathy. "I'm sorry. This happened because I pressed you yesterday on the doll story. This is my fault."

"It's not your fault, and I would like to point out that they weren't normal dolls," I said. "They were as big as us, there were hundreds of them, they had glowing red eyes and they wouldn't stop laughing at me."

Kade stilled. "They laughed at you? Like the doll from when you were a kid?"

I scowled. "I know what you're getting at, but it's not a big deal. I didn't mean to frighten you."

"We're a team. I'm supposed to be here if you have a bad dream." Kade stroked my mussed hair. "I'm sorry about the doll dream. I do feel it's partially my fault."

I exhaled a shaky breath and forced a smile. "It's fine. I'm fine. Let's forget about it and shower, huh? I'm starving."

Kade didn't look convinced, but he let it slide. "Sounds like a plan."

I WAS BACK TO MY normal self when I carried a container of eggs to the kitchen area an hour later. Kade followed with bacon, bread and a bag of pre-cut hash browns. I could feel his eyes burning holes into my back as we walked, but he wisely kept from pressing me on the dream.

He was either biding his time or he'd honestly opted to let it go. I was hopeful it was the latter.

"There you are." Luke was impatient when we arrived. "I thought you were getting up for sunrise yoga? I'm starving, by the way. Make my eggs scrambled."

Kade frowned as he rested the food items he carried on the picnic table. "I believe you meant 'Poet, will you please cook me breakfast.' Because, if you didn't, I will totally thump you in about five seconds flat."

"Listen, Prince Testosterone, Poet likes cooking me breakfast," Luke argued. "She doesn't feel complete unless she does it."

That was a gross exaggeration, but I was too irritated to call him on it. "Scrambled eggs. I've got it."

Kade shot me a look before returning his focus to Luke. I realized what he was going to do a split second before he did it, but it was too late to stop him.

"She had a bad dream and woke up screaming, Luke," Kade barked. "Don't treat her like a servant."

Luke immediately sobered. "You had a bad dream?"

Great. By the time these two were done the entire circus would know I hated dolls ... and why. "It was nothing."

"It was something," Kade argued. "She scared the crap out of me. I thought we had an ax murderer in our trailer or something."

"I've always wanted to be an ax murderer," Nellie announced, joining us under the tarp we set up to keep the kitchen area dry during rain. "I figure I would make a good one."

"You would definitely make a unique one," Kade said dryly. "I don't know many ax murderers who attack in evening gowns."

"Norman Bates wore dresses while attacking with a knife," Nellie pointed out. "It's not that far off."

"No, but the ax is a colorful detail that will add to your mystique," Kade drawled before turning his attention back to Luke. "Be nice to Poet. She had a rough night."

Oh, geez. "My night was fine. It was just a dream. I think you're more upset about it than I am."

"That might be," Kade conceded. "You didn't hear your screams from my point of view, though. I swear my blood turned to ice. That means Luke had better be nice to you because I'm feeling a bit helpless. I'm totally fine with smacking the crap out of him to feel better."

Yup. Prince Testosterone sounded just about right. "Do whatever you want. I'm staying out of it. In fact ... ." Whatever I was about to say died on my lips when I caught sight of a harried-looking woman picking her way through the trailer aisle and heading in our direction.

"What were you saying?" Kade asked, shifting so he could follow my gaze. "Who is that? Do you recognize her?"

I shook my head. The woman was largely nondescript, short dirty blond hair and sad-looking eyes offsetting a rather plain face. She headed directly toward us, exuding purpose and worry with each step. I opened my mouth to greet her, briefly wondering if she thought the circus was already open and expected to find the big show ready to go down under the main tent, but something about the way she carried herself had me changing course before any words escaped.

"Can we help you?" Kade asked, stepping forward.

I remained where I was, watching with a mixture of worry and curiosity.

"I hope so." The woman didn't bother faking a smile. "My daughter went missing last night and I'm hoping very much that you'll be able to help me find her."

And just like that, my day took a turn.

8
EIGHT

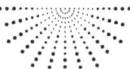

Pamela Dobbins was on the edge. She was ragged, exhausted and ready to burst into tears. I read it all, including her name, within a split-second of her arrival because it lingered on the surface. The moment she got close enough to touch, her emotions whipped through me, barreling into my heart and almost knocking me over. Kade was so distracted by the distraught woman he didn't notice my reaction, instead hurrying to her side so he could lead her to the picnic table.

"Please, sit down." Kade is gallant under every circumstance. He's very rarely rude or crass (unless Luke eggs him on and they've been drinking). I often wonder if that's a product of being raised by a single mother. It's a nice trait, whatever the cause.

"Here's some coffee," Luke offered, sliding a mug in front of Pamela. His face was lined with concern as he exchanged a quick glance with me.

We were all thinking the same thing: Would we be blamed for the missing girl? It was a callous first conclusion, but we'd been blamed for crimes more times than I could count. Still, there was something about Pamela's demeanor that shook me to my very core.

"I'm sorry for troubling you." Pamela twisted her fingers as she tried to get comfortable at the table. She introduced herself on a shaky breath. I already knew who she was, but the others didn't. It was good to have a bit of normality, even if it were sandwiched between bouts of panic.

Naida appeared out of nowhere, her eyes on Pamela as she took the spatula from me. As a pixie, Naida was in tune with people's emotions. Whatever she sensed when walking the row of trailers, she instinctively understood that Pamela wasn't to be trifled with.

"I'll finish breakfast." Naida's voice was low. "Nixie is walking the boardwalk to make sure there are no surprises. Once that's done, we should probably talk about this."

Naida was rarely serious. In fact, when she was close to water she was generally in a good mood and downright giddy for days. Still, her agitation was evident now, and that made me edgier.

"Why is Nixie walking the boardwalk?" I asked.

"In case there's a body to be discovered." Naida was matter-of-fact. "We don't want a mother to discover it, do we?"

That was undoubtedly true. "Good thinking." I wiped my hands on a towel before moving to the picnic table. What Naida left unsaid while we talked near the grill was that the best way to figure out what happened to Pamela's daughter was for me to read her. Yeah, that whole "circus fortune teller" shtick I run on show days isn't merely an act. I can read people ... and it isn't always a welcome gift.

Kade spared me a glance as I sat on the bench next to him. Most of his attention went to Pamela, but he managed a tight-lipped smile for my benefit. I had no idea what he was thinking.

"Tell us what happened, Ms. Dobbins," Kade prodded. "We can't help if we don't know what we're supposed to be looking for."

"It's my daughter, Katie," Pamela said. "She was down here hanging out with her friends last night and ... well ... she didn't come home."

"How old is she?" I asked.

"Seventeen. She's a good girl. She never misses curfew, and she's always on time. I didn't wait up for her last night. She's older now, so I don't do that like I used to. I thought for sure she was home, but when

I went to check her room … ." Pamela broke off, chewing on her bottom lip.

"She wasn't there," I finished, cocking my head to the side. "Did you call her friends?"

"Not yet. It's early. I didn't want to wake the other parents. I thought I was probably overreacting, so I decided to come down here and check. But she's not here."

Pamela looked lost … and my heart went out to her. "Well, we'll help you look." I reached across the table and grabbed her hand. To an outside observer, it would look as if I were comforting a woman upset about her missing daughter. Those in the know would realize I was reading her.

I narrowed my eyes as I tried to absorb the series of images zooming through my head. They were scattered and non-linear, but I saw enough to cause my blood to run cold as I stood on shaky feet. "My friends here will help you contact Katie's friends. You need to do that right away … and then we'll contact the police."

I sounded wooden, robotic even. That was all the energy I could muster.

"Where are you going?" Kade asked, pinning me with a worried look.

"To wake some of our co-workers. We need to search the area."

"Uh-huh." Kade didn't look convinced, but he offered a solid smile for Pamela. "Luke will be right here while you make calls. I'll only be gone a minute. Then we'll continue looking."

Kade followed me out of earshot as I headed toward the far end of trailer row. That's where Melissa – who had some of the same abilities I did, although not quite as honed – put her head on a pillow every night. I needed reinforcements for what I had planned, and Melissa and Raven were my first choices.

"What aren't you saying?" Kade challenged, grabbing my arm and spinning me so I faced him before I could put too much distance between us.

"What do you mean?"

"You know exactly what I mean." Kade clearly wasn't happy with my diversionary tactic. "You saw something when you touched her hand. What was it?"

Now that right there was a loaded question. "I saw several things."

"Is her daughter dead?"

I opened my mouth to answer but ultimately shook my head, holding my hands palms up as I shrugged. "I'm not sure. What I saw didn't answer that question."

"So why didn't you go deeper?" Kade asked. "I know you can do that if you put a little effort into it."

Admitting that I was afraid to go deeper because the vision flashes were altogether terrifying wasn't going to help my street cred, but lying wasn't an option. "I saw ... a dark room ... and blood ... and I heard crying ... and screaming ... and laughing."

Kade arched an eyebrow. "Laughing?"

I nodded as I licked my lips. "I heard laughing like the laughing I heard in my dream."

Kade was understandably confused. "So ... what? Do you think it's dolls or something?"

That was too simplistic. "I think whatever we're dealing with is evil. I don't know what else to tell you."

"So where are you going?"

"To get Melissa and Raven. I'll need help if we're going to magically search the area for Katie."

"Do you think she's dead?"

There was that question again. "I don't know. I don't think she's safe. I don't think Pamela will find her with a friend. I don't think a sheepish apology for forgetting to come home – or at least call – will fix this."

"What do you think will fix this?"

"Maybe nothing. I know it'll take more than me to get answers. You need to let me do this. I need a power boost to figure things out."

Kade released my arm and nodded. "Okay. If you need me, you know where to find me."

I gave him a quick kiss. "Take care of Pamela. I think things are going to get worse for her before they get better ... if they ever get better."

I RAPPED ON MELISSA'S trailer door before turning the handle and pushing inside. It didn't occur to me that I should wait for Melissa to invite me in – that's not really how we do things at Mystic Caravan, after all – but one look at Melissa told me I should've rethought my decision.

The girl – it was hard to think of her as anything but a girl even though she was technically an adult – sat on the couch, head in her hands. The look she shot me was pure venom as I pulled up short.

"Do you knock?" Melissa rasped.

"I did knock." That was true. I simply didn't wait for an answer. "Are you sick?" I took a concerned step forward until the expression on Melissa's face told me it would be a mistake to crowd her.

"I'm not sick," Melissa gritted out. "I'm ... having a hard time waking up this morning."

I took a moment to give her a longer look – taking in her disheveled hair, ashen features, the same clothes she wore the night before and a distinctive odor emanating from the couch – and pursed my lips as I debated how to handle the situation.

"You're hungover," I said after a beat.

"So?" Melissa's frustration was evident. "Why does that matter?"

"You're not old enough to drink." The answer was out of my mouth before I thought better about uttering it. I wasn't Melissa's mother. And, as for underage drinking, I'd done my fair share of it. I wouldn't have reacted well to anyone bringing that up to me – I was taking care of myself, after all – and I expected Melissa to balk. I wasn't disappointed.

"Like that's important." Melissa rolled her eyes. "I met some of Paige's friends down by the waterfront last night. They had a keg. It's not a big deal."

One look at Melissa's wan features told me it most definitely was a big deal. "Well, we have a situation. You should probably get some coffee in you and then meet me by the kitchen area so we can come up with a plan of action."

Melissa knit her eyebrows. "What kind of situation?"

"A missing girl. Her mother stopped to ask if we'd seen her. We think there's a very real possibility she was either taken or found trouble on her own."

"So what?" Melissa made an annoyed face. "People go missing all of the time."

Her vitriol caught me off guard. "That doesn't mean we shouldn't look ... or try to help."

"And what if we can't help?"

I shrugged. "We can only do what we can do. Right now that means helping Pamela Dobbins."

"Well, I didn't sign up for the circus so I could help the PTA keep tabs on their kids," Melissa drawled, leaning back so her head rested against the couch as she rubbed her forehead. "I think I'll pass."

I was floored. "You'll pass?"

Melissa nodded. "I'm not really into looking for a kid who probably took off for a day or two to have a good time."

"And what if she didn't take off voluntarily?"

Melissa shrugged. "Bummer for her, I guess."

"Yeah, bummer." My anger flared, but I kept it to myself. Melissa's attitude needed an adjustment, but I didn't have time for it. "I have to get Raven."

"Yeah, you should probably do that." Melissa refused to look at me. "Close the door on your way out. Oh, and next time, wait until I invite you in, please. I'm entitled to a little privacy."

I stared at her for a long moment. "Right. I'll try to remember that."

I WAS FUMING WHEN I descended the steps and hit the pathway in front of Melissa's trailer, scuffing my feet against the packed earth as I tried to rein in my annoyance.

I remembered well what it was like to be Melissa's age. I was a teenager when Max plucked me from the streets of Detroit – after I attempted to pick his pocket and read his mind, of course – and I remembered having attitude to spare. I also remembered being grateful for what he did for me and showing him a modicum of respect.

I stepped in to help Melissa because she was a gifted girl languishing away in middle America. She had no one who really cared and no prospects. I wanted to help her.

Given the attitude I just bore witness to, I couldn't help but wonder why I did that in the first place. She clearly wasn't thankful for the chance I'd given her ... and I kind of wanted to smack her around a bit for the attitude.

I was about to settle into a self-righteous internal monologue when something at the back of trailer row caught my attention. I slipped between Melissa and Luke's trailers so I could get a better look, dropping to my knees and peering close at the footprints.

I'd almost missed them. I was so caught up in Melissa angst I almost didn't see the prints. I wasn't a tracker by any stretch of the imagination, but the indentations clearly belonged to heeled shoes. In fact, if I had to guess, I believed they signified a chunky heel and flat sole. Most men didn't wear shoes like that, so it had to be a woman.

"Hmm."

I studied the shoeprints a bit longer, shifting my neck and scanning the trail. It followed a parallel track, as if someone had been walking behind the trailers the previous evening. The tracks didn't go all the way up to the trailers, stopping a good ten feet short. In fact ... . I cocked my head to the side and pictured the dreamcatcher lines in my head, my stomach twisting when I realized my initial reaction was right.

The footprints indicated a straight path behind the trailers, but whoever it was never crossed the dreamcatcher line. That couldn't be a coincidence, right?

That was the only thought plaguing me when I straightened and returned to my trek. I figured I would have Raven look at the tracks before we started looking for Katie Dobbins. The odds of the tracks and the missing girl being tied together were slim, but I couldn't completely rule it out.

I climbed the steps to Raven's trailer and knocked with brisk efficiency. I hadn't spent much time with Raven in her trailer – that was a personal choice, for the record – but I knew Kade had wasted an hour or two (or ten) inside when we were trying to figure things out. The thought still stuck in my craw.

I heard a muffled sound from inside and assumed it was Raven inviting me in. I pushed open the door, a friendly smile on my face, and pulled up short when I realized that whatever Raven said wasn't an invitation to enter. In fact, it very well may have been an admonishment to leave.

"What are you doing?" Raven screeched, crossing her arms over her chest to cover her nudity.

"Um ... ." My mind went blank.

"Poet!" Raven was furious. I couldn't blame her. Yet I couldn't make myself look away from the scene in front of me.

Percival Prentiss, Raven's new boyfriend and our one and only fake-accent clown, stood dressed in an odd sort of outfit. It was almost impossible to describe – there was a colorful ruffle, a big red nose, oversized shoes ... his fish belly-white ass cheeks protruding from leather chaps that reminded me of a western gone wrong – and my mind had trouble processing what I was seeing.

"Poet! Get out of here," Raven barked.

That's exactly what I wanted to do, but I couldn't find my voice ... or the ability to control my muscles. Instead, as if trapped in a hazy dream, I slowly turned to the door at the sound of footsteps. Nellie, his favorite ax in his hand, poked his head through the door, glancing from face to face.

"What needs killing?"

I didn't know how to respond, so I merely pointed at Percival's chaps. "I can see his butt."

"I can see it, too." Nellie smirked at my reaction, cocking an eyebrow when Raven scorched him with a "you're going to die" look. "This looks like a fun trailer. What are we doing this morning, kids?"

"You're getting out," Raven shot back. "This is a private moment."

"Then why did you invite Poet?" Nellie asked pragmatically.

"I didn't invite her. She let herself in."

"I thought she invited me in." I felt mildly sick to my stomach ... and completely disconnected from my body. "I think I need to sit down."

"Not in here," Raven snapped. "You need to take your ridiculously judgmental behind out of here. I'm not joking. I don't have to put up with this."

"Of course not." I licked my lips. "This is just not my morning."

As if on cue, Kade appeared in the open doorway and poked his head inside. "I heard someone scream. Is everything okay?"

"Son of a ... !" Raven narrowed her eyes until they were nothing more than glittering slits. "I'll make you pay for this."

I had no doubt that was true.

9
NINE

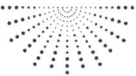

"I'm going to kill you if you don't get out of here, Nellie!"

Kade and I stood in front of Raven's trailer, listening to her shrieking at Nellie – who refused to leave – and steadfastly avoiding making eye contact.

"So, that was ... interesting," Kade said after a few moments of silence.

"It was," I agreed. "It was so interesting I was rendered deaf and dumb for a bit."

"Well, I don't blame you." Kade scratched the back of his neck. "I didn't even know they made chaps with clowns in mind. What do you think those hanging pompoms were supposed to signify?"

"I don't want to know."

"Yeah, me either." Kade scuffed the toe of his boot against the dirt. "You didn't see them like ... doing it ... did you?"

I scowled as I forced my eyes to his. "No. They were playing some sort of game."

"And the clown outfit was part of the game?"

"How am I supposed to know?" I barked. "You're going to give me nightmares if you don't stop."

Kade held up his hands in mock surrender. "Sorry. The last thing I want to do is give you nightmares."

I knew that was true, and yet … . "Why do you think she was holding the riding crop?"

"I'm trying to forget that part myself." Kade took me by surprise when he pulled me close and gave me a hug. "That kind of puts the doll nightmare you had last night in perspective, huh? Things could be so much worse."

"Yeah, I'm not sure how much worse they could be." I rested my cheek against his chest. "I need to flush out my eyes with acid or something. Maybe that will erase what I saw."

"It's something to consider." Kade swayed, shifting his movement only when Nellie trudged down the metal steps. "I'm glad to see you're still alive. I thought there was a real possibility she'd kill you if you didn't leave within the next ten seconds."

Nellie let loose a derisive snort. "I'm not afraid of her. She's all talk."

I knew that wasn't true. "Did you ask her what the riding crop was for?"

Nellie nodded. "She likes to ride her clowns hard and put them away … um … wet."

That was way too much information. "Okay, well … I need to focus on something other than what I just saw. Apparently I'm meant to work alone this morning because I'm zero for two in my recruitment efforts."

Kade turned serious. "What do you mean?"

"Melissa has a hangover and Raven is … otherwise engaged."

"Melissa has a hangover?" Kade made a face. "She's not old enough to drink."

Something about his demeanor made me feel better about my earlier reaction. I patted his arm. "Were you twenty-one the first time you got drunk?"

"I was fifty-six," Nellie offered. "Of course, people age differently where I come from."

Kade was intrigued. "How old are you now?"

Nellie winked. "Wouldn't you like to know?"

"I believe that's why I asked."

Nellie shrugged. "Let's just say I'm old enough to know Raven isn't a threat to me and leave it at that." He flicked his eyes to me. "Have you recovered from seeing Percival's bare butt?"

"I guess." I wasn't sure I would ever truly recover. "I don't know a lot about butts, but his seemed really white, right?"

Nellie chuckled. "I think he used his clown makeup on his lower extremities to … enhance something or other. That caught me off guard, so I had to look closer. By the way, they didn't like that."

"I don't imagine so." Kade rolled his neck. "But back to Melissa. How do you know she was hungover?"

"Because she looked like death, smelled like stale beer and basically admitted it to me," I replied without hesitation. "She seemed agitated that I'd dare question her actions."

"She's got a lot of nerve," Kade muttered. "You're the only reason she's here."

"And I remember what it was like to be that age. You think you know everything and it's not until later that you realize you knew next to nothing. Plus, well, if it's her first hangover she's bound to have a raging headache. I know from personal experience that it's easy to be bitchy when you have a headache."

"I know that from personal experience, too." Kade poked my stomach. "I'm talking about you, not me, by the way. I'm always a delight."

"Ha, ha." I pressed the heel of my hand to my forehead. "Where is Pamela?"

"Luke is helping her call Katie's friends. They were halfway through the list when I left. I'm assuming you don't think they're going to get anywhere with that."

"No, I don't," I confirmed. "I don't know where she is, but I don't think she's with friends."

"Do you think she's dead?" Nellie turned somber. He liked to have a good time, but he also enjoyed hunting for beasts that needed slaying. "I heard something about that wall of missing girls you found. Do you think this Katie girl is part of that?"

I held my hands palms up and shrugged. "I don't know. The things I saw in Pamela's head ... well, they were jumbled. I couldn't make much sense out of it."

"Plus, I wouldn't be surprised if it melded with the nightmare you had last night," Kade added. "When you told me about the images you saw – and the laughing – the first thing I thought was that you were mixing the two."

I pursed my lips as I stared. "I don't often mix things up." I knew I shouldn't be agitated, but I couldn't stop myself. "I can separate the real world from a dream."

"Uh-oh." Nellie wrinkled his nose. "I sense trouble in happy land. Now isn't the time for you two turn on each other."

Kade was affronted. "What do you mean?"

"You've upset her," Nellie pointed out. "You insinuated she didn't know what she was doing."

"I did nothing of the sort," Kade protested. "I just ... don't even think about making this a thing." He extended a warning finger. "That's not what I was doing and you know it. You're just trying to stir up trouble."

"Ah, well, you caught me." Nellie's eyes twinkled. "I do like being the resident pot stirrer. Still, I'm not sure what the dream had to do with the vision."

"It didn't have anything to do with the vision," I said. "The vision was disjointed, as if something ... magical ... was trying to keep me out."

Nellie used the ax to balance his weight and leaned forward. "Do you think something magical took these girls?"

"I think it's a distinct possibility."

"Okay, then how do we figure out what sort of magical being we're dealing with?"

I exhaled heavily, searching my brain. "I have no idea. I was going to take Raven and Melissa with me to walk the boardwalk, perhaps create a net to search for magical remnants, but that doesn't look as if it's going to be a possibility."

"Melissa is hungover," Kade argued. "She's not dead. Why can't she help?"

"Apparently she doesn't want to."

"That doesn't make any sense."

"That's what I said, but I can't force her," I supplied. "I didn't give it much thought right after it happened because I got distracted by footprints behind the trailers. I was going to show them to Raven, but I'm guessing she has no intention of talking to me today."

"I think that's a fair bet." Nellie squared his shoulders. "Show me the tracks. Maybe I'll see something you didn't. I'm not magical, but I understand how tracks work."

"Okay, but I think the most interesting thing about the tracks is that they run parallel to the trailers but are on the other side of the dreamcatcher."

Kade's arm shot out and grabbed my wrist before I could move more than a few inches. "Does that mean whatever was out there recognized the dreamcatcher?"

"I don't know. It seems curious, though, doesn't it?"

"Yeah, I'm definitely not liking it."

Kade and Nellie followed me to the spot where I'd identified the footprints. Unfortunately, they seemed to have disappeared.

"I don't understand." I was flustered as I walked up and down the small area. "They were right here." I pointed for emphasis.

"They don't appear to be here now," Kade said. "Are you sure you really saw them? I mean … you were upset over what Melissa said. Maybe you imagined them or something?"

"Yes, because that sounds completely plausible," I drawled, rolling my eyes. "Why would I possibly imagine footsteps behind the trailers? What possible reason would I have to do that?"

"I don't know." Kade's temper flared thanks to my tone. "I don't think you need to take this out on me, though."

"I'm not taking it out on you."

"That's not how it sounds."

I crossed my arms over my chest and focused on Nellie. "Am I taking this out on him?"

"I stopped listening ten minutes ago," Nellie admitted, his eyes trained on the ground as he moved back and forth over the area where I was certain the footprints existed only twenty minutes earlier. "Do you smell that?"

The question caught me off guard. "Smell what?"

"I ... don't ... know." Nellie lifted his nose and inhaled. "It almost smells like ... licorice or something."

"Like anise or licorice?" I pressed.

Nellie shrugged. "Does it matter?"

"Probably not, but I'd still like to know."

"I guess anise would be the correct term," Nellie said after a beat. "That's black licorice, right?"

I nodded.

"Then definitely anise."

"So what does that mean?" Kade asked, holding my gaze as he licked his lips. "What are we dealing with?"

I hated the way he asked the question. I hated even more that I didn't know how to answer. "I have no idea. This whole thing is weird, and there's definitely something going on."

"Then we'll find out together," Kade said. "We're still a team, right?"

The leading edge of my anger softened. "Yeah."

"Then we'll work together to find the answer."

My smile was rueful. "Sorry I bit your head off."

"Sorry I questioned your memories."

Nellie let his gaze bounce between us. "You guys are so cute I totally want to throw up all over you. There is such a thing as a sweetness limit ... and I think you've hit it."

I wasn't bothered by the statement. "You'll live."

"Yeah, yeah."

SETUP OPERATIONS WERE ONGOING, so I left Kade to discuss security procedure with his men and drafted Luke to search the boardwalk with me. He wasn't exactly happy about it, but when he realized I was distracted and he could complain to his heart's content, he embraced the shift in plans rather quickly.

"I can't believe you saw Percival's naked rear end," he said after we'd been walking for what felt like forever. In real time it had been only an hour, but it felt infinitely longer. "Did it look different?"

The question threw me for a loop. "Look different how?"

"Like ... did it look British?"

"Percival isn't really British," I reminded him. "He's faking being British, although we're not supposed to bring it up. As for the question, what does a British butt look like?"

Luke shrugged, noncommittal. "I don't know. I've never seen one. I was merely curious."

"It looked like a normal butt ... other than the clown makeup, of course."

Luke grabbed my arm before I could continue walking. "He had clown makeup on his butt? Oh, that's so weird! I'm never going to let him live this down!"

I pictured the riding crop Raven carried and silently congratulated myself for leaving that part out of the story when retelling it for Luke's amusement. "So, how did things go with Pamela once I left?"

If Luke was bothered that I purposely changed the subject, he didn't show it. "Not well. She called all of her daughter's friends. None of them had any idea where Katie ended up after the beach party."

I shifted my eyes to the sandy expanse on our right. We'd stuck to the boardwalk's designated path for most of the walk, but the beach was close enough that we could search it, too. "Perhaps we should head out there."

Luke followed my gaze. "If you think that's necessary, I'm willing to do it, but I want to know what you're thinking first."

"I'm not sure what I'm thinking," I admitted. "The flashes, the things I saw, they're hard to put into words."

"But you heard the laughing, right? It was the same laughing you heard in your dream. That has to mean something."

"How do you know about the laughing?" I was honestly curious. "I don't remember going into great detail about the laughing."

"Kade told me while we were waiting for Pamela to talk to the police," Luke replied. "He seemed worried."

"I didn't know you guys were on speaking terms."

"It comes and goes." Luke was blasé. "The thing is, he's right about both of us loving you. We like to irritate each other – in fact, we turn it into a game at times – but we both want you to be happy. We're willing to work together for that."

"That was almost touching. If I didn't know you better, I'd think you meant it."

"I do mean it. Just because I want to beat him up most of the time, that doesn't mean I don't want you to be happy. Those things aren't mutually exclusive."

"Fair enough." He had a point. "As for the dream ... I'm not sure what to make of it. Kade blames himself because he pressed me on the doll story, but I'm not sure that was it. Er, well, I'm not sure that was completely it."

"And you didn't even tell him the full doll story," Luke drawled.

I stiffened, slowly turning my eyes to Luke. "What do you mean?"

"Oh, don't do that," Luke chided as he wagged a finger. "I know that's not the entire doll story."

Crap on toast. "I thought you didn't remember the story."

"I don't. I only remember bits and pieces of it. But I know that the very abbreviated version you whipped out last night isn't everything."

"If you don't remember, how can you possibly know that?"

"Because I remember laughing really hard when you were telling that story, and what you told Kade last night wasn't funny," Luke replied. "I can't remember exactly what happened, but I know there's more to that story."

"Not much."

"But there's more."

I thought back to the day I destroyed the doll. "There was more. You're never going to hear it again, so it's probably best if you let it go."

"Yeah, that sounds nothing like me." Luke followed me toward the beach. We'd been up and down the boardwalk four times. Not once did I sense a displaced spirit or hidden human remains. The search was obviously starting to wear on Luke because he groaned in frustration whenever I stopped to extend my senses. "Do you think she's out here?"

"I don't know." I kicked at the sand before turning my attention to the water. "The truth is, she could be out there. The odds of finding her if she went into the water aren't great."

"This isn't a normal water pattern," Luke reminded me. "I'm not sure that's true. Still, if you want someone to search the water, Naida is the obvious choice. She was out here skinny-dipping all last night."

I definitely didn't need to know that. "Tapping Naida is a good idea. Of course, if someone died and was dumped in the water last night, we would probably already know because Naida would've detected it."

"Just out of curiosity, what makes you think Katie is dead? She could've taken off on her own. That's not unheard of with teenagers."

"I didn't say I thought she was dead."

"Then what did you say?"

"That something was wrong with the scenario ... and I stand by that."

"Okay, so what do we do next?" Luke asked. "She's not here. If she was taken, she was moved to another location. How do you suggest we find her?"

"I have no idea."

"What do you know?"

"Absolutely nothing."

"Oh, well, at least you seem on top of things." Luke made a face. "Do you want to get some ice cream? I'm hungry and I think I might pass out if my blood sugar gets any lower."

I'd heard worse offers. "Okay, but you can't question me about Percival's naked butt again. I'm declaring a moratorium on that conversation."

"Oh, I'm definitely going to talk about Percival's butt. Get used to that."

10

TEN

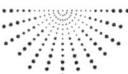

Melissa sat with the rest of the group around the picnic tables when we returned. She looked marginally better, although her color remained off and she seemed a bit surly.

"Must you be so loud?" she challenged Nellie, who appeared to be in the middle of a re-enactment of the scene from this morning.

Nellie wasn't the type to bow to anyone, especially a young woman who created her own ailment. "Yes."

"Well, I don't have to listen to it."

"You certainly don't," Nellie agreed, returning his attention to Seth and Dolph. Seth worked as muscle when it came to setting up and breaking down camp. He also served as our resident tiger because he was a shifter. Dolph was our strong man, and even though he towered over Nellie by a good two feet he often deferred to the gregarious dwarf. "Now, where was I?"

"The makeup on his behind," Seth answered automatically. "I'm still unclear on that, by the way. Did he draw a face or was it simply white?"

"I wish he'd drawn a face," Nellie replied. "That would have made things so much more entertaining."

"I heard that," Raven snapped, moving toward the kitchen. She didn't look happy – although I couldn't blame her – and I wondered if this was the first time she showed her face since the incident in her trailer. "If you keep telling that story, Nellie, I'll make you choke on it."

As a lamia, Raven possessed powers and a certain skillset of her own. I knew it wasn't an empty threat. Nellie didn't look bothered in the least, though.

"Well, if I'm going to choke I want to make sure I've got things right," Nellie drawled. "With that in mind, why did you have a riding crop?"

Raven scowled as she shifted her eyes to me. "This is your fault."

I could see how she might feel that way. "I honestly thought you told me to come in."

"Well, I didn't."

"That wouldn't have stopped her anyway," Melissa noted, her tone sour. "She didn't even wait for me to speak before entering my trailer this morning."

I clenched my jaw to keep from blowing up, a hundred different ways to slap back the girl on the tip of my tongue. Ultimately, all I did was shrug. "I didn't realize it would be such a big deal. I'm sorry. I will wait for an invitation next time."

"Whatever." Melissa rolled her eyes and sucked down half a bottle of water.

"What's going on here?" Raven asked, her gaze bouncing between Melissa and me. "Are you two fighting?"

"I think 'fighting' is the wrong word," I replied. "We're merely seeing things differently."

"How so?"

"Well, for starters, she thinks she's my mother," Melissa drawled. "She's decided that she needs to tell me what to do ... and when."

That was hardly the way I remembered things. "Do you have something you want to say to me?"

Instead of backing down, Melissa doubled down. "I believe I already said it."

"Great." I sat on a bench and grabbed a bottle of water from the cooler at the end of the table. "We searched the boardwalk but came up empty."

"This is for the missing girl?" Raven furrowed her brow. "What did you expect to find?"

I shrugged. "I didn't expect to find anything. I was hoping to find something – even if it was just a whiff of something – but it didn't work out."

"She's a teenager. Teenagers take off."

"That's what I told her," Melissa grumbled. "But she didn't listen to me. Maybe you'll have better luck."

Raven shot her an unreadable look. "I know you don't want to hear it, Poet, because you felt bad for the mother, but it's not unheard of for teenagers to take off without telling their parents."

"The mother described her as a good girl," Luke argued. "She gets good grades and never misses curfew. She made it seem like taking off was out of the ordinary."

"I'm sure there have been plenty of mothers who said that about kids who really run away," Raven pointed out. "Sometimes it's the good ones who keep things bottled up for so long that they explode and do the unthinkable."

"What's unthinkable about it?" Melissa challenged. "Maybe she simply got sick of an overbearing mother and wanted to be on her own. I can relate to that."

Raven snapped her head back to Melissa. "What is your deal?"

"Just ignore her." I waved off Raven's concern. "She's hungover and upset because I entered her trailer without waiting for her to invite me in. It's not a big deal."

"It sounds like a big deal." Raven pinned Melissa with a look. "Is it the hangover making you act as if you're possessed or is it something else?"

"Possessed?" Melissa rolled her eyes. "How is this my fault? She's the one who didn't knock."

"She's second in command here. She doesn't have to knock."

"That's not what you said this morning," Nellie pointed out.

Raven ignored him. "You're the new element on our magical periodic table, Melissa. You're only here because Poet took pity on you and invited you to join us. Just for the record, I would've left you behind … but I'm not a people person."

Melissa balked. "Why are you telling me that?"

"Because your attitude leaves a lot to be desired. You shouldn't talk to her that way."

Raven's matter-of-fact manner caught me off guard. She was the last one I expected to rush to my defense.

"You talk to her that way," Melissa snapped. "Isn't that a little hypocritical?"

Raven refused to back down. "Not in the least. Do you want to know why?"

"Not really."

"I'll tell you anyway." Raven leaned over so Melissa would have nowhere to look but her face. "Poet and I are equals. Technically she's the boss, but we've been working together for a long time. We don't always get along, but we do respect each other.

"Your problem is that you want to be an adult, yet you refuse to grow up," she continued. "You want to drink like an adult? Then suck it up. It's not our fault you have a hangover. It's not our fault that you feel like crud."

"I didn't say it was your fault." Melissa jutted out her lower lip. "I was trying to … have a little fun."

"Well, you had fun, didn't you? Now you have to deal with the consequences. If you choose to deal with the consequences by being the devil, my vote is going to be to leave you behind when we pull up stakes. That's just me, though."

Melissa licked her lips. "I … ."

Raven rolled her eyes at the girl's hesitation. "Either grow up or be a child. Straddling both worlds is how you end being like Luke." Her eyes flicked to me. "I'll help you after dark if you want to cast a spell to find the girl. We might get lucky."

I was surprised. "Thanks. I might take you up on that. Kade mentioned heading over to the food trucks for dinner. I'll check around when we get back."

"Great." Raven moved to leave, stopping long enough to glare at Melissa one last time. "You cannot be both a child and an adult, no matter what Luke has taught you. Be one or the other. When you decide, make sure you tell us so we can either wave you goodbye or fully accept you into the group. The decision is yours."

And just like that, Raven slapped back a child and left a petulant adult in her wake.

"I don't have to listen to her crap," Melissa groused as she got to her feet. "I'm not the one in the wrong here."

Nellie made a tsking sound with his tongue as he shook his head. "You didn't hear a thing she said, did you?"

"I heard all I needed to hear."

I WAS HAPPY TO get away from my new position as circus mommy for the night. Luke threatened to ruin my date with Kade by tagging along, but instead he took off with Dolph and Nellie. I had no idea what they were planning, but ultimately I figured it wasn't my business. I wasn't their mommy, after all.

"You're quiet tonight," Kade mused as we wandered the food truck area. There were a lot of choices, so we took our time selecting.

"I'm sure you heard what happened this afternoon. Mystic Caravan is nothing if not crawling with gossip."

"I might have heard something. Nellie likes to talk."

"Nellie does like to talk." I sighed. "I don't know what to do about Melissa. It seems that her attitude shift came out of the blue and I'm out of my depth."

"Why do you think it's your responsibility to take her on?"

I shrugged. "I brought her in."

"And you did her a favor by doing it. You went out on a limb for her. In fact, you've gone out on several limbs for her. It's not your job to make things easy for her. At a certain point, she needs to stand on her own two feet."

Was that what I was trying to do? "She's powerful."

"So are you. That doesn't mean we can't do without her. We did without her for a long time."

I pursed my lips to keep from laughing. "You joined like five minutes before she did. We did without you for a long time, too. That doesn't mean I want to do that going forward."

"And there we agree." Kade slipped his arm around my shoulders and pressed a kiss to my temple. "Listen, I know you're worried about Melissa, but I think you're looking at this the wrong way."

"And how should I look at it?"

"I told you I was a good boy when I was younger, right? I followed all the rules and joined all the teams. I gave my mother very little trouble."

"And I was the exact opposite," I noted. "I found trouble and caused constant headaches for my parents before they died. They were always worried about me. What's your point?"

"My point is that when I joined the military and went overseas I kind of fell off the rails. I drank, went a little crazy, and tried to be as rowdy as I could possibly be. I was the same age as Melissa. Do you know what I learned?"

"Hangovers suck?"

Kade snickered. "I definitely learned that. I also learned that fitting in with the crowd wasn't what I wanted to do. So, I had a few wild months and then I got myself together and became a better man."

"And you think that's what Melissa is doing?"

"I don't think the situations are exactly the same," Kade cautioned. "I do think Melissa is testing her boundaries. You have to wonder how things are for her. She's the youngest one here. She's the new face on the block.

"We do things she doesn't understand, like drinking around a fire and messing with one another," he continued. "She wants to fit in, but she's not quite there yet. Then we land here and she meets someone her own age – someone you claim might be a witch – and maybe they're bonding.

"That doesn't mean Melissa will turn into some monster," he said. "It means she's feeling things out. Don't write her off yet. I'm willing to bet, much like me, she'll realize she wants to live her life a certain way and that constant hangovers – and that bad attitude she put on display today – won't be a part of it."

I couldn't help being hopeful he was right. "You have keen insight into the minds of teenagers," I said, offering up an amused grin. "I had no idea you were so worldly."

"Ha, ha." Kade smacked a kiss against my lips. "Let's not dwell on it for the rest of tonight, huh? Let's get dinner instead. I'm thinking we should get small meals at like eight different places. I'm feeling the need for variety."

I smirked. "Just when it comes to food, right?"

"Absolutely."

"Okay. Well, I want to start with the Lebanese place and then I totally want to try that bourbon chicken at the Chinese one before swinging over to the creole offerings at that one over there."

"And that right there is exactly how you get in the spirit of food trucks."

I WAS STUFFED BY the time we finished, so full that I thought I might bust a button on my cargo pants.

"Let's take a stroll and see if we can walk off some of this gluttony," Kade suggested after tossing our empty food containers.

I took his extended hand and groaned getting to my feet. "We ate enough for ten people."

"Yes, well, it was good. I have zero regrets."

Other than the potential stomachache, I didn't either. "Let's walk down by the water. We don't get ocean views very often."

We lapsed into companionable silence, both of us simply happy to be together. We walked a good way along the boardwalk before turning in toward the beach, breaking from our reveries when a couple of excited boys – they couldn't have been older than thirteen – started exchanging information in loud voices.

"She's naked, dude!"

"She's not naked. She clearly had underwear on."

"That wasn't underwear. That was seaweed. She was naked. I totally saw her tits!"

I jolted at the crude language, sliding a sidelong look in the direction of the boys. Their faces were flushed with excitement and they kept looking toward the surf.

"You guys saw a naked woman?" Kade asked. "Where?"

One of the boys pointed toward the water. "She's right over there ... and she's freaking hot."

Kade exchanged a quick look with me, worry evident. "Naida?"

"That's exactly what I was thinking." I picked up my pace and hurried toward the water. "Why couldn't she wait until after midnight? No one would've seen her then."

"You know how she gets about water. Maybe she couldn't stop herself."

That wasn't much of an excuse as far as I was concerned. "Well, she'd better hope we can explain this away. In fact ... ." I didn't finish what I was going to say. I couldn't even remember what it was. My eyes were drawn to the rolling surf, a body caught in its push and pull, and all previous thoughts simply evaporated.

"That's not Naida," Kade said after a beat.

I shook my head. It was a woman. That much was obvious. I couldn't see a face, though. It was obliterated by long hair, brunette waves spilling over what looked to be young features.

"Katie Dobbins had long brown hair, right?"

"Yes."

I felt sick to my stomach. "We should probably call the police."

"I was just thinking the same thing."

11
ELEVEN

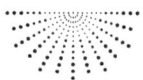

"So, how did this happen?"

Detective Rick Walker pulled a notebook from his pocket and stood in front of Kade and me. Things became chaotic after the body discovery. It only took the kids a few minutes to realize they hadn't seen a live naked woman but rather a nude dead one. They reacted with screams, which carried over to onlookers, and before we realized what was happening we were involved in a full-blown panic.

Kade had to stop onlookers from trying to resuscitate the girl – it was obvious she was dead given the state of the body – and after that we had nothing to do but wait for the police to arrive.

It didn't take long.

Walker took control of the scene, called in the medical examiner. He segregated us to the side and made us wait while he walked the beach and talked to several uniformed officers. It was clear he was trying to exert control, which was normal, but I didn't like his attitude all the same.

"How are we supposed to know how it happened?" Kade challenged.

"You called it in, right?"

"Yes, but that doesn't mean we know how it happened," Kade replied. "We heard a couple of kids talking about a naked woman in the water. We thought perhaps someone got drunk ... or something else happened ... so we came to take a look. We knew right away that it wasn't some random drunk."

"No, definitely not." Walker checked his notebook before turning to me. "You're with the circus, right?"

Part of me felt as if I should be insulted he looked to me when he asked. "We are. Mystic Caravan. Why? Do we look like circus folk or something??"

Walker shook his head. "No, but you're ... unique ... looking. We've made it a point to get to know everyone setting up for the festival. The one place we haven't stopped is the circus grounds."

Unique looking? I was fairly certain that wasn't a compliment. "Well, you're welcome to stop by whenever you want. I'm second in command. Tell whoever meets you at the front that Poet said it's fine for you to explore. Just make sure to ask for a guide when going to the animal tent. We have very expensive liability insurance."

"Right." Walker nodded. "Anyway, what can you tell me about the girl?"

That had to be a trick question. "Not much. We saw her in the surf. We realized she was dead. We called you."

"And that's all you know?"

"Yes."

"Okay, well ... you can be on your way." Walker was dismissive when he moved to turn from us, but Kade wasn't keen to let him escape without answering a few of our questions.

"Is it Katie Dobbins?"

The question caught Walker off guard. He shuttered his surprise quickly, but it was too late to completely cover. "And how do you know that name?"

"Her mother stopped by the grounds today with a photograph of her," Kade replied. "She said her daughter was on the beach with friends last night but didn't come home. She was distraught. We helped her call her daughter's friends, but none of them knew where

Katie was. Then we called your department and a uniformed officer showed up to ask a few questions. We haven't seen the mother since."

"We don't know that it's Katie Dobbins," Walker cautioned. "The medical examiner needs to make the identification."

He was lying. He was good at keeping his emotions in check, but there was a veneer of rage bubbling near the surface. I didn't need to poke into his head to see he was frustrated. He was also keen to dole out some justice, which I found interesting.

"You know it's her," I argued, playing a hunch. "I saw her face when the medical examiner moved the body. It was pretty obvious."

"But you only saw a photograph, right?"

"What is that supposed to mean?" Kade asked, his temper flaring. "What exactly are you accusing us of?"

"I'm not accusing you of anything." Walker made a big show of being pragmatic. "I'm simply wondering how you managed to identify a teenage girl from fifty feet away after only seeing one photograph."

"We might have only seen one photograph, but Pamela was with us for hours," Kade supplied. "She was upset ... and crying ... and falling apart. That isn't easy to forget."

"We also promised to be on the lookout for Katie," I added. "We thought there might be a chance that she visited the circus grounds if she really did leave voluntarily. It looks like that's not the case."

Walker cocked a challenging eyebrow. "What makes you say that? She could've accidentally drowned. We don't have a cause of death yet."

The fact that he insisted on talking down to me, as if I were blind and couldn't see what was obvious, set my teeth on edge. "Really? You think those marks on her wrists and ankles were made by accident?"

I felt Kade stiffen next to me, but he wisely remained silent.

Walker, on the other hand, opted to play dumb. "What marks on her wrists and ankles? I didn't see any marks."

"She had open wounds," I said. "Those weren't made by ocean nibblers. They were big, wide and ugly. They were also made before she died."

"And how do you know that?"

"I've seen my fair share of wounds."

"You see a lot of wounds like that in the circus, do you?"

I shrugged. "I've seen a few in the circus. We have tigers and bears, after all. That's not where I saw wounds like that before, though."

Walker leaned forward, intrigued. "And where did you see wounds like that?"

"Back in Detroit. I grew up there. I was on the streets when I was a teenager, in the city, and I lived in a park for almost a full year. They had this bridge that went over an abandoned road, and to keep warm during the winter we camped under it during chilly months.

"We had these barrels we filled with wood for fires and used to warm food on the rare occasions we could find some," I continued. "It wasn't just homeless teenagers and rootless adults. There were also quite a few ... I guess the term would be 'mentally unstable' individuals as well, the ones the system failed and turned out on the streets."

"I'm familiar with how the homeless population works," Walker said. "I'm sorry you were part of it as a youngster. I guess that's how you ended up with the circus."

"Not like you think."

"That doesn't explain how you recognize those wounds," Walker pressed. "Have you seen them before? Have you seen them here?"

I saw another flash from his mind. This one involved another body, a different body. It had the same wound pattern, and it was equally ravaged by time in the water.

"Not here." Lying on that front wouldn't get me anywhere. "It was in Detroit. It was winter, and it was under the bridge, and there was a fight for warmth. I wasn't very big, so I was hyper-vigilant. It was late in the winter, so I was really thin because I was going days without food. I knew better than getting too close to the barrels, so I kept my distance.

"There was this guy named Big Joey," I continued. "He decided who got to stand next to the barrels – generally people who provided him with food. He was big – huge really – and he liked to fight. One day he took on this little guy who showed up out of nowhere. That guy's name was Aaron.

"Now, no one knew much about Aaron except that he talked to himself and had scars on his wrists from being strapped down at whatever hospital he was most recently kept at," I continued. "Mental health in Michigan underwent quite the upheaval in the years right before that happened and a lot of people were turned out on the streets.

"Aaron was quiet and kept to himself most of the time," I said. "No one knew his story ... until one night Big Joey told him he couldn't stand next to the fire and Aaron decided he was done doing what Big Joey wanted.

"Aaron might have been small, but he was terrifying," I said. "He knocked Big Joey out, threatened anyone who tried to come near him with a knife, and then drove spikes through Big Joey's wrists and ankles ... just like what I saw on Katie Dobbins' body. They were almost identical marks."

Walker pursed his lips. "Do you know why he did that?"

"No, but I figured out why when I woke the next morning and saw Big Joey's body hanging off the side of the bridge. He used the holes to run rope through the wounds and strung him up like a marionette."

"But ... why?"

"To serve as a message," I replied. "He wanted everyone to know there was a new sheriff in town."

"What happened then?"

I shrugged. "I have no idea. I got out of there as soon as I could and found a different park to live in. There's crazy ... and then there's crazy."

"I don't doubt that." Walker tucked his notepad in his pocket. "I doubt very much the cause of death was accidental. That doesn't mean I'm willing to theorize on it right now."

I saw another flash in his mind and this time I forced the fissure wider so I could see what he was really hiding. I almost reeled back at the images, but I managed to hold my footing with a little help from Kade, who wrapped his arm around my waist to lend me a bit of his strength.

Walker furrowed his brow. "Is something wrong?"

"No. I'm fine."

"Well, that was an interesting story." Walker forced a smile. "I'll keep it in mind and ask the medical examiner if someone could have been trying to hang the body. If that's all … ."

Kade opened his mouth to argue, but I offered up an almost imperceptible shake of my head to still him. Now was not the time. He caught on to my non-verbal cue and instead returned Walker's tight smile. "I guess we'll see you around."

"I'm certain you will."

KADE WAITED UNTIL WE WERE far enough away that there was no risk of Walker hearing before questioning me.

"First, that was a horrible story and I'm glad we both stuffed our faces with endless piles of food tonight because otherwise I would have to take you someplace and fill you with warm soup right now," he said. "Second, what did you see in his head? I know you saw something."

"Katie's is the third body found. They have at least fifteen other missing girls – the ones we saw on the bulletin board – and Walker is convinced more than that are missing. Apparently the mayor doesn't want people to think this is an unsafe area, so he's forcing the cops to rule most of the missing person cases as runaways even though there's no evidence to support that."

"That's … not unexpected." Kade slid a strand of hair behind my ear. "What else did you see?"

"All three bodies were marked the same way Katie was."

"And you think it's because someone wanted to string her up?"

"Or tie her down so she couldn't move," I replied. "I lied a little bit at the end there because I didn't want to draw things out. I did hear what happened to Aaron after Big Joey's death. It was the talk of the streets for a month straight."

Kade grimaced. "I'm almost afraid to hear it. If you think the rest of the story was okay to tell and this last part somehow isn't, it must be bad."

"It is." I swallowed hard. "There was this girl under the bridge named Crystal. She was mentally ill, too. She needed medication to balance her moods, but she couldn't get it. When we left the bridge, we tried to get her to go with us, but she wouldn't. She didn't do well with change, got confused and lost easily."

Kade ran his hand over the top of my hair to smooth it, perhaps sensing the story couldn't possibly have a happy ending. "And what happened to Crystal?"

"Aaron thought she was too loud and active. He didn't like her, so he decided to keep her quiet while tying her down," I replied. "He put the same holes in her wrists and ankles and tried to use wire to pin her down. Apparently she lived twenty-four hours like that because he missed her major arteries by going in at those locations."

"Oh, geez." Kade pressed his forehead to mine. "I'm sorry."

"I didn't see it. I only heard about it."

"And yet it tortured you all the same." He pulled me in for a hug. "I still kind of want to feed you. How do you feel about dessert?"

I chuckled at his determination. "If I eat another thing I'll throw up. Instead, how about you promise to buy me ice cream tomorrow and we head home? I'm tired ... and I want to run everything I saw in Walker's mind through my head. I might've missed something."

"I doubt you did."

"He thinks they have a serial killer," I supplied. "He thinks that all the girls are dead and were dumped in the ocean. They simply lucked out when the three washed to shore."

"What do you think?"

"I don't know. I'm not sure the answer is as easy as he wants to believe it is."

"Then we'll find the truth." Kade released me and linked his fingers with mine as we turned back toward the circus grounds, pulling up short when Paige and Melissa popped into view.

The two young women, each clutching an ice cream cone, stood about twenty feet away as they watched the police officers and medical examiner work. As if sensing my presence, Melissa slowly turned her eyes in my direction.

"What's going on?" Melissa asked nervously.

"The girl from earlier today, the one who went missing, she washed up on the beach," Kade replied. "She's dead."

"Oh." Melissa's voice was barely audible. "I guess she didn't take off after all, huh?"

"No." Kade glanced at me and then squared his shoulders. "You should come back to the circus grounds with us. We're calling it a night."

Melissa looked as if that was the last thing she wanted, and when she turned to Paige to see what the other girl thought of the idea Paige merely rolled her eyes.

"I'm not in the mood to go back," Melissa said. "It's not as if we're in danger. We're together, so … I think I'll stick with Paige."

"But … ."

Kade shook his head to cut me off. "She's an adult. She wants to be treated like an adult."

"Yeah, she's an adult," Paige echoed, her voice so high and girly it was like nails on a chalkboard. "She doesn't need a mommy."

I ground my teeth to keep from lashing out.

"We're going back." Kade squeezed my hand as we started walking. "Be safe. I expect you to be on time for work tomorrow morning, Melissa. If that's not part of your plan, don't bother showing up at all."

Melissa's eyes widened. "Are you firing me?"

Kade shook his head. "No, I'm treating you like an adult. Adults have to turn up to work on time. You haven't been on time for work since … well … ever. You don't want to be treated like a kid. Congratulations, you're officially an adult. That means you're responsible for your own actions."

"I'll be on time," Melissa said. "I won't be late. You don't need to worry. I can handle myself."

"Oh, I'm not worried." Kade's tone was breezy. "If you're late, we'll simply replace you. You wouldn't believe the stack of applications we get every week from people who want to join our outfit. It's not as if you'll be hard to replace."

Melissa balked. "I'm not just any worker."

"No, but you're hardly special given the group we've already put together," I said. "Kade's right. Be on time tomorrow or don't bother coming at all. Do you understand?"

Melissa mutely nodded.

"Great." I turned my full attention to Kade. "Believe it or not, now I think I could eat some ice cream."

"You read my mind."

12
TWELVE

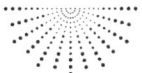

K ade wrapped himself around me so tightly when we climbed into bed that I thought he might squeeze the life out of me. Neither of us were in the mood to frolic – stumbling across a dead teenager on the beach basically kills the idea of romance – but I was grateful he was close because I thought I might need his proximity to beat back the nightmares.

As if sensing my worry, Kade rolled behind me and pressed his body flush against mine. He kissed the back of my neck and gathered me close, not moving the entire night and serving as something of an anchor.

I did dream, but the fear was nowhere near as overwhelming compared to the previous night, and it allowed me the chance to explore the nightmare landscape rather than run from it. I woke with the odd giggling echoing in my ear and a sense of dread coursing through my stomach. I wasn't alone, though, and Kade's breath was warm on my ear as I stirred.

"Morning," Kade murmured, kissing the ridge of my ear and causing a chill to shoot down my spine. "How did you sleep?"

"Okay." That wasn't a lie. "The dolls were back, but … I wasn't as afraid of them this time."

"Why do you think that is?" Kade moved my hair away from my neck so he could rest his chin on my shoulder.

"I think it was you being close."

"I think that was a good answer, but you don't need to placate me."

"I'm not placating you. I honestly think that." I rolled to face him, smirking when he nudged up my leg so we could snuggle. "I felt you the entire night and somehow I knew I wasn't alone. It was weird. I mean ... I was in a different place and yet I knew you were there."

"I don't want you to ever feel alone." Kade was earnest. "That story you told last night ... ."

I cut him off. "It doesn't matter. It was a long time ago."

"It matters to me. I didn't even know things like that were real until you told the story. I was so angry when I found out about Max being my father that I convinced myself no one had ever suffered as much as me."

"That was jarring for you."

"Yeah, but it was hardly the end of the world. You lived on the streets after both of your parents died when you were a kid. The freaking streets!" His eyes went so wide it was almost comical. "They weren't just any streets either. They were streets in Detroit. You're lucky to be alive."

"I think you're being a bit dramatic, but I get what you're saying ... and I appreciate it."

He opened his mouth to say something more, but I waved him off. If we weren't careful, this would turn into something of a mutual admiration society and we'd lose the entire morning. "The truth is, I had an edge over the other kids who were out there. I could read minds and safely steal to survive."

"You still slept under a bridge."

"I did, but I managed to get out. How many of the people I knew back then do you think are still out there?" I involuntarily shuddered. "Even worse, how many do you think are still alive?"

"Poet, I don't like this conversation." Kade made a face as he kissed my forehead and stroked the back of my head. "It makes me uncomfortable."

"Good. It makes me uncomfortable, too." I forced a bright smile. "Are you up for breakfast?"

Kade knew I was purposely changing the subject, but he didn't fight the effort. "I could eat. It's funny, after all the food we chowed down on last night I thought we'd never eat again. Now I'm actually hungry."

As if on cue, his stomach growled, causing us both to burst out laughing.

"I'm a little hungry, too," I admitted, tilting up my chin. "We should probably check on Melissa before stuffing our faces."

Kade didn't overtly react, but I felt an agitated ripple run up his flank.

"We're not checking on her," Kade said after a beat. "I told her to be on time for work. If she's not, she's fired."

I balked. "I thought you were just threatening her to threaten her."

"That's not really how I roll."

"But ... she's a kid."

Kade cocked a challenging eyebrow. "Is she? I thought she was an adult. That's what she's been whining about. It's time we treated her like one."

He was obviously agitated, although I couldn't figure out why. "Did she say something to you yesterday when I wasn't around?"

Kade shook his head. "No. That doesn't mean I'm happy with her."

"But ... she's young. You make mistakes when you're young." I had no idea why I was standing up for Melissa. I was sick of her mouth and attitude. Still, I remembered what it was like to be that age and make a mistake. It felt as if the world was ending. That's not what I wanted for Melissa. "I don't think she should have to pay for a mistake for the rest of her life."

"No, but she needs to learn from her mistakes," Kade countered. "She wants to be treated like an adult. That's what she says even though, in reality, she really wants to be treated like a kid. She wants all of us to bow down and treat her as if she's special. Well, she's not special."

"She is, though," I hedged. "She has a gift. She might be stronger than me when it comes to some of her abilities."

"I don't believe that, but it's hardly important. She needs to learn respect. You went out of your way for her. You invited her along. Heck, you've been trying to come up with something to keep her mentally engaged during circus showings because she wants something of her own to do. You didn't have to do any of that."

"No, but ... ."

Kade shook his head. "I grew up privileged, or at least not wanting. You clearly had some rough years. I don't think Melissa understands what it's like to suffer, even though she acts as if she's suffering now. I'm not going to put up with it. She needs to face some consequences."

I licked my lips, uncertain. "But you can't just abandon her here. I mean ... she doesn't know anyone. We're all she has."

Kade stared into my eyes, his expression unreadable. "You don't want her to end up under a bridge."

"No, it's just ... ."

"It's okay." Kade ran his thumb over my cheek. "I didn't consider what you were really worried about. I wouldn't just abandon her, Poet. But she needs to own up to her responsibilities. If she's not on time for work, she's fired. I'm holding firm on that. I won't leave her here. I'll arrange for her to get a flight home."

Well, that at least was something. "She's just going through something. She'll get better."

"You have a big and giving heart. I like that about you. She's still an adult and she wants to be treated like one, so ... she needs to suck it up."

I pursed my lips and nodded. Apparently that made my mouth a target because Kade swooped in and gave me a kiss.

"I don't want you worrying about this," he said. "Melissa will either shape up or ship out. That's something my mother used to say when I wouldn't clean my room." He adopted what I'm sure he considered a feminine voice. "'You're going to either shape up or ship out, Mister.' She thought that was an original saying."

"I'm sorry I never got the chance to meet her." I meant it. "As for Melissa ... ."

Kade pressed a finger to my lips to silence me. "We're not going to argue about Melissa. It's going to be okay. I need you to trust me on this."

"I do."

"Good." Kade gave me another kiss. "So ... where did we land on breakfast?"

"We should definitely have some." I rolled to a sitting position and shifted my legs so they were hanging over the edge of the bed. "It's kind of weird, huh?"

"What?"

"We went from deciding to move in together to having a teenage daughter almost overnight."

Kade poked my side. "Don't rush things. I want to enjoy living together before we even talk about stuff like that."

His reaction gave me pause. "I'm not ready to just wash my hands of Melissa. I know you want me to be strong and do that tough love thing, but I can't just abandon her."

"You wouldn't be who you are if you could. Don't worry about it. I promise everything will be fine."

I hoped he was right. I wasn't sure I was equipped to deal with more than what was already on my plate.

THE MAJORITY OF OUR GROUP was already at the picnic table when we joined them. A quick look at Luke told me he was a little worse for wear – his eyes red-rimmed and his skin pale – and I instantly knew he'd been out carousing until late into the night.

"Hungover?"

Luke shot me a derisive look. "What do you think?"

I leaned closer so my hand brushed against his. He wasn't interested in shielding his mind, so it was easy to get a glimpse. "It seems you, Nellie and Dolph had quite the night. How exactly did they talk you into going to a strip club?"

"It wasn't all that hard," Nellie said dryly, sipping his coffee as he offered a lazy grin. "I told him there were free drinks, good food and some really interesting body glitter designs. He was all for it."

I patted Luke's shoulder while making sympathetic sounds. "I'll make you a big breakfast. How does that sound?"

"Like you'd better make sure I have sausage and bacon," Luke replied, rubbing his forehead. "Seriously, I haven't been this hungover since … I can't even remember when."

"I can." Nellie hopped to his feet, his eyes sparkling. "I believe it was the morning after you did that keg stand last week."

Luke scalded him with a dirty look. "You make me want to punch you."

"I'm fine with that." Nellie was surprisingly upbeat as he followed me to the kitchen area, where Raven was already at work. "I heard you found a body last night, Poet. You need to learn the proper way to take a night off. We did it the right way. You did it the wrong way."

"Thanks for the tip." I flicked my fingers in Nellie's face, causing them to spark a bit so he'd back up. "You're invading my space."

"I'm hungry and I figure this is the best way to get you to cook faster."

"Good to know." I reached for the bacon. "We did find a body, though. It washed up on the beach. We heard some kids talking about a naked woman in the surf and thought it might be Naida. We were wrong."

"I can see that." Nellie leaned against the counter. "Was it the girl from yesterday? The one whose mother was here."

I nodded. "They didn't identify her in front of us, but I saw her face. It was her."

"How long do you think she was in the water?" Raven asked. That was a good question. "I don't know a lot about body decomposition, but she looked as if she'd been dead the whole time." I looked to Kade for confirmation. "What do you think?"

"I think she was only in the water an hour or two." Kade sat next to Luke and slid him a sly smile. He clearly meant to mess with my hungover best friend. "I can't be sure, though. Her skin still had pigmentation. That makes me think she wasn't in the water long."

"If she didn't die right away, where was she?" Nellie turned serious.

"I don't know, but I think something was done to her wherever she was." I explained about the marks on her wrists and ankles. "Detective Walker was kind of a jerk, but I saw in his head, and he's worried. He thinks they have a serial killer."

"How many bodies have they found?" Raven asked, sparing a glance for a sullen-looking Melissa as she skirted the edge of the dining area and took a seat across the table from Kade.

"Three bodies."

"So what happened to the others?" Dolph asked, adjusting his big frame so he could stare at me. "Why have they found only three?"

"There are several possibilities," Kade replied. "The first is that all the bodies were dumped in the water and only three washed ashore. There are big fish and whatnot out in the ocean. Sharks could've eaten the others or they could've washed out to sea."

"I don't think that's the way it works with these tides, but I can conduct more research," Luke offered, pouring himself another mug of coffee. I had a feeling he was going to need a vat of it to get him going. "I think it's more likely that only three bodies were dumped in the water."

"See, that doesn't make a lot of sense to me," I said, lining up the bacon on the grill before reaching for the sausage links. I was nothing if not an efficient multitasker ... and with a touch OCD. "They have fifteen missing girls ... and that's only the girls they're owning up to. They have quite a few others who are missing, but the mayor leaned on the cops to deem them runaways because he didn't want the story leaking to the media."

"Yeah, right before a big festival, that wouldn't be good for tourism," Nellie agreed. "How many girls are we talking about?"

I pictured the bulletin board at the grocery store. "Like, one-hundred ... and that's only the ones who have parents who cared enough to put up fliers. I'm sure there are some girls out there who didn't have people care enough to report them missing."

Kade stared at me for a long beat, his expression unreadable. "That's too many to ignore. We need to come up with some answers. How do you suggest we do that?"

"I don't know." I rolled my neck. "I think we have to start with someone local."

"The cops?" Kade's opinion of the suggestion was obvious. "Detective Walker isn't going to help us."

"Not the cops."

"She's talking about a local psychic," Raven supplied. "She's right. Someone local is probably already working on this while trying to avoid the cops. If we find the right psychic, we'll be ahead of the game because he or she will have information for us right from the start."

"Okay, that sounds like a plan," Kade said. "What do you want me to do?"

"Come up with a plan to make sure no girls are taken from these grounds," I replied. "We open tomorrow. The festival is only half open right now. It goes into full swing tomorrow. That means this will be a target-rich environment."

"We can't keep them all safe," Kade said. "I wish that were the case, but … the area is just too big. There's only so much we can do."

"Then we'll have to figure out a different way to catch a killer." I shifted my eyes to Melissa. She appeared to be listening but not participating in the conversation. "Why don't you take Melissa to help you today?"

Melissa balked. "Why? I'm here and on time."

Raven snickered. "It's not a punishment. We all work together at Mystic Caravan."

"It feels like punishment," Melissa grumbled, lowering her eyes.

"I think that has to do with the guilt you're carrying," Raven noted. "You might want to learn from that." She flicked her eyes to me. "We'll search for psychics during breakfast and pick the top three. Hopefully we'll be able to tell who the real deal is right away. It will slow us down if we have to deal with a fraud."

"At least we have a place to start."

That was something, although it didn't feel like nearly enough.

13
THIRTEEN

Raven and I narrowed our choices to five psychics and then shoved the list in front of Naida and Nixie so they could lodge their opinions. By handing it to them blind, they knew nothing about the individuals in question and chose using their instincts only.

"I like her," Naida announced, pointing at the name "Desdemona Freeman."

Nixie cocked her head to the side and narrowed her eyes. "I like her, too, although this one jumped out at me." She tapped the space next to the name "Michael Bentley."

"That's a man," Raven pointed out, wrinkling her nose.

"Why is that important?" Kade read the list over my shoulder, confusion evident. "Are real psychics only women or something?"

I shook my head. "No, that's not it."

"Then what is it?"

"It's … difficult to explain." I searched for the right words. "Most men who are truly psychic don't advertise it. For some reason, it's a stigma for men. Women embrace it – and are more often public with their abilities – while men try to hide it. I don't know why."

Kade shifted his eyes to Raven. "What isn't she telling me?"

"What makes you think I'm not telling you everything?" I protested.

"Because you do this squinting thing with your eyes when you're trying to keep something from me," Kade replied without hesitation. "Before you get worked up, I'm not calling you a liar. I think it's more that you think I can't understand something about magical folk and you don't want to confuse me. It's fine."

It didn't sound fine to me.

"Raven," Kade prodded.

"She's too delicate to say it like it is, but I don't have that problem." Raven's smile was mischievous. "Here's the thing: Male psychics are rare because the gift tends to pass through female genes."

Kade held his hands palms up. "That doesn't sound too confusing."

"There is one notable exception," Raven said. "Mages."

"Mages? Like Max?" Kade furrowed his brow. "Does that mean Max is psychic?"

"He has psychic abilities," I cautioned. "Max's powers are much broader than those held by the rest of us. In fact, he could take all of us on without breaking a sweat. We're good, but he's magnificent."

"Maybe you should be dating him," Kade teased.

"That's not what I meant. It's just ... mages are rare."

"How rare?"

"Like almost nonexistent," Raven replied. "Mages were created to act as supernatural peacekeepers, for lack of a better way to explain it. It's not beneficial for any side if good or evil takes over. That's why we need the balance."

"I guess I don't understand," Kade hedged.

"It's a lot to absorb," I offered. "I thought Max would be the one to explain it to you when you were more comfortable with him, but ... it's not easy to explain. It's very convoluted and the history is all kinds of whacked out.

"The thing is, mages are kind of like angels in a weird way," I continued. "They're identified as children and taken from their homes. There aren't as many of them as there used to be, and their day-to-day activities are conducted in secrecy."

"But Max is out in the open."

"He is," I confirmed. "He's also not a chosen mage. He's a born mage."

"I don't know what that means." Kade's frustration mounted. "Just spell it out in English."

"Fine." I heaved a sigh. "Chosen mages aren't supposed to mate. It's one of the rules. On rare occasions – we're talking very rare occasions here – two mages fall in love and procreate. That's where born mages come into play. They're different ... and stronger."

Kade's eyebrows rose. "So that's what Max is? He's a born mage."

"Exactly."

"That's why he has psychic abilities." Kade seemed more intrigued than agitated. "I definitely need to do some reading on this subject. I feel as if I'm behind. Now isn't the time for that, though. We need to focus on the missing girls, so if the male psychic is an issue ... go to the woman."

"I think that's probably the best plan," I agreed, rolling to the balls of my feet and giving him a quick kiss. "I'm leaving you in charge. Don't let the power go to your head."

Kade smirked. "Don't worry. The only thing I plan to do is punish Melissa."

I opened my mouth to argue, but Kade shook his head to quiet me.

"It won't be terrible, but I'm going to have a long talk with her," Kade said. "That's not your concern. I've got Melissa under control. You handle the psychic and see what information you can dig up."

"Okay, but if she's crying when I get back I'm going to make you dry her tears."

"Duly noted."

DESDEMONA FREEMAN'S SHOP looked like something out of a movie. It was only two blocks from the beach, so the breeze was stiff as we approached, and the purple walls and pink trim were enough to turn my stomach.

"Are you sure about this?" Raven made a face. "This is a bit too … um … on the nose."

I focused on the neon sign advertising palm and tarot readings in the window. I couldn't help but worry we'd made a huge mistake. "Maybe we should've gone for the dude."

"We could still do that. In fact … ." Raven didn't get a chance to finish her sentence because the store's front door opened, allowing a breathtaking woman with a scarf over her head and vibrant green eyes to hover in the threshold.

I instinctively straightened my shoulders as I met the woman's gaze. "Oh, um, hello."

"Hello." Desdemona's gaze was long and studied as she glanced between our faces. "I believe I've been expecting you."

"You have?" Raven cocked a dubious eyebrow. "Who told you we were coming?"

"No one told me. I just knew." Desdemona was matter-of-fact. "I cleared my schedule. I believe we have a few things to talk about."

Raven and I exchanged a quick look. Desdemona was clearly putting on a show, but the thing is, she was good at it.

"Great. We're looking forward to it." Raven's tone was breezy as she moved toward the door. "You know your decorations are ostentatious and annoying, right?"

Desdemona shrugged. "You have to know your market, and I know mine." She gestured for me to enter before turning the sign in the window to "closed" and pointing us toward the table in the center of the room. "I steeped some tea. I hope that's okay."

"That sounds great." I was more nervous than I probably should've been. Desdemona was a master at taking control of a room. I couldn't help but be impressed. "Your space is nice, other than the colors, I mean."

"I happen to like the colors, but that's neither here nor there." Desdemona poured three cups of tea before taking her seat and focusing on me. "You found the body last night."

This was hardly the first local psychic I'd crossed paths with. Some were more adept than others. She was, however, the first who seemed to think she could control us. I found the turn of events interesting.

"I did," I confirmed. "How did you know?"

"I read it in your mind."

Raven and I snorted in unison.

"You most certainly didn't," Raven countered. "You may be strong … and even good at reading people … but you're not strong enough to read Poet."

Desdemona pursed her lips. "Maybe I was at the beach last night when the discovery occurred," she conceded.

"So why lie?"

"Because it makes the story better." Desdemona shifted on her chair. "I saw you with a man. You seemed close. You were talking to Detective Walker. I don't suppose you want to share with me what he had to say, do you?"

Desdemona might have been good with visions and reading people, but she was bad at communicating. I could hardly hold that against her – my communication skills were lacking at times, too – but if she thought we were going to supply her with information for nothing in return, she was sadly mistaken.

"Okay, I think we need to set some ground rules." I rested my palms on the table. "We'll share a piece of information, and then you'll share a piece of information. This isn't going to be one-sided."

Desdemona tilted her head to the side, considering. "Fair enough. No lying, though."

"We don't lie," Raven said. "By the way, if you lie to us, you won't like what happens."

Desdemona stared for a long moment, perhaps testing if she could get inside Raven's head. It was impossible. There was no way she was strong enough. Heck, I wasn't strong enough. Perhaps Max wasn't even strong enough. That didn't stop Desdemona from trying … and ultimately failing.

"I won't lie," Desdemona promised. "I think we both want the same outcome, so there's no reason to lie."

"Great. Go ahead and ask your question."

"What did Detective Walker say to you?"

"Not much." I leaned back in my chair and stretched out my long legs in front of me, giving the appearance of relaxation. "He asked how we discovered her and then essentially dismissed us."

"And how did you discover her?"

"We heard several boys talking about a naked woman in the water. We thought perhaps it was a drunk and went to help. That's not what it turned out to be."

"And ... ."

Raven cut off Desdemona before she could ask a third question. "It's our turn. What do you know about the missing girls?"

Desdemona wrinkled her nose. "I know there are more than what the police are admitting."

"We know that, too." Raven crossed her arms over her chest. "You've seen things. Don't bother denying it. This game – whatever it is – grows tiresome and we've barely started. How about we cut through the crap and focus on the important stuff?"

"And what did you have in mind?"

Raven didn't hesitate when she reached across the table and grabbed Desdemona's hair. I realized what she was going to do a split second too late.

"Raven, no!"

Raven didn't stop, instead jerking the hair and causing a wig to tilt and slip from Desdemona's head. Underneath, the woman had short hair – more peach fuzz than hair – that was clearly growing back after being clipped or falling out.

Desdemona grappled for the wig but it slipped through her fingers. "What do you think you're doing?"

"Cutting to the thick of things," Raven replied. "You're dying. You know that, right?"

I widened my eyes. "Raven, what has gotten into you?"

"Let me handle this," Raven instructed, never breaking eye contact with Desdemona. "You can't see into our heads – although you've tried a few times – but I can see into yours. You're not strong enough to shield, though you're giving it a valiant effort.

"I'm sorry you're dying and I'm sorry it's made you so ... bitter," she continued. "It's not fair. You're young and you're giving, often trying to help others, and it's definitely not fair. Before this you were an optimist. Now you can't see past your pessimism.

"I get it, and I'm not sure I'd feel differently in your position," she said. "That's not why we're here. We can't help you. The cancer invading your body will overwhelm it. You're resigned to it, yet you continue to work ... you also continue to investigate even though you can't quite understand why."

I chewed my bottom lip as I waited for Desdemona to respond. Raven did a much deeper scan than I allowed myself to conduct. It's considered rude to probe someone's mind without invitation. I didn't catch the cancer bit, but I sensed something eating the woman from the inside. I couldn't stop the pity from building.

"People are dying," Desdemona said. "Young girls are dying. If it were only that, I might be able to look away. But something else is going on, and I can't ignore what I feel inside. Trust me. I've tried. I can't ignore the nightmares any longer.

"So, you figured out my secret," she continued. "I'm dying. Before I go, I'd like to stop others from dying. Is that such a terrible thing?"

Raven handed back the wig. "No. We want to stop it, too. But there's no need for theatrics. We're not frauds. This is hardly the first ... monster ... we've come up against. We're not afraid of monsters. We are afraid of time. We only have so much of it. No more games."

Desdemona snagged the wig. "Fine. For the record, I wasn't trying to play games. I was simply trying to feel you guys out. You're obviously powerful."

"We are," I agreed. "What can you tell us about the girls?"

"They're all young, between the ages of sixteen and twenty," she answered. "They don't look alike. They're not all blonds or anything. They're all thin."

"That means what you inferred from that bulletin board is correct," Raven said. "It's not exactly earth shattering, but it is confirmation."

I nodded. "How long?"

"Six months."

"And there are no leads?"

Desdemona shook her head. "I've poked around in Walker's head. There's not a lot there. He's aware something bad is happening. He knows the young women in this area are in danger. The mayor has severely limited what Walker can do."

"Is that why no warnings have gone out?" Raven asked.

"Exactly." Desdemona sipped her tea. "The mayor knows better than holding a news conference and announcing that possibly one-hundred girls have gone missing."

"That seems like a large number," I noted. "Surely some of the girls who have gone missing have done so voluntarily. The area is too big for it to be otherwise."

"Oh, I wouldn't argue with that. But most of them have been taken. I've tried to meditate in an effort to make contact with them – usually doing it as soon as possible after I find out someone has disappeared – but I haven't come up with much."

"Do you think they're all dead?"

"No. However, I think they're all changed."

That was an odd phrase. "What do you mean?"

"I can't sense who they used to be," Desdemona explained. "Usually that's not a problem for me. At first I chalked it up to the cancer weakening me, but I don't think that's it. Something else is happening that somehow alters their minds."

That was mighty interesting. "Drugs?"

"I can't rule that out."

"It could also be magic," Raven suggested. "Someone could be putting spells on them to keep them docile. Even if you knock that big number in half and assume only fifty girls have been taken, that means forty-seven are still out there. How do you control that many kidnapped girls?"

"This area is thick with witches," I noted. "Maybe we should try to track down one of the covens."

"That never goes well." Raven made a face. "You know how I feel about witches. It's the same way your boyfriend feels about clowns."

Desdemona shuddered. "Who doesn't hate clowns?"

I pointed at Raven. "Her boyfriend is a clown."

"For real?" Desdemona cracked a genuine smile. "Maybe I should visit the circus this weekend. It sounds like you guys have fun."

"We definitely have fun, and I have tickets for the big show if you want them. I think it's a good idea for you to visit. We can keep each other updated."

"So what are you going to do?" Desdemona asked. "How will you find who is doing this?"

"I don't know yet. We'll figure something out, though."

"We always do," Raven said. "By the way, you look better without the wig. Be bold. Wear the scarf over your real hair."

"But … people will stare."

"That's not necessarily a bad thing." Raven got to her feet. "We'll be in touch. This one is going to take more legwork. We need to come up with a plan to track the missing girls, and I don't think it's going to be easy."

"No," I agreed. "Whoever did this put a lot of thought into it. We're not going to luck into a solution. We need to think hard and fast if we're going to outsmart him or her. We don't have a lot of time."

The serious nods from the other two women told me on that we could all agree.

14
FOURTEEN

After leaving Desdemona's shop, we headed for the beach where Katie's body washed up. Raven, who always preferred wearing black, seemed a bit overdressed, but she ignored the curious stares and doffed her shoes so she could wade in the water.

The immediate area where Katie washed ashore was cordoned off with police tape, but the beach was open down the way, so we picked a spot close but not near enough that we'd make people suspicious.

"Do you sense anything?" I curiously watched Raven slosh through the water. She seemed to be having a good time.

"No, but I didn't really expect to. That would be too easy." Raven bent over and slid her fingertips through the water. "I grew up by the ocean. I like when we visit a spot close to the beach like this. Of course, it would be more entertaining if we weren't looking for a killer."

"What did you think of Desdemona, other than the obvious, I mean?"

"I like her, but she's not long for this world and she knows it. She's weak, but holding on because of this case. It eats at her in ways she doesn't understand. It also bolsters her. Once this is done, she will go … and I'm not sure she realizes it."

"We can't stop trying to help these girls because of her."

"I didn't say we should. It's just … I hate it when I'm faced with mortality. It always leaves me feeling … blah." Raven exhaled heavily as she shook off the heavy musings. "Well, enough of that. I hate deep thoughts."

Despite the serious nature of our conversation, I found myself smiling. "You are an enigma."

"I am," Raven agreed. "The water is full of energy, and very little of it is good. I can't follow magic in water. I think we need Naida for that."

"Now there's an idea." I brightened. "We can send her out after dark tonight. She might be able to follow the trail."

"That was my idea, too. The thing is, she wasn't taken in the water. That means she left a trail on land. Because she's dead, we might be able to follow it."

"Is that a lamia thing?"

"Kind of. I can follow the trail of the dead if I put my mind to it. We're dealing with a limited timetable, so I figure it's worth a shot. I'm not guaranteeing anything, but it won't hurt to try … especially because Kade promised to make Melissa work in the House of Mirrors all afternoon. That means she's doing my work and I have time to waste."

I was surprised. "When did he promise that?"

"When I cornered him after breakfast. You were off getting your computer so we could look up area psychics."

"You cornered him?"

Raven slipped on her shoes and marched up the beach. "Don't get your panties in a bunch. It wasn't like that. In case you haven't noticed, I have a boyfriend of my own."

I pictured Percival's flabby white cheeks sagging out of the chaps. "Oh, I noticed."

Raven's smile was impish. "I saw what flashed through your mind just now. It was right on the surface. That was a breathtaking view, wasn't it?"

I wasn't sure how to answer. "It was ... unique."

"I'm guessing you and Kade don't roleplay, huh?" Raven was breezy as she pointed us toward the crafts fair. "You should try it. It's ... invigorating."

My discomfort was almost overwhelming. "I don't think we should be talking about this."

"Please. You're such a prude." Raven rolled her eyes. "If you think I'm embarrassed, I'm not. I like a guy who can think outside of the clown car."

Now there was a troubling vision. "Well ... good for you then."

"Yes, I think so."

We lapsed into silence as we walked past the various booths. It wasn't exactly a comfortable feeling, but it was hardly taxing. Finally, Raven broke the quiet.

"I sense ... something."

"Do you want to be more specific?"

"I'm not sure I can. I'm not even sure it's Katie. It's just ... something."

"Like ... ?"

"Like a whisper under the wind." Raven pressed her eyes shut and cocked her head. "It's voices, more than one – I can't really tell how many because they overlap – and they're asking for help."

I pushed thoughts of Raven and Percival's rather unique relationship out of my mind. "Do they say anything about what happened to them?"

"No. It's more a plea than anything else." Raven stepped forward. "I'm lost. Please find me." She took another step. "It's dark. I can't find my way." Another step. "There's someone here. We are not alone." She turned to her left and focused on a booth. "We can't get out without help."

Raven's voice was so eerie, nothing more than a raspy whisper, that it turned my blood to ice. "Is that what they're saying?"

"They're saying a lot of things, and it's hard to make out." Raven shook her head and focused on the booth. "I think Katie was in this area right before she disappeared. I've been trying to pick her out of the din, but it's difficult."

"So let's look around here." I allowed my gaze to land on the booth and internally cringed when I realized it was the doll booth. "Oh, well, great."

"You don't like dolls, do you?" Raven was amused.

I pictured the doll from my childhood and shivered. "Not particularly."

Raven snapped her head in my direction. "What happened with that doll?"

I couldn't shut down my shock. "You saw that?"

"You had a visceral response. You couldn't hide it fast enough."

"I killed that doll." I offered up a hollow laugh. "I know that's a weird way to put it, but I'm convinced it was alive."

"I've heard weirder things. They made those Chucky movies for a reason. I'm sure something inspired them."

"I think we would've heard if a doll went on a murderous rampage," I pointed out dryly.

"Not that part." Raven wrinkled her nose. "I'm talking about the part where the killer transferred his soul into the doll. I can guarantee that's happened before."

The notion caught me off guard. "But ... how? Dolls aren't real."

"They're not, but look at those voodoo dolls Nixie sells. They're real humans before she shrinks them down and offers them for purchase. Granted, they're evil humans, but they're still alive. What do you think happens to those souls after the bodies are rendered inert?"

I opted for the truth. "I don't like thinking about it. I know the people she uses her dust on have done wrong – most of them are murderers and rapists ... oh, and the occasional sociopath thrown in for good measure – but it's still weird to think about them trapped as dolls."

"I think it's fun." Raven was never one for sentiment. "They're also still stuck in there. As perhaps an unintended consequence of the pixie magic, the souls are trapped. They don't escape ... ever."

"They don't?" That was news to me. "So they're stuck in there forever."

"Or at least until the doll is destroyed. Then the soul is freed. Those dolls are technically possessed until that happens. I'm guessing that's what happened to the doll from your childhood."

"But how would that happen?"

Raven shrugged. "How does any of it happen? How do we do the things we do? You'll probably never know how it occurred. That doesn't mean it didn't happen."

I drifted closer to the doll booth, glaring at the one that caught my attention the first time I strolled through the area. It sat on the counter, its leg hanging over the side, and it seemed to be watching me. "I was never much of a doll person."

"Me either. When I was a kid, dolls were made of corn cobs and looked even weirder than these things." Raven picked up the doll and stared into its button eyes. "No soul here."

That was a relief. "I swear I saw it move the other day."

"That's because you're predisposed to be suspicious of dolls. This one is empty. Katie was here, though. I don't know if it was her last stop. In fact ... ." Raven trailed off when the man behind the counter straightened and fixed her with a curious look. "And who are you?"

If the artisan was insulted by Raven's direct approach, he didn't show it. He seemed amused more than anything else. "My name is Charles Bates."

"Bates, huh?" Raven dropped the doll on the counter, keeping her full focus on him. "Are you like Norman Bates?"

Bates chuckled, causing his eyes to cross a bit and give him a mildly sinister look that made me think of a bad horror movie. "Not last time I checked."

"And you made these?"

I let Raven keep up the conversation, mostly because I was too distracted by the odd ragdolls hanging about. They sat patiently on shelves, waiting for someone to come and give them a forever home, yet I couldn't shake the idea that they were watching me. I knew it was ridiculous, but I felt it all the same.

Raven flicked the spot between my eyebrows. "Stop that. They're not watching you."

My mouth dropped open as I rubbed the spot. "Did you just flick me?"

"Shutter better or stop complaining." Raven turned back to Bates. "I have to ask ... why dolls?"

Bates shrugged. "Why not?"

"Because you're a grown man and no one trusts an adult male who makes dolls for a living," Raven replied, refusing to back down.

Bates barked out a laugh that was so hoarse it caused my stomach to turn. "You're funny. I like that."

"Don't even think about getting perverted," Raven warned. "I'm already dating a clown. I draw the line at doll maker."

Bates clutched at his heart. "You wound me."

"At least you have a good sense of humor." Raven was droll. "You'll need to hold onto that as long as you insist on making dolls. Still, what's the story with these things? What gave you the idea to make them in the first place, let alone sell them at a crafts fair?"

Bates shrugged. "I made the first one for my daughter when she was three. My mother taught me to sew as a young boy and it's a skill I never forgot. I didn't have a lot of money, but I did have some crafts supplies around, so I made my daughter a doll ... and she carried it everywhere until she was five. She even had it with her when she tried to cross the road by herself – without looking – and was struck down. I buried it with her."

I was horrified. "That's awful. I'm so sorry."

Raven made a face. "He's making it up. That didn't happen."

Bates widened his eyes. "Are you calling me a liar?"

"No, but you're a masterful storyteller," Raven replied. "I bet you dust off that story whenever you're in danger of losing a sale, huh?"

"It's the truth."

"You've never been married," Raven countered. "You've never had a daughter, at least to your knowledge. You've spent the better part of your life staring down the bottom of a bottle. You're fine with that and are not inclined to change."

"You're good." Bates folded his arms over his chest. "How is it you know that?"

"I was struck by lightning as a child and ever since I've been able to see the pasts of others," Raven replied wryly.

"Why really?"

"Because I'm with Mystic Caravan Circus," Raven explained. "We all have a bit of ... shine ... to us."

"I can see that." Bates' friendly demeanor had all but disappeared. "I would appreciate it if you minded your business where my dolls are concerned."

"That's no problem at all." Raven nudged me to the left with her hip. "Make sure you stick to touching dolls and nothing else."

Bates was offended. "I would never ... !"

Raven waved off his outrage. "Keep it that way. I'll know if you break from your promise. I'm good when it comes to stuff like that."

"And now you know why I stick to dolls," Bates sneered. "Real women are way too much work."

Raven offered up a half salute. "On behalf of the female population, we thank you."

"WHAT WAS THAT?"

I barely managed to contain myself until we were out of earshot.

"I don't like him." Raven's response was simple. "We need to watch him. He managed to shutter his mind relatively well after I conducted my initial reading, which shouldn't be possible for a mere mortal without a bit of coaching. I saw a few things before that."

"Like what?"

"Like he'd be more than happy to be the salami in a sandwich if you and I wanted to be the bread."

Ugh. That was stomach turning. "So he's a pervert."

"He's also a champion liar. That story he spun was well thought out, and I'm sure he's sold more than a few dolls on the back of it."

"We're technically liars, too," I reminded her. "We lie to protect ourselves. Maybe he does the same."

"Yes, but I don't think the things he wants to hide can be misconstrued as altruistic by any stretch of the imagination. It hardly matters." Raven slowed her pace and glanced over her shoulder. "And look who he's talking to now."

I followed her gaze, frowning when I caught sight of Barney and Paige. The young woman looked bored, but her father was in the middle of some story – that seemed to be his favorite hobby, after all – and Bates appeared to be listening even though his gaze was fixed on us.

"It's probably just a coincidence. Barney's booth is only two down. They've most likely been hanging out."

"Yeah, but I don't like Barney either," Raven supplied. "He's hiding something, too. He's much better at it than Bates. Also … there's something up with that kid."

I felt the same way, so I was understandably intrigued. "She's a witch."

"Interesting."

"I don't know that she knows she's a witch," I added. "She heard the lullaby when we unleashed it the night of the dreamcatcher spell. She kept tilting her head, as if she was trying to pick up the refrain and couldn't quite do it."

"Do we know anything about her mother?"

"No."

"Witch lines run through women, just like psychic lines. I'm guessing her mother isn't around any longer. That's probably why she isn't trained."

"She seems to have latched onto Melissa," I pointed out. "Maybe she's simply playing dumb. I mean … Melissa is powerful. Maybe Paige sees something in her she likes."

"Melissa may be powerful, but she's young and dumb," Raven countered. "She would be a prime mark if Paige were playing that game. The thing is, I don't think Paige is any smarter than Melissa. They've become best buddies because there's no one else in their age group. It's not power calling them together, it's a lack of options."

I scratched the side of my nose as I regarded her. "You have an unbelievably sunny attitude. Has anyone ever told you that?"

"No one I care to spend time with." Raven was blasé. "It's the truth. Melissa is surrounded by older people. It might not seem like a large age difference, but in this line of work it can feel overwhelming. She'll survive. In fact, I think Kade is probably beating the resistance out of her even as we speak."

That was a sobering thought. "I think our best bet is to put Naida into the water after dark. She might be able to sniff something out. If she can't, we'll have to figure something else out."

Raven cast a final glance in Bates' direction. "Yeah. I'm still going to watch him."

"Do you believe he's involved?"

"He's involved in something. Odds are it's not this. Still ... he's more than he seems."

"Then we'll both watch him."

"Won't that be fun?"

15
FIFTEEN

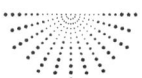

I found Kade in the House of Mirrors, more specifically in Raven's office. He looked as if he was enjoying his tenure as circus hard ass. He leaned back in Raven's chair, his feet propped on her desk, flipping through a magazine. At first I thought he was alone. Then I heard the whining.

"This is so gross!" Melissa complained.

I couldn't see her, but her screeching was coming through just fine.

"That's why it needs to be cleaned," Kade said dryly. "Raven left a list of things that need to be done, by the way. You still have two left when you're finished with that closet."

Closet? I turned myself at an angle, remaining in the hallway while peering inside, and found an open door. I couldn't see the contents, but the grunts and groans Melissa emitted were enough to make me bite the inside of my cheek to keep from laughing.

"It's almost dinner," Melissa groused. "You can't expect me to work through dinner."

"You'd already be done if you hadn't spent two hours crying as if I stole your favorite Barbie doll." Kade didn't look up from the magazine. "Perhaps we should consider having you attend some efficiency classes."

Melissa's expression was murderous when she poked her head out of the closet. "You're getting off on this, aren't you? You can't make me work through dinner. It's inhumane."

"Ah, but that's a child's way of thinking," Kade countered. "You're an adult. Adults often work through dinner."

"Not you," Melissa spat. "Why am I working while you're sitting there reading a magazine?"

"I'm supervising." Kade was blasé. "Now ... back to it. That closet won't clean itself."

"I could quit," Melissa warned. "No one would blame me."

My heart rolled at the words and I opened my mouth to say something, although I had no idea what words I could use to better the situation. I didn't get the chance.

"I'd blame you," Kade said. "I'd blame you a lot. More importantly, I think you'd blame yourself once the dust settles. You might be able to muster some righteous indignation for a few days – maybe even a week – but afterward you'd realize you'd made a mistake.

"The thing is, you know you're acting like a complete and total idiot, but you can't seem to stop yourself," he continued. "You know that Poet went out of her way to help you, give you a job, make you part of our community. The fact that you're so ungrateful might be new, but you're not dumb enough to pretend it's acceptable."

I leaned against the wall, arms folded, and listened intently. Melissa couldn't see me from her position, and Kade wasn't looking. Eavesdropping was often frowned upon in our circle, but I didn't care. I wanted to hear Melissa's response.

"I'm not ungrateful," Melissa sputtered. "I'm ... I'm not ungrateful."

"You're certainly not thankful for the opportunity you've been given," Kade countered, flipping a magazine page. "You've been nothing but mean and surly since we stopped here. Is that because of your new friend?"

Melissa balked. "I'm not some idiot teenager who gets bowled over by peer pressure."

"Huh."

"Why did you say 'huh' in that tone of voice?"

"Because I'm not sure what else to say. You claim you're not an idiotic teenager, but that's exactly how you've been acting the past few days. You claim you're not easily manipulated, but you weren't this way before we arrived, and the only difference here is that you've been spending all your time with Paige. I'm not sure how you want me to react."

"I'm really starting to not like you," Melissa groused.

"I'm fine with that." Kade flicked his eyes from the magazine and found me watching him. "I don't need to be liked."

"All you care about is Poet liking you," Melissa added.

"That is my top concern," Kade agreed, smiling. "Speaking of Poet … how was your day, darling?"

I had no choice but to step into the room. Melissa's eyebrows flew up her forehead when she saw me. "Long and somewhat interesting," I answered.

"Thank the Maker you're here," Melissa said. "He's been working me like a slave all day. You need to force him to cut me loose."

I pursed my lips. "Why would I want to do that?"

"Because he's being unreasonable."

"I think you're the unreasonable one," I countered. "Clean your closet. I need to talk to Kade." I sauntered across the room, internally crowing about Melissa's unhappy expression. She looked downright furious … and surprised. It was the surprise I relished. She expected me to be a pushover, and when I refused she was forced to regroup. The entire endeavor was entertaining.

"Have a seat." Kade patted his lap and wiggled his eyebrows suggestively. "I believe I have a spot right here for you."

That seemed a dangerous prospect when we had an audience, so instead I sat on the edge of the desk and faced him. "How was your day?"

Kade briefly shifted his eyes toward the closet before moving them back to me. "You know how we weren't crazy about having a teenager this morning?"

I nodded.

"That still stands."

I pressed my lips together to keep from laughing. "I see. I guess that means you've been having fun being the boss all day, huh?"

"I've had better days," Kade said dryly. "I missed you. What did you do?"

I told him about our meeting with Desdemona, not leaving anything out. When I was done, Kade was impressed.

"You and Raven have spent the past month getting along – at least when you don't invite yourself into her trailer and interrupt weird clown games, that is," he said. "It's kind of nice when you guys aren't fighting."

I shot him a "whatever" eye roll. "We're both working toward a common goal. I hardly think we're going to start braiding each other's hair and having sleepovers."

"That's too bad. My dreams will never be the same again."

"Ha, ha." I poked his stomach before sobering. "This is big. There are a lot of missing girls. We need to figure out what's going on here."

"I don't disagree with you. How do you intend to do that?"

"We're sending Naida into the water tonight."

Whatever response he expected, that wasn't it. "Excuse me?"

"The water," I repeated. "Raven and I stopped by the crafts fair after we were done at the beach. She heard ... whispers ... for lack of a better term. She doesn't think all the girls are dead."

Melissa poked her head out of the closet. "Have you ever considered that you're exaggerating and none of them are dead?"

"They've found three bodies," Kade reminded her. "Obviously some of them are dead."

"Yes, but Poet thinks there are, like, a hundred missing girls out there." Melissa's disdain was evident. "That's just ridiculous. There's no way one-hundred girls could go missing without it hitting the news."

"There is if the police are being forced to keep it quiet," I countered. "Most of the girls have been listed as runaways because the mayor doesn't want to incite a panic. That's probably going to come back and bite him before it's all said and done, but I get the feeling that this festival is very important to the city's bottom line. That's all he can see right now."

"I still don't buy it."

"You don't have to buy it." I forced my attention from Melissa and back to Kade. "Raven said the whispers were weird and disjointed. She almost felt as if something was … muting … the girls' feelings. That could be drugs or something else. We simply don't know."

"And how does Naida fit into this?" Kade asked. "I don't understand what you're planning."

"Katie was found in the water. The other bodies were, too. Naida might be able to find something if she looks … like a trail to a house or something. I'm not guaranteeing it will work, but we won't know unless we try."

"Fair enough." Kade slipped a strand of hair behind my ear. "What if it doesn't work? What if we have no idea where to search next?"

"Then we'll have to get creative."

"Do I even want to know what that means?"

"Probably not."

Kade heaved out a sigh. "That's what I was afraid of." He focused on Melissa. "Start working faster. I'm hungry and you're infringing on my dinner hour."

"Why can't I just finish tomorrow?" Melissa asked, petulant. "Why can't I be done?"

"Because the circus opens tomorrow and you'll be busy with other stuff." Kade stretched his back as he stood. "Oh, and because I said so." He extended his hand to me. "How does dinner sound?"

I shifted an uncertain look to Melissa. "What about … ?"

"She'll be fine." Kade was firm. "Melissa, I left the list you have to finish on the desk. Try not to take all night."

Melissa's expression was murderous. "You think this is funny, don't you?"

"Not really." Kade's expression was hard to read. "That doesn't mean I haven't found portions of this afternoon enjoyable. Hopefully you've learned something. If so, this won't have been a wasted effort."

Melissa rolled her eyes. "Whatever."

Kade refused to sink to her level. "Give it some thought. I'll be checking to make sure you finished your chores before going to bed. If you don't ... you're fired."

"I'm really starting to dislike you," Melissa hissed.

"I'm fine with that." Kade squeezed my hand. "Shall we? I'm still not done stuffing your face after last night. I'm thinking another trip to the food trucks is in order."

I beamed. "You read my mind."

THE ENTIRE MYSTIC CARAVAN CREW – sans Melissa, of course – opted to eat at the food trucks. The circus opened the following day, so we had to be up early. No one wanted to cook a heavy dinner, and because we had so many options within easy walking distance, the mood was jovial.

"What did you do today?" Luke asked as he grabbed an onion ring from my plate. "Did you miss me?"

"More than life itself," I said dryly, shaking my head. "What did you do today?"

"We went to the woods," Seth volunteered. "We spent the entire afternoon out there."

I furrowed my brow. "Doing what?"

"We shifted," Luke answered, taking me by surprise.

"You shifted this close to people?" Kade was beside himself.

"Why don't you say it a little louder," Luke drawled. "I don't think the teenagers in the corner heard you. Oh, wait, they're looking in this direction. I guess they did hear you after all."

Kade scowled. "Sorry. It's just ... what were you thinking?"

"They were thinking that their noses were better in animal form," Nellie supplied. "We were hopeful they'd pick up the scent of the girls – or at least someone who wasn't supposed to be out there – and maybe we could help."

"Oh." I scratched my cheek, guilt rolling through my stomach. "Did you find anything?"

"No, but ... the whole thing was weird," Luke replied. "It's almost as if someone cast a spell so we wouldn't scent anything."

That was an interesting take. "Why would you say that?"

"Because we couldn't scent anything," Seth replied. "I mean ... nothing. No rabbits. No deer. No bears. The entire woods were somehow ... empty. That's the only word I can think to describe it."

"Huh." I cut into my coney dog. "What would do that?" I turned to Raven for answers.

"I don't know." Raven, Percival smiling happily as he ate a salad with lemon juice dressing at her side, tilted her head. "That sounds almost like a witch thing."

"You've mentioned witches several times," Kade noted. "Are they dangerous?"

"Not usually," I replied. "Most self-identified witches are really Wiccans. That basically means they don't have legitimate power and are essentially militant environmentalists. They love nature ... and occasionally dance naked in it. They're not often dangerous.

"Real witches are a different story," I continued. "Some lines are born with actual power. There's a family in Michigan, for example, that is supposed to be ridiculously powerful ... even though, apparently, they spend most of their time cursing each other rather than evil-doers.

"Most witches are active members of covens and, by design, covens are supposed to promote sisterhood and peace," I said. "There are a few that go the opposite way."

"Did she just explain something?" Nellie asked, his agitation evident.

I ignored him. "Evil covens have been known to do a lot of damage. If we are dealing with a coven ... members would be capable of casting a spell to cover up scents in the woods. That's not beyond their scope."

"But why?" Dolph challenged. "Why try to cover up the scent?"

"Perhaps they knew shifters would come looking for them," Kade suggested.

"But how would they know that?"

"Because they probably knew we were coming," I supplied. "No, think about it. We're famous in certain circles. Humans don't know exactly what we're capable of, but the paranormal population lives in fear of our visits. It's entirely possible a coven found out we were coming and cast the spell just in case."

"Then what are we supposed to do?" Luke asked. "There are too many girls missing to ignore this. We only have a few more days in this location. We can't simply leave before this is sorted out."

"I don't disagree with you. That's why we're sending Naida into the water."

Naida, who sat between Dolph and Nellie, happily ate her vegetarian pita.

"How is that going to work?" Nellie asked curiously.

"All three bodies were dumped in the water," Raven supplied. "If we're lucky, Naida should be able to figure out which direction the killer was coming from when he or she dumped the bodies. At the very least we should get a more accurate location for where the bodies were dumped."

"And then what?"

Raven shrugged. "We don't have all the answers yet. We might have to put our heads – and magic – together to create a trail. If we are dealing with a coven powerful enough to remove scents from the woods it could be an interesting couple of days. Of course, no matter how strong they are, we're stronger."

"You sound awfully sure about that," Nellie said. "I want to believe you, but you weren't in the woods. The entire place felt ... empty. Like everything was gone."

"That doesn't sound good," I admitted. "We can only tackle one problem at a time, though. Tonight we're sending Naida into the water. We'll figure out a way to handle the woods after that."

"And how will you get Naida into the water without anyone noticing?" Luke asked. "This area is thick with people and they're all interested in us. I don't think it'll be as easy as you think."

"We've taken all that into consideration," I supplied. "It's under control."

"Did anyone else just feel a tremor in the Force?" Luke asked. "I'm pretty sure the Dark Side is coming to smite us."

I flicked his ear. "You're ticking me off."

Luke flicked me back. "Right back at you."

"Don't make me wrestle you down," I warned.

"I'm fine if you want to try. It's been a long time since anyone has cursed my coven. That will be the most action I've seen this month."

"How sad for you," Raven said dryly.

"It is," Luke agreed. "I'm thinking of getting some chaps to liven up my social life, though. I hear they're all the rage."

Raven narrowed her eyes to murderous gray slits. "You're going to want to tread carefully."

Luke refused to adjust his cheerful demeanor. "That sounds nothing like me."

"I can make you tread carefully … and beg for reprieve before it's all said and done," Raven warned.

"Bring it on."

16
SIXTEEN

Naida was practically vibrating with unrestrained excitement when we hit a remote part of the beach. It happened to be surrounded by large and jagged rocks, making for a dangerous situation should someone slip into the water and be pummeled against the shore, but that meant the curious would be less likely to follow us.

"Anything?" I asked Raven as she surveyed the surrounding landscape, her back to us.

"Give me a second," she murmured, closing her eyes.

I could feel the power rippling through her as she cast a net. The spot where we stood was relatively hidden thanks to the rocks, but a tall bluff about five hundred feet down the beach allowed for spies … if someone was so inclined. Since finding out that someone purposely cast a spell to mess with us, it was hard to believe we weren't being followed or spied upon.

"What do you want me to look for specifically?" Naida asked, stripping out of her clothes.

Kade instinctively jerked his head to the side so he couldn't see Naida's naked body. It was a rather deliberate – and hilarious – reaction. Percival, on the other hand, didn't bother looking away.

"I'm glad there are no scales," he said after a beat. "I imagined scales."

Raven didn't open her eyes, but her agitation was evident. "How often have you been imagining her?"

"Not very often." Percival shrugged, unbothered by Raven's tone. "It was merely a curiosity."

"Stop looking at her," Kade ordered, clutching his hands into fists at his sides.

"Why?"

"Because it's rude."

"I'm fine with it," Naida said. "Where I come from we rarely wear clothes. If we do, it's only because we're feeling in a mood to wear glittery stuff."

"Oh, well, joy." Kade focused on me. "You could've left me behind for this."

"You're head of security."

"I'm aware of that."

"We might need you to secure us."

"You don't need me to secure you." Kade made a sour face. "You're perfectly capable of securing yourself."

"We definitely are," Raven agreed, cocking an eyebrow as she turned to face us. "That doesn't mean we don't like eye candy when we're doing the heavy lifting."

Kade scowled. "You are … just a delight. Has anyone ever told you that?"

"I believe you told me that one night when you were visiting my trailer."

Kade jolted, panic washing over his features. "She's making that up, Poet."

I considered messing with him, but it seemed unbelievably cruel given the circumstances. "I'm well aware."

"Well, great." Kade pressed the heel of his hand to his forehead. "There are times I hate hanging around you people. You know that, right?"

"We do. You'll survive, though." I patted his arm and focused on Naida. "Look for anything out of the ordinary."

"That could be anything in this area," Naida pointed out. She wasn't shy in the least and refused to cover her bare breasts as she excitedly wiggled her bottom. "I don't know much about this area, so everything will seem out of the ordinary to me."

"I'm guessing that you'll know if you find something. Just ... swim up and down the coast. Don't go too far out. There's land on the other side, so take time to at least breeze past that. I'm not sure what you're looking for. You'll know it when you see it, though."

"Okay." Naida offered a saucy salute. "I'll probably be back late. Don't wait up."

"If you find something, come back and track us down right away," I instructed. "We don't have a lot of time on this one."

"I'm on it."

Kade remained facing away until he heard Naida splash into the water. Then curiosity got the better of him and he swiveled, his eyebrows rising when he caught sight of Naida's newly-formed fin gleaming under the moonlight. "Holy ... !"

"Yeah, she looks like a mermaid," Raven said dryly. "Water pixies started that legend. Blah, blah, blah."

I pressed my lips together to keep from laughing. "Are you done staring, boys?"

Percival and Kade had the grace to look abashed.

"Great." I held out my hand for Kade. "Come on. We need to do rounds at the festival. If someone is hunting we want to make sure he or she doesn't get a clear shot at anyone but us."

Kade linked his fingers with mine. "Sounds like a plan."

"THE FESTIVAL DOESN'T EVEN start in earnest until tomorrow," Kade noted as he handed me an ice cream cone. We stood in the center of the crafts area and scanned the crowd. "The grounds are only half full, but there are hundreds of people already. Why do you think the crafts people started selling early?"

"They have different margins than we do," I explained, licking my ice cream. "They get a lot of exposure from events like this, but the competition is fierce. Much like the circus, people on the crafts circuit turn this into a lifestyle."

"You seem to know a lot about it."

"I've always enjoyed crafts. Luke and I used to have a weekly craft night, in fact."

"Really?" Kade was understandably dubious. "You made crafts with Luke? Why am I picturing the two of you sitting in the middle of the trailer floor gluing Popsicle sticks together?"

I rolled my eyes. "That's not what we did."

"Oh, yeah? What did you make?"

"Mosaics. We made candleholders."

Kade opened his mouth and then closed it. I could practically see his mind working.

"Yeah, it's not so funny now, is it?" I challenged. "We did a real craft."

"I've never seen any of these candleholders around the trailer," Kade pointed out. "You light candles all the time. I've never seen a mosaic one."

"Oh, well ... hmm."

"Yeah, now I need to hear the story." Kade leaned closer. "Did you use glue?"

He thought he was funny, but the story of the mosaic candleholders probably wasn't far from what he was imagining. "Let's just say I found I'm not a very crafty person." I took another lick of my cone. "That doesn't mean I don't wish I was somehow talented with stuff like that."

Kade slid an arm around my waist. "You're talented in other ways. You don't need mosaic candleholders." His lips twitched, telling me he wasn't quite done teasing me.

"Thank you, but I've always wanted to be good with my hands rather than just my mind. You're good with your hands. You know how it is."

Kade grinned. "I'll take that as a compliment."

"It was meant as one."

"You're very good with your brain, though," Kade said. "You're also good with your hands, even if it's not the way you want to be. As for the candles ... you know you can buy a mosaic candle holder for, like, five bucks, right?"

I rolled my eyes. "It's better to make them yourself."

"I'll take your word for it." Kade leaned forward and licked my ice cream cone. "Now, how about we take a look around and see if you find someone who gives you the willies? I wouldn't mind narrowing our suspect pool."

"I get the willies from a lot of people. That doesn't mean they're all serial killers. Sometimes they're simply random perverts."

"Well, I'm fine taking out a random pervert, too." Kade cracked his neck. "Let's start looking around. I think it's going to be a long night."

BATES WAS HOLDING COURT at his booth when we passed. He mimed tipping an invisible hat in my direction and winked.

"I think one of these little beauties is right up your alley, circus girl." He gestured toward the ridiculous and freaky dolls.

Kade shot me a curious look. "What is that about?"

I told him about our earlier conversation, taking delight in recounting Raven's part in the tale. When I was done, Kade laughed.

"I'm sorry I missed that." He shot a pointed look over his shoulder and caught Bates' eye, something unsaid passing between them. "I don't like him ... and it's not simply because he's a grown man who spends all of his time with dolls."

"You sound like Raven."

"I'm fine with that." Kade directed his attention in front of us. "They're supposedly having a bonfire on the beach tonight. I heard some of the carnies talking about it when they were visiting with the clowns. I'm guessing that would be the sort of gathering that could draw a killer."

"Probably."

We strode through the crowd, pausing here and there to listen and look. I opened my senses, doing my best to explore with my magic, but it was a busy night and picking one thought out of the din wasn't easy. On the surface, everyone appeared to be having a good time. Even when I sought out strife, most of what I found was of the emotional variety rather than the physical.

"Do you know what I find interesting about young people?" I asked as we started walking again. "They're so sure they're right even though they can't possibly understand how wrong they are."

Kade chuckled as he swung our joined hands. "Did you pick up something?"

I nodded. "That boy over there likes that girl." I pointed for emphasis. "He's convinced she likes him because she keeps looking at him. The problem is, she really likes his brother and doesn't understand why the brother is more interested in staring at the boy across the way."

"Ah." Kade squeezed my hand. "Young love is twisty, isn't it?"

"I guess. I often forget what it was like to be that age."

"Were you ever that age?"

"I was. My life didn't change until I was a bit older. When I was fourteen, I felt the sting of young love keenly. In fact, I thought at one point my heart would break and I'd never get over it."

Kade's eyes twinkled. "What was his name?"

"Tom Crawley."

"And what did he look like?"

"Big brown eyes, short brown hair, cheekbones chiseled from granite. No, seriously, I went completely gaga over him. He was a football star, making the varsity team our freshman year. He made my heart race and my cheeks burn."

"I'm not sure I want to hear more," Kade admitted.

"Don't worry, you did the same things to me when I met you. Even though I was older and thought I understood men – and how to control them – I was wrong. You made my heart sing when I saw you, which left me feeling uncomfortable."

"Oh, that was too sweet to mock even though it was a bit sugary," Kade said. "Sadly, I felt the same way. I'm not sure what that does for my standing in the male community, but I felt it all the same."

"That's nice to hear." I beamed. "Thank you for saying it."

"You don't have to thank me. I'm always happy to be schmaltzy when it's just the two of us. Still, tell me what happened with you and Tom Crawley."

"I thought he was going to ask me to the homecoming dance, but he asked Sybil Harper instead. She had bigger boobs, a smaller waist, and her father was loaded. We hated each other on sight when we met. I was crushed beyond belief."

"Did you ever get a chance to date him?"

"No. Once my parents died the trials and tribulations of romancing Tom Crawley took a backseat."

"Still, I bet you wish he could see you now," Kade prodded.

"Because I run the circus?"

"Because you're the best woman I've ever met. You're strong, funny, obstinate, occasionally obnoxious ... and yet you're a complete person. Why wouldn't he kick himself for letting you slip through his fingers?"

"Well, when you put it like that ... ." I leaned forward and pressed a kiss to the corner of his mouth. "Come on. This isn't a date. We're supposed to be keeping the populace safe from a serial killer. We won't be able to do that if we're too busy staring at each other."

"Very good point."

ONCE WE GOT TO THE BONFIRE, I was dumbfounded to find what had to be at least one- hundred teenagers milling about. I performed a cursory scan of the crowd – and then a longer study – and tilted my head as I turned in a circle.

"There are no adults here."

Kade followed my lead and looked over the teenagers. "Huh. You're right. How did that happen?"

"I don't know." The sound of hysterical laughter caught my attention and I focused on two young women near the fire. Melissa and

Paige looked to be a bit drunk by the way they listed to their sides. "I guess I shouldn't be surprised."

Kade followed my gaze, a muscle in his jaw working. "We're not her parents."

"No."

"We're still her superiors." Kade strode forward, not stopping until he was directly in front of Melissa. He jerked the bottle from her hand and lifted it to his nose.

"What are you doing?" Melissa sputtered, surprised.

"Just checking." Kade drank from the bottle. "Hard cider. Nice choice."

Melissa's eyes flashed. "Great. Can I have it back?"

"Oh, we can't have that," Kade drawled. "I'm your boss and you're underage. I don't know much, but all the books I've read about getting underlings to fall in line are pretty strict when it comes to supplying people with alcohol."

Melissa made a face as Paige rolled her eyes.

"And you said they weren't your parents," Paige taunted.

"We're not her parents," Kade clarified. "We're her bosses. Both of us."

"Well ... how great for her." Paige had her role as mean girl down pat. "I thought my father was a pain until I met you guys."

"Your father is a pain," Kade said. "At least he's friendly. He obviously didn't pass on that trait to you."

"I didn't know I needed to be friendly to make it in this world."

"I don't really care what you do." Kade opted for honesty. "You're not our problem. Melissa is."

"I'm an adult," Melissa repeated for what felt like the hundredth time.

"Then act like one." Kade tipped the hard cider bottle upside down and emptied it before tossing it in the nearest trash receptacle. "If you get arrested, Melissa, you're on your own. Keep that in mind."

Kade slipped his arm around my waist and prodded me away from the fire. It took everything I had not to grab hold of Melissa and drag her with us. Not only would she fight me, it would very likely make things worse.

I waited until Kade moved us closer to the water to speak. "She's spiraling."

"I don't think things are as bad as that. She's just going into party mode. It happens."

"You were hard on her."

"She needs it."

"I guess, but ... ." Movement from the corner of my eye caught my attention and I jolted when I realized it was Naida, her hair still wet from her swim and her eyes keen. She was hurrying in our direction. I pushed worry about Melissa out of my head and focused on the problem at hand. "You're back early. Did you find something?"

Naida ran a hand through her damp hair and nodded. "There's a current of death under the water. I followed it."

"That sounds ominous," Kade said.

"It is." Naida was serious. "I followed the current. It led to a cave."

I knit my eyebrows. "An underwater cave?"

"Yup ... and it's warded."

I felt as if the air was being sucked from my lungs. "And that right there is a game changer."

SEVENTEEN

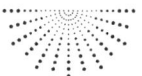

"Warded how?"

I did my best to remain calm while Naida ran her fingers through her hair and chatted loudly, ignoring the people casting her curious looks as they passed.

"I don't know." Naida took the time to pull on her shorts and a T-shirt, but she'd forgone her panties and bra, which happened to be poking out of her pocket for anyone to see. If the three teenagers watching from about fifteen feet away were any indication, she was starting to cause a stir.

That wasn't good given our location.

"How could you tell it was warded?" Kade asked, his expression unreadable. He clearly didn't understand what Naida was trying to say, and explaining it to him would be difficult.

"Because I was smacked in the face with black magic when I tried to get closer to the cave," Naida replied without hesitation.

"How did you sense the cave in the first place?"

"It's a little gift of mine," Naida said. "It's kind of like sonar, if you will. My senses pick up rock formations so I can avoid them when I'm swimming in the dark. The formation pinged more than ponged, though."

Kade turned to me, incredulous. "Did she just explain something?"

It took everything I had not to laugh. It was a serious situation, after all. "I believe she thinks she did." I kept my gaze on Naida. "Could you hear anything from the cave?"

"No, but it's not empty." Naida shook her hair. "The thing is, I couldn't really see inside, but there was a lot of bad juju outside."

"Creature?" I asked, intrigued.

"What kind of creature lives in a cave in the water?" Kade was legitimately curious.

"All different manner of creatures live in water caves." Naida acted as if she were talking to a child. "It's generally not a big thing. Most of them are harmless. But what I felt in that cave was pretty far from harmless, and it wasn't ... otherworldly."

Kade's frustration was evident. "Meaning?"

"Meaning that the energy feels more human in origin," I supplied.

"So ... a person managed to ward a cave?"

"Or a witch," Naida said. "The wards were drawn in blood. I don't know much, but I do know that."

Kade often struggled with patience and this was no exception. "How do you know that?"

"I smelled it."

"Under water?"

"Oh, geez." Naida rolled her eyes until they landed on me. "I know you like this guy, but ... come on."

I pressed my lips together and forced my eyes to Kade. He didn't look happy. "I'll explain it to him when we get back to the circus. Can you tell me anything else about the cave?"

"It looks as if it had an entrance from underwater so you can swim beneath and go up through the hole. I believe there are places inside untouched by the water.

"It was hard to see, but if the cave hadn't been warded I believe I could have swum through the hole and then climbed onto dry land," she continued. "You know what that means, right?"

I nodded, thoughtful.

"I don't know what that means," Kade pointed out.

Naida patted his arm in a soothing manner. "It really is a good thing you're handsome."

Kade scowled. "You guys make me tired."

"Yeah, get used to that," Naida said, flicking her eyes back to me. "I'll draw the wards I remember and take a photo and text it to you. I know you have books. Maybe we can narrow our suspects through the wards."

"Good idea. Thanks for looking."

"No problem." Naida waved off my gratitude. "Oh, one other thing." She stilled before leaving. "The way the formation was designed, I think there's probably another entrance on land."

Now that was intriguing. "Do you think you could find the spot during daylight hours?"

"I think I could find the formation," she clarified. "My guess is the door is hidden, but I'm sure if you and Raven put your minds to it you'll find a way to discover the door."

"I'm sure we will, too." I forced a smile. "Thanks, Naida. You've given me a lot to think about."

"That's good, because I'm going to have nightmares. Whatever is down there is evil, Poet. I think it's strong, too. When we decide what to do … I think we'll have to do it together if we want to win."

I was thinking the same thing. "We'll figure it out."

I watched her go with a mixture of enthusiasm and trepidation. We were finally getting somewhere, although I had no idea what to do with the information she supplied.

"What are you thinking?" Kade asked after a beat.

"I'm thinking I want to see inside of that cave."

"Because you think the girls are being kept there?"

The question caught me off guard. "I really didn't think about that," I said. "I guess, in theory, it could happen. Wards are meant to keep someone out of a space, not in. I'll need to give that more thought before I come up with an opinion either way. I assumed the cave was for the creature and the girls were either somewhere else or … dead. I haven't allowed myself to think about that too much."

"Fair enough. But what about the cave? What do you think it means?"

"I think that someone is trying to hide some black magic stuff inside. You don't ward a cave unless you're serious about keeping busybodies away from your business. I have no idea what's going on inside, but I'm guessing it's something big ... and dark."

Kade didn't seem nearly as keen to see the cave. "Can you break wards?"

"I hope so. I need to see the photos Naida sends me first. Hopefully I can do a little research before we go to bed."

"See, I was hoping we could do a little something else first," Kade teased, poking my side as he tried to lighten my mood.

"I'm sure we'll have time for both."

The sound of high-pitched giggling caught my attention and I shifted my head to stare at Melissa and Paige. They'd moved from their previous location and were surrounded by at least eight boys as they twirled their hair around their fingers, flirting.

Kade followed my gaze, his smile slipping when he realized what I saw. "They're drawing quite a crowd, huh?"

That was an understatement. "I wasn't popular when I was a teenager. Is it normal for that many boys to talk to two girls like that?"

As if reading my mind, Kade gripped my shoulder to give it a reassuring squeeze. "Do you want me to get her?"

I balked. "I'm not her mother."

"I know that."

"You're not her father."

"I definitely know that."

"We can't stop her from having a good time," I reminded him. "She's an adult and she's allowed to do whatever she wants in her off time."

"She is," Kade confirmed. "The thing is, I checked her work from earlier before we left the grounds tonight and she half-assed the last two tasks on her list. In my mind, that means she needs to go back and fix it."

I understood. Unfortunately, I wasn't sure I was completely comfortable letting him torture my protégé. "Um … hmm."

Kade leaned closer and lowered his voice. "If you're worried about Melissa being out here with those guys … and whatever else is hunting the area … I have no problem being the bad guy and forcing her back to the circus grounds."

I was intrigued but torn. "What do you think she'll do?"

"I really don't care."

I wished I shared his attitude. "I'm worried she'll blow up and quit because you embarrassed her in front of her friends," I admitted.

"She won't do that."

"You seem convinced of that. I would like to know how."

"She wants to be you," Kade answered easily. "Right now she's having a good time, but ultimately she wants to be you. She's not stupid enough to let that slip through her fingers."

"Are you sure?"

Kade nodded.

I made up my mind on the spot. "Get her … and make sure you scare the life out of those boys. In fact, I'll help you do that."

Kade arched an eyebrow. "How?"

"Don't worry. It will be entertaining, though. Trust me."

MELISSA WAS SPITTING MAD, so I left Kade to deal with her once we returned to the circus grounds. I conducted a quick circuit, testing the dreamcatcher boundaries before hitting my trailer. By the time I changed into comfortable shorts and a T-shirt, Naida texted with the symbols and I had something to research.

What I found was … disturbing.

Kade stomped his feet as he entered an hour into my research, but I didn't bother looking up from my computer screen.

"I don't know how anyone deals with kids of a certain age," he groused, kicking off his shoes and unbuckling his jeans. "I know she's technically an adult, but right now she's acting more immature than most ten-year-olds I've met."

"Where is she?"

"Cleaning the main tent."

"I thought that was already done."

"Yeah, well, I didn't think it was clean enough, and now she has something to keep her busy for a few hours." Kade dragged off his shirt before lifting the covers and sliding in next to me. "I think she's been taking lessons on effective complaining from Luke. I almost gave up and told her to get out three times while explaining exactly what I wanted. But I knew that was what she was trying to get me to do, so I held strong."

"Good for you." I absently patted his knee.

"That's it? I thought you'd thank me with kisses or something."

I flashed a wry grin. "I will in a few minutes. Naida sent her drawings of the wards she remembered, and I'm trying to see what I can find."

Kade turned serious. "Anything good?"

"I guess that depends on how you define 'good.'"

"Do you want to expand on that?"

"Sure." I tapped the screen. "See this one?"

"Yeah. It looks like a square with small circles in three of the corners."

"Right. It's an old symbol."

"Okay." Kade wasn't up on magical mystique, so explaining things to him was often an exercise in patience. "Why is it important?"

"I believe I've already told you that most modern witches are really Wiccan and they stick to the basic symbols from those tenets," I started. "So, for example, a pentacle represents the four earth elements and symbolizes the connection between them.

"You also have things like the Triple Moon, which represents the three phases of the moon," I continued. "The first symbol is the new moon, which represents new beginnings. The middle is the full moon, which is when magic is most powerful. The last is the waning moon and is supposed to signify the best time for sending things away.

"Now, that's not technically important to this discussion, but it's essentially a way to give you an example of the symbols modern witches use when exploring the craft," I said. "Most Wiccan folk believe one tenet: Whatever energy you put out comes back to you threefold. That means they essentially want to be good people because they believe they will be rewarded for it."

"Okay, I think I'm following." Kade rubbed the back of his neck. "You're saying the symbols Naida found are different."

I nodded. "Definitely different ... and darker."

"Darker how?"

"Keep in mind, these symbols aren't necessarily bad by themselves," I cautioned. "When used together, though, they're troubling."

"Okay. Lay it on me."

"This is the symbol for water, which is fairly obvious," I supplied. "This is a protection symbol for a child, but it's inverted. This is a sleep symbol ... and a crone symbol ... and a death symbol, which also happens to be inverted ... and the purification symbol, also inverted."

Kade studied the stick drawings. "What's the significance of the symbols being inverted?"

"If they're upside down, that means they're being used for the opposite of their intended use ... or at least a strong variation. Also, since they're drawn in blood, they're supposed to be stronger."

"If the death symbol is inverted, that means that no one is dying, right?"

"In theory, but that's not always the practice. That symbol is often stolen and used for different things, including mind control. The person isn't dead, but they're not essentially living either."

Kade knit his eyebrows. "Like zombies?"

"Not necessarily. We don't know enough about that symbol. I'm more interested in the crone, child protection and purification symbols."

"Does the crone mean we're working against a woman?"

"Maybe. We could also be working against a coven. The purification symbol being inverted makes me believe someone is trying to pollute something – maybe a soul – rather than cleanse it."

"Okay, I think I'm following," Kade said. "What does all of this mean together?"

"I have no idea." I felt mildly defeated. "I want to show it to Raven tomorrow. She's older than me – by a long shot – and she might have some idea what these symbols mean together."

"What's our next step?"

"We need to find the cave."

"How do you plan to do that when the circus opens tomorrow?"

That was a very good question. "I don't know." I closed the laptop and shifted it to my nightstand. "We'll figure it out. It would be easier in some ways to do it during daylight hours."

"People might see us during daylight hours, too," Kade pointed out.

"I know. That means we might need to go after dark no matter what might feel easier ... or safer. Are you going to argue if that's what we decide?"

Kade shook his head as he slipped his arm beneath my waist and shifted me so I had no choice but to roll partially on top of him. "No."

I was dubious. "Are you sure?"

"I'm sure I'm not going to put up a fight."

"That doesn't seem like you. No offense, but I've noticed that you like to argue when we make plans to do something you think is stupid."

"Then don't be stupid." Kade kissed the end of my nose. "You know what you're doing. You're strong. I don't want to be cut out of any decisions, but I'm not going to pretend that this is my area of expertise. If there are girls out there who need help, I know you'll find them and offer help. You can't stop yourself even if it means you'll be at risk ... and I wouldn't want you to pull away from something like this."

I didn't bother to hide my relief. "That makes things so much easier. I thought I might have to manipulate you."

Kade pursed his lips. "How were you going to do that?"

"I believe nudity was going to be involved."

Kade chuckled. "Well, in that case, I'm putting my foot down. Under no circumstances are you to search for that cave."

I stared at him for a long moment.

"That's your cue to make me see things your way," Kade prodded.

I didn't want to encourage him, but I laughed all the same. "Fine, but you should know that manipulation is often pleasurable and painful at the same time."

"I can live with that."

Something told me he was telling the truth.

18

EIGHTEEN

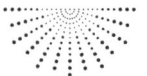

Evil dolls infiltrated my dreams again. This time they wore scuba gear and darted through the water, attacking legs and feet while people – including me – attempted to swim. It was almost more terrifying than *Jaws*. It was also a bit ridiculous, so I didn't wake feeling cranky and out of sorts.

I took the research I uncovered to the communal dining area and placed the computer in front of Raven while I set about making breakfast with Naida and Nixie. "What do you make of that?"

Raven furrowed her brow as she sipped her coffee and stared. "I don't know. What am I supposed to make of it?"

I ran through the story, casting the occasional glance toward a petulant-looking Melissa as she purposely sat pouting by herself at the end of the table. When I was done, everyone was intrigued. Even Melissa, who I'm sure wanted to avoid talking to me, seemed to have questions.

"A cave?" Nellie wrinkled his nose. "Caves are gross. I don't want to go into a cave."

"I'm pretty sure no one said you had to," Raven shot back. "Still, you're a dwarf. Don't dwarves like caves?"

"You've been watching too much *Lord of the Rings*. That's a myth."

"The dwarves in our realm like caves," Nixie argued. "In fact, they prefer caves to direct sunlight. And they're all really pale and twisted. They look like little yellowish potatoes."

Nellie heaved out a disgusted groan. "Those are gnomes."

"I'm pretty sure they're dwarves."

"And I'm pretty sure that you're an idiot."

I held up a finger to still Nellie. "Now is not the time to argue the difference between dwarves and gnomes."

"Fine," Nellie gritted out, resigned. "I'll pick a time later to explain the difference. And I expect all of you to be there with pen and paper so you can take notes."

"That sounds like the worst classroom experiment ever," Luke said. "Go back to the cave. I can't say I'm a fan of caves either. Will we have to go inside this cave?"

"You're a wolf when you want to be," Kade pointed out.

"And you're a manly man with broad shoulders who shaves his chest," Luke fired back. "What's your point?"

"I thought wolves liked dens."

"Oh, we definitely need to have a class to eradicate the myths," Luke complained. "Poet, how can you let him say things like that to me?"

This was not how I envisioned breakfast going. I thought I'd show Raven the symbols, she would come up with a brilliant idea and everyone would rally for a plan.

"You don't have to go into the cave, Luke," I offered. "No one has to go into the cave. I'll go into the cave by myself."

"You say that now, but when you get captured who do you think is going to have to go into the cave to save you?" Luke challenged.

"I think that falls under my job description," Kade said dryly. "I'll go into the cave."

Luke made a face. "I think you do that as often as you can anyway."

It took Kade a moment to realize what Luke referred to. "Do you have to be such a complete and total pervert?"

"She's my best friend and I don't even like the parts she's sporting," Luke said. "How is that perverted?"

"You just said ... ."

"What did I say?" Luke feigned innocence. "I think you heard something I didn't say and your head went to a dirty place. That makes you the pervert."

Kade shifted a slit-eyed look to me. "He's in our lives because of you. It's your job to deal with him."

"I already told you I'm not getting involved when you guys decide to thump your chests," I shot back. "We have more important issues than your fake drama."

"Yeah." Raven's eyes flashed as her lips twisted into an impish grin. "Grow up. My boyfriend is a clown and he's ten times more mature than you guys."

"Oh, thank you." Percival beamed as he gazed at her adoringly, his fake accent on full display. "That's a lovely way to start the day, my dear."

Luke stared at them a beat before rolling his eyes. "Whatever. He fakes his accent and wears chaps. If you think I'm holding him up as some iconic man hero, you've got another think coming."

"What's a man hero?" Nixie asked, curious.

"It's a man who happens to be a hero."

"Do you say it that way because here at the circus most of the heroes are women?"

"No. That's ridiculous."

"Really?" Nixie was clearly spoiling for a fight. She occasionally enjoyed a good row and Luke was almost always willing to oblige. "I don't hear the women complaining about going into a cave."

"She has a point," Naida said. "Only the men are doing that."

Luke made an exaggerated face only a best friend could love – and I totally enjoyed it, for the record. "That's not true at all. Nellie is wearing a dress and he complained first. He's practically a woman."

Nellie's expression shifted. "Don't make me thump you with my ax."

"There will be no ax play," I warned.

"I totally thought she was going to say something else," Luke offered with a snicker, causing Nellie to grin.

"And you're back to being a pervert," Kade complained. "This conversation went full circle in less than two minutes, and that's including the time we spent talking about chaps and ax play."

Luke snorted. "Living in a community like this is fun, huh?"

I could tell Kade didn't want to smile. That would only encourage Luke, who needed no prodding when he wanted to be a pain. He couldn't stop himself. "It has its moments."

I tapped the spoon I held against the lip of the bowl I was using to scramble eggs for the grill. "We have a serious problem," I reminded them. "We have a bunch of missing girls and we need to find them. This cave is our best shot."

"So what's the plan?" Raven asked. "We can't swim like Naida. I've heard about a few oxygen-deprivation spells but they rarely end well."

"That wasn't my plan." Truthfully, I'd heard about the same spells and would never risk it. "Naida thinks there has to be a cave entrance on land."

"Oh." Raven perked up. "So you want to access the cave via a different route. If we can find it, that means we can take more people."

I nodded. "Exactly."

"I don't understand what you think you're going to find there." Melissa spoke for the first time, her voice clear but her expression hard to read. "There was a police officer on the boardwalk last night and I asked him about the missing girls. He said that's a rumor and nothing more."

I focused my full attention on her. "Of course he said that. They're trying to cover it up."

"But ... why? What good does that do them?"

"This festival is a big deal for the city," Kade explained. "They want people to come from all over just because of the festival. Tourism is a big boon to local economies, and this festival has clearly been planned for a long time."

"How does admitting there are girls missing change that?"

"If tourists knew that there were more than one-hundred girls missing, they might choose to go somewhere else," I supplied. "That would take money away from the local economy. Also, the city officials spent a lot of money to set this thing up. They did it because they thought they would earn it back – and then some – through high turnout. If people take off and don't attend the festival, what do you think that means for them?"

Melissa opted to remain stubborn. "Yes, but if girls were really missing, that's more important than money."

"Of course the girls are more important than money," Raven said. "The city officials have chosen to pretend that the girls are running away instead of disappearing. That helps them keep their consciences clear."

"You don't know that." Melissa refused to back down. "You're assuming that. Maybe the girls did run away. It's been known to happen."

"It has," I agreed. "That doesn't mean that's what happened here."

"There are too many girls missing, Melissa," Kade prodded. "If it were one or two girls, I'd agree with you. But it's one-hundred girls."

"This is a big area."

"Not that big."

Melissa opened her mouth to say something and then snapped it shut, ultimately folding her arms across her chest as she shook her head. "I think you guys are seeing things that aren't there."

"And I think you're being willfully blind," Raven shot back. "We've been at this a lot longer than you. We know when something is wrong – even if we don't exactly know how something is wrong at any given moment – and we know when to act. We need to act now."

The silence hanging over the table was weighted, everyone expecting Melissa to push things further. Instead, a man cleared his throat behind us and everyone snapped to attention, worried someone had managed to sneak up on us and eavesdrop. It was Max.

"This looks like a serious discussion." Max forced a watery smile as he moved to the table, his eyes briefly landing on Melissa before moving to other faces. "Does someone want to tell me what's going on?"

"How much time do you have?" Raven asked.

Max shrugged, opting to sit in the spot across from Melissa before pouring himself a mug of coffee. "I have all day if need be. What seems to be the problem?"

I launched into the tale from the beginning, highlighting the salient points but keeping things brief. When I was done, Max was thoughtful.

"So you think it's witches?"

"Witches are nature-loving peaceniks," Melissa argued.

Max spared her a look. "You're cute." His expression reflected amusement. "This is why I enjoy spending time with young people occasionally. I forget that they can see the world in such … novel ways."

Melissa balked. "Are you saying I'm naïve?"

"I probably wouldn't use that word."

"Good."

"It's not the wrong word, though." Max wasn't the type to back down and he clearly had no intention of doing that with Melissa. She was used to barreling over people. He wouldn't allow that. "Your youth is not a bad thing. Maturity is good. Wisdom gained through age is good. Young people can see possibilities those more set in their ways cannot see. One age is not necessarily better than another."

Melissa, thankfully, had the good sense not to put her newly-discovered attitude on full display for Max's benefit. "I'm not sure those girls are missing. Everyone else seems to think I'm crazy for believing that."

"I see. What do you think happened to them?"

"I think they ran away."

Max cocked an eyebrow. "All of them?"

"Why not? They're all young. Running away holds appeal when your whole life is about other people bossing you around."

Max swished his lips, his amusement growing. "I see." He slid his eyes to me for a beat and then back. "I understand you're having a few growing pains."

Now it was my turn to be nervous. "Who told you that?"

"I hear more than you realize. Just because I choose to spend most of my time in my trailer doesn't mean I don't know what's going on."

Uh-oh. I flicked my eyes to Kade, but he looked as clueless as I felt. "And what have you been hearing?"

"That Miss Melissa feels put upon."

Melissa made a protesting sound deep in her throat. "That's not what I said."

Max held up his hand to quiet her. He was a patient man, but Melissa's tone told everyone she was about to start whining. If there was one thing Max hated, it was whining.

"You're in an awkward place," Max noted. "You're the youngest one here. The group you're assigned to isn't exactly full of gregarious partiers – Luke's keg stand notwithstanding."

Luke blanched. "All right, who has the big mouth?"

I pressed my lips together to keep from laughing.

Max studied Melissa with intent eyes. "The paranormal part of this team plays, but they focus on work first. The other groups tend to focus on play first, but they're nowhere near as interesting to you. You came here and found someone your own age who could do both. You're feeling a bit … intrigued. No one blames you for that."

Melissa widened her eyes. "What do you mean?"

"Your new friend has powers," Max replied. "I saw you with her the other night. I could practically smell the witch on her."

"I knew it," I muttered, shaking my head. "I should've followed up on that."

"We don't know that she's involved in this," Max reminded me. "She's barely more than a child. Heck, she's traveling with her father. Plus, well, I smelled witch. I didn't smell power."

The distinction caught me off guard. "What do you mean?"

"She was born a witch, which means her mother was probably a witch," Max replied. "I have been watching her since that first night, but haven't seen or felt her use her powers. Have you noticed her exhibiting powers, Melissa?"

Melissa shifted, uncomfortable. "No."

"Are you sure?"

"I'm sure. I don't like talking about her behind her back. It doesn't seem fair. That's not what a good friend does."

Luke made a derisive sound in the back of his throat. "Honey, that's a child's way of looking at things. Adults know that everyone talks behind his or her back. It's the way of the world and human nature. I talk behind Poet's back all the time and she's my best friend."

I wrinkled my nose. "What do you say behind my back?"

"Mostly stuff about how you're whipped for Kade. You know, normal stuff."

How was that normal stuff? "We'll talk about that later," I warned, shaking my head. "For now we need to focus on the problem at hand. Melissa, if you know anything about Paige using her powers – perhaps being involved in all this – you need to tell us now."

Melissa hopped to her feet, outraged. "How could she possibly be involved in this? She travels the country with her father. She's only been here a week. I'm not even sure where she lives most of the year because she says they're on the road a lot."

"That's a good point," Raven said. "She hasn't been here since this started."

"I wasn't saying that I thought she was involved," Max added. "I was merely trying to massage Melissa's psyche to find out why she was so attached to Paige."

"I like her because she's fun and doesn't always want to talk about work and whatever monster we're fighting this week," Melissa shot back. "All we do is hang out and gossip. Do you know how long it's been since I've been able to do that?"

"No one is stopping you from doing that now," I argued. "You simply have to finish your work before you do it."

"Sometimes we gossip and have fun while working," Luke added. "It's not easy, but we manage."

I shot him a withering look. "Sometimes I think you talk just to hear yourself talk."

"And sometimes I agree with you." Luke was blasé. "Have you noticed Paige exhibiting magic?"

"No." Melissa was firm. "She's just a normal girl."

"She's far from normal, and you know that," Max countered. "I'm not sure Paige knows, though. Either way, it very likely doesn't matter. She's clearly not involved in abductions from six months ago."

"No," I agreed. "We need to make finding the cave our first priority. In fact … ." I trailed off when I caught sight of a figure hurrying in our direction. "It's Barney."

Everyone shifted and stared, our conversation coming to an end as we prepared for what looked to be an intense interaction. I expected Barney to meander until getting to the point, but apparently he wasn't in the mood this morning.

"Have you seen Paige?" Barney's attention was on Melissa, who appeared surprised by the question.

"Not since last night," Melissa replied. "Why?"

"She didn't come to our tent."

"Maybe she met someone," Luke suggested. "Maybe she spent the night in someone else's tent."

Barney pinned Luke with a hateful look. "Paige wouldn't do that. She knows it would drive me crazy. That's not it."

"But … ."

Barney vehemently shook his head to cut off whatever Luke was about to say. "She's missing. My daughter is missing. I think someone took her."

And just like that, things officially got worse.

"Oh, well, that can't be good," Nellie said. "That can't be even a little bit good."

19

NINETEEN

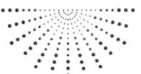

Melissa's bewilderment, fear and fury lashed out and slammed into my stomach like an angry fist.

"What are you talking about?"

She was on her feet and staring down Barney as if he were the enemy before I could recover.

"Melissa, you shouldn't take that tone with him." Max's voice was full of warning as he stood. "I don't believe we've had the chance to meet. I'm Max Anderson. I own Mystic Caravan."

Barney glanced between Melissa and Max, confusion warring with anger. It was clear he had no idea how to react. Finally, he extended his hand for Max to shake. "Barney Tolliver. I have a stained-glass booth in the crafts area. I've visited your bonfire a time or two."

"That's lovely." Max had no intention of dillydallying. "Tell us what happened with Paige."

Barney ran a hand through his disheveled hair, misery washing over his features. "She didn't come home last night."

"I understand that." Max's tone was soothing. "We need more specifics, though. When was the last time you saw her?"

"Last night." Barney leaned his hip against the picnic table. "I was working the booth during the late shift. She left with your girl and said they were going to that big bonfire down at the beach."

"She was there," I volunteered. "Kade and I walked through that area before bed and she was down there."

"You saw her?" Barney looked hopeful. "Is there a chance she came back here to sleep?" He flicked his eyes to Melissa. "Did she stay in your trailer?"

Melissa shook her head. "I left early."

"You left early?"

Melissa swallowed hard and nodded. "I had to come back and do some cleaning."

"So you just left her down there by herself?" Barney's tone was accusatory. I didn't blame him. That didn't mean any of this was Melissa's fault.

"That's on me," Kade interjected, drawing Barney's attention to him. "Melissa had work to finish and I put my foot down. We made her leave early."

"You made her abandon my daughter, is what you're saying?" Barney's temper ratcheted up a notch. "How great for your girl, huh?"

Kade was calm. "I'm sorry you're under duress. I didn't know it would turn into such a big deal."

"Obviously," Barney said dryly. "So you have no idea where she is?"

"No. I'm sorry."

"That doesn't mean we can't figure out where she is," Max offered. "What time were you at the bonfire, Poet?"

I did the math in my head. "We left shortly before ten."

"And Paige was there when you left?"

I nodded. "She was ... talking to some boys."

"Boys?" Barney clearly wasn't thrilled by the revelation. "What boys?"

"Melissa was talking to them, too," Kade said. "What can you tell us about them, Melissa?"

Melissa's face twisted. She obviously didn't like being put on the spot. "I don't know. They were just ... boys."

"You had to hear names," Max pressed.

"I did, but … I didn't hear last names." Melissa shrugged. "The tall one with the dark hair, the one who looked like Robert Pattinson, his name was Toby."

"Wait." Luke held up a hand. "Is looking like Robert Pattinson a good thing? What? I can't keep up with teenagers today."

I ignored his interruption and kept my attention on Melissa. "What other names?"

"Josh. Dakota. Matt. Brian."

"Anything else that you recall?" Max asked.

Melissa shook her head. "No. We only talked to them a few minutes. I know that Paige liked Toby. She called dibs on him the second she saw him."

"Dibs?" Barney arched a confrontational eyebrow. "What is that supposed to mean? Are you insinuating that she planned to have sex with that boy before she'd even met him?"

Max held up his hand to draw Barney's ire. "I don't believe that's what she was saying at all. I'm guessing Paige merely said that so she could flirt with Toby and Melissa could flirt with whatever other boy struck her fancy. Unless teenage girls have changed since I was that age, I believe that's how it has always worked."

Barney was placated, but only marginally. "I'm sorry. You have to understand, she's my daughter. I'm a single father. She's all I have."

"I do understand." Max made sympathetic noises. "Just out of curiosity, what happened to her mother?"

I widened my eyes, surprised. It wasn't like Max to veer off on a tangent when the stakes were so high, so I knew he must have his reasons.

"She died a long time ago," Barney replied. "We owned a store in Phoenix. It was one of those kitschy places that has a little of everything. You know, pop culture items, shirts, purses … candles and stuff. It was fairly successful.

"She was closing up one night and there was a fire of some sort," he continued. "The medical examiner said she suffered a blow to the back of her head, but the fire was accidental. He thinks she tried to extinguish the fire and accidentally got hurt in the process. That was eleven years ago."

"I'm sorry," Max said. "That must have been hard on Paige."

"She's a trooper." Barney puffed out his chest, pride evident. "She's a good worker and we've been running this circuit together for almost eight years. She knows the rules and doesn't break them. That allows me to grant her certain privileges. She wouldn't take off with a guy and simply not call me. That's not how she is."

"I don't believe anyone is suggesting that's what happened," Max said. "In fact, I believe your initial instincts were correct. I think it's far more likely that someone took her."

"Oh." Barney deflated a bit. "I don't know what to do. I've never had to grapple with something like this before." He took everyone by surprise when he grabbed the front of Max's shirt, desperation rolling off him. "You have to help me. I can't lose her. She's too important to me. I ... please!"

Max patted his wrist. "I'm going to help you." He extended his hand and pointed at the expensive trailer at the far side of the property. "That is my trailer. Head that way. We'll call the police and I'll help you search."

Barney looked so profoundly grateful my stomach twisted with anxiety.

Max waited until Barney was on his way to the trailer, well out of earshot, to speak again. "If Paige was taken by the person or entity who took the other girls, she could be in real danger. I will handle Mr. Tolliver and the police. You all have duties to attend to."

Melissa was furious when she slapped her hands on the table. "Duties? You expect us to work when Paige is missing. That's just ... ridiculous!"

"I expect you to fulfill your responsibilities." Max chose his words carefully as his eyes hardened. "I understand you're upset, bereft even, but the show must go on."

"Screw you." Melissa's face flushed with rage. "I'm not simply going to abandon my friend. She's out there somewhere and she needs help."

"You will do your duty," Max shot back. "You will leave Paige to me for the time being. When I have more information I will be back and we'll make search decisions then."

"I don't have to listen to you." Melissa's eyes glinted with something I couldn't quite identify. "You're not my father."

"No, but I am your boss."

"It doesn't have to be that way."

"It certainly does not."

I cleared my throat to get Max's attention and hopefully ease the tension. "Now is not the time for this. Max will get information on Paige. You have to trust him, Melissa."

Her face twisted with conflicted grief. "You know what? No. I'm looking for her myself. You can't stop me." She turned on her heel and stalked away, heading in the direction of the beach.

I made to go after her, but Kade stopped me with a hand on my wrist.

"Leave her be," he instructed. "She's upset and her emotions are all over the place. You'll only make things worse if you track her down and attempt to force her to see reason."

I didn't see how things could get worse. "She shouldn't be out there wandering around alone."

"No one is going to take her in broad daylight, especially once we get the cops down here," Kade argued. "Let her be. She'll be okay."

I hoped he was right. I pressed the heel of my hand to my forehead. "Okay, no matter what, we need to search for that cave once the circus closes down tonight. I don't care who hates caves or why, we're putting together a team ... and I don't want to hear any crap."

"You won't hear crap." Luke was earnest. "You've got our support. You always do."

I knew that was true, yet it didn't make me feel any better. What in the holy hell is going on around here?

I WASN'T IN THE MOOD TO tell fortunes, but I had no choice. After breakfast I changed into my costume, tucking my hair under a brightly-colored scarf before sliding into a skirt that had bells hanging from the drawstrings. Usually I enjoyed the sound I made when I walked. Today was another story.

The circus opened at noon and guests were lined up twenty minutes before that. I didn't have a lot of time to worry about Melissa – who was apparently still out searching for Paige on her own – yet she was never far from my mind. So when I recognized one of the boys from the previous night I decided to play fast and loose with the magical rules to entice him to my tent.

He was with a group of boys, so I was forced to wait until he was alone. That meant following him for a full ten minutes before I found an opening. When it happened, I didn't waste time and immediately started working on him.

I let loose a different sort of lullaby, one that weaved its way through the boy's mind – this was the infamous Toby, I found out within seconds – and drew him to my tent. There was a line, but I politely informed everyone that things would move quickly and Toby had won a free reading at the bonfire the night before. Then I drew him into my web and forced him to sit in one of the chairs across the table from me.

In general, I'm not one to exert undue force on an unsuspecting young man. I had no proof Toby did anything wrong – and I mostly believed he was innocent – but I needed as much information as possible and I didn't want to waste time being polite. I also didn't want to risk falling for a lie because Toby was uncomfortable with the truth.

"Do you remember me?"

Toby's eyes were glazed and unfocused. "You were at the bonfire last night. You took that Melissa girl away."

"How did that make you feel?"

Toby snorted at the question, as if there was something funny about it. "How was it supposed to make me feel?"

I clamped down tighter on the magic wafting through his brain. "How did that make you feel?" I repeated, keeping one eye on the closed tent flap should someone try to push inside while I was essentially using a magical vise on this kid's brain.

"Angry," Toby barked out, his features twisting. "I was angry when it happened because she was hot. I wanted to take her to the beach for a private swim session."

I poked his brain with a deliberate needle, enjoying the way he whimpered. "She's too good for you. Stay away from her. In fact, if you see her again, you're going to wet your pants. Do you understand?"

Toby was horrified. "Why would I want to do that?"

"You won't be able to stop yourself. Do you understand?"

Toby squirmed on his seat but nodded. "I understand. I don't want to talk to her."

"That's good." I returned my voice to a soothing tone. "Once Melissa left, Paige stayed behind. "What happened after that?"

"We talked for a bit and I asked if she thought Melissa would return."

I hadn't spent much time talking with Paige, but I was fairly certain her ego wouldn't like that reaction one bit. "What did she say?"

"She told me that Melissa was a tease and I was wasting my time."

That sounded about right. "Did you stick with Paige?"

"For a time, but she was kind of annoying," Toby replied. "She kept flirting with me and then she got upset when I ignored her."

"Why did you ignore her?"

"She's not really my type. She's too ... out there, if you know what I mean."

"She was aggressive?"

"Yeah." He nodded. "She kept putting her hands on me and I was uncomfortable. She asked if I wanted to go for a walk with her. I said I was happy hanging out with my friends, but she said she thought we could walk alone together. I didn't want to, so I told her that."

"And how did she react?"

"She was angry. She didn't yell or anything, but you could tell she was ticked off. Once I told her no, she turned her attention to Dakota and tried to get him to walk with her. He wouldn't. He thought she was crazy too."

"Then what happened?"

"Then ... I don't know. She got sick of us and took off. She didn't even say goodbye. We were kind of happy about it, because she was weird. We only started talking to them in the first place because of that Melissa girl."

"Was that the last time you saw her?"

"Um ... I think so."

Well, that was disappointing.

"No, wait. We saw her again right before we left," Toby volunteered. "She was on the beach talking to someone."

"Was it another boy? Did you recognize him?"

"No, she was talking to a woman."

Now things were getting more interesting. "Did you recognize the woman?"

"I don't know. She looked familiar, but I'm certain I didn't recognize her."

I poked through his brain, searching for an image, but his memory of the night was clouded by alcohol, and by the time he'd decided to leave he was truly drunk. The woman he saw on the beach with Paige was a blur. There were no clues in her clothing either – simple jeans and a plain black shirt – which left me very little to go on.

"What time did you leave again?"

Toby shrugged. "I think it was around midnight."

"And Paige was on the beach at that time with the woman?"

"Yes."

"Did she look like she was enjoying the conversation with the woman?"

"I don't know. They were just talking. No one was angry or anything. They stared out at the water and talked. That's all I saw."

"Okay." I let loose a sigh. "Remember what I said about staying away from Melissa. She's too good for you."

Toby involuntarily shuddered when I pushed an image of him

standing in front of Melissa with a notable stain on the front of his jeans.

"You don't want that to become reality, right?"

"Absolutely not!" Toby was adamant. "I don't want to ever see her again."

"That's probably a good idea." I licked my lips before pushing a more pleasant fake memory into the young man's head, this one involving him sitting down for a reading with me. I made it a reading he'd enjoy because I didn't want him dwelling on our interaction for too long. Then I released him and pasted a fake smile on my face.

"Have fun at the circus today. Make sure you stop at the midway and play a few games. I'm sure you'll enjoy spending money there."

Toby stood on shaky legs, his eyes focused but his mind working overtime to come to a resting stop. "I ... um ... okay."

"Thank you for stopping by my tent. Have a nice day."

20
TWENTY

I steadfastly worked my way through the line until lunch, when it was time for my mid-afternoon break. It had been a long day and I knew it would feel endless by the time we wrapped things up.

There was nothing I could do about that, so I persisted through readings in the hope that I would find hints to … something. So far the only thing I'd been tipped off to was that one woman was about to get a rude awakening when she went home early to surprise her husband and a husband was about to get the shock of his life when his wife announced she was pregnant.

That was it.

Kade surprised me with takeout containers from the food trucks and directed me toward the picnic tables shortly after noon. Raven, Naida and Nellie were already seated and deep in conversation.

"Anything?" I asked hopefully.

Naida shook her head. "I've tried a few scans, but I haven't run across outright evil yet. I did find a woman who is plotting the death of her husband's secretary – who also happens to be his future baby mama – but she's too stupid not to get caught, so I gave her a fake potion and sent her on her way."

I wasn't sure how I felt about that. "Are you sure that's the way to go?"

Naida shrugged. "It's not as if I can tell the cops how I know she's planning to kill the secretary."

"How do you know?" Raven queried. "You can't read minds."

"She told me."

Kade arched an eyebrow. "You can tell the cops that. Do you remember her name?"

"Danielle Studebaker."

"Write it down. And what she looks like," Kade instructed. "I'll pass it on to the police."

I poked at my food with my fork as I listened, my stomach arguing with the thought of trying to digest fried food. I'd been on edge all morning and the acid rolling through my tummy seemed to indicate that it was on strike ... at least until Melissa returned and I could stop worrying.

"You need to eat," Kade prodded, tapping his fork on the side of my container to get my attention. "You'll need your strength later."

I forced a smile, but it was purely for his benefit. "I know. I have a little news, by the way." I related my run-in with Toby and what I saw in his head. When I was finished, Kade's expression was hard to read.

"How often do you do that?"

I shrugged. "As often as is necessary."

"Hmm."

I wasn't a fan of his shuttered expression. "If you have a problem with it ... ."

I didn't get a chance to finish because Kade cut me off with a shake of his head. "I didn't say I had a problem with it. I simply wasn't aware you could take things that far. I thought you could only read minds."

"I told you about the rapist and murderer I put into a trance before Luke and I pushed his truck into the lake right after we met," I reminded him. "You were worried that it would be tied to us, but we got away with it. How did you think I did that?"

"I didn't know." Kade flashed a smile. "It's okay. I'm more impressed than anything else."

It didn't feel that way. "He won't remember. He'll be fine."

"Okay." Kade's eyes flashed as he held up his hands in mock surrender. "I was merely asking a question. I didn't mean to step on your toes."

I scowled as I stared into my food. "I'm on edge. It's not your fault."

"You're worried about Melissa," Kade surmised. "She's okay. You don't have to worry about her."

"I know she's an adult, but ... she was upset. She could do something stupid while trying to find Paige."

"No, I mean you really don't have to worry," Kade clarified. "I sent one of the security guards to find her. He's been following her all morning. She's been walking up and down the boardwalk and asking people if they've seen Paige. She's safe."

"Oh." I felt a bit stupid for overreacting. "Well, that's good." I dug into my food with gusto as my appetite came roaring back. "That was smart. Good job." I shot him an enthusiastic thumbs-up with one hand while shoveling food into my mouth with the other.

Kade merely shook his head as he dumped cucumber sauce on his kebab. "I guess I should've told you that hours ago, huh? You're much more relaxed."

"You definitely should have," I agreed, flipping my eyes to Raven. "What about you? Have you come up with anything?"

"I enchanted one of the mirrors to show me the guests' true faces," Raven replied. "The worst thing I've seen is a housewife who used to be a man and hasn't told her new husband the truth yet."

Kade knit his eyebrows. "Wait ... how does that work? Isn't it obvious?"

Raven shrugged. "Apparently not."

Kade flicked his eyes to me. "There's nothing you want to tell me, right?"

I managed a genuine smile. "You're safe."

"Good to know." Kade pressed a quick kiss to my cheek and lowered his voice. "Melissa will be fine until we can get through this day and tackle her together. I promise."

I should've known he wouldn't allow her to wander around

without watching her. That wasn't his way. "I'm not worried." I rested my hand on his knee under the table. "I was worried earlier, but I'm not any longer. In fact ... I feel a lot better."

"Good." Kade shoveled some rice into his mouth. "We need to come up with a plan to find that cave," he said after swallowing. "Does anyone have any ideas?"

"I'm working on a pixie dust spell that might be able to help, but we'll need to be close to the door before we cast it," Naida offered. "I mean ... close. We're talking ten feet."

Raven made a face. "If we're within ten feet of it we won't need a spell."

"Unless it's hidden," Nellie pointed out. "I mean ... why would you have a secret cave to do whatever gross things you like to do and then have a door that everyone can see? That's not how it works."

"You seem to know a lot about how gross caves work," Raven pointed out, wrinkling her nose.

"I am a fount of useless information," Nellie agreed. "The magic pixie dust isn't a bad idea."

"We still have to get close for that to work," I pressed. "Naida, how sure are you that you can find the area on land rather than water?"

"Very sure." Naida said the words, but her expression reflected otherwise.

"How sure really?"

Naida's shoulders hopped up and down. "Like ... fifty percent."

I didn't like those odds one little bit. "There has to be a way for us to increase those odds."

"There is," Raven supplied. "Max is going to get us an item of Paige's clothing. I asked him about it before he went off to help Barney talk to the police."

"What good will that do?" Kade asked. "I mean ... can you use her clothes to cast a spell to find her?"

"Not that I've ever accomplished," Raven replied. "But that's not what I have planned."

"What do you have planned?"

Raven slid her eyes to me. I already knew. I also knew that the answer probably wouldn't go over well with one specific person.

Kade slid his gaze to me. "Am I missing something?"

"The clothing will have Paige's scent on it," I replied. "Luke is a wolf and has a heightened sense of smell when he's in his shifter form. Raven is hoping he'll be able to track Paige to wherever she's being held."

Kade brightened. "I didn't know he could do that."

"He's not exactly fond of it."

"Well, he'll live." Kade wiped the corners of his mouth with a napkin and pointed to my lunch. "Eat that. We're going to have a long day ahead of us and then an even longer night. You need some fuel."

"Yes, sir." I mock saluted before attacking my lunch. "I'll talk to Luke this afternoon and let him know what he's going to have to do. He won't be happy, but he'll eventually do what we want."

"And I'll work on the pixie dust spell," Naida said.

"Keep reading people as they move through the circus," I instructed. "We might get lucky and happen upon someone who knows something."

"When have we ever gotten that lucky?" Raven asked.

"There's a first time for everything."

THE FLOW OF GUESTS through my tent was slower during the afternoon. I was thankful for that. It allowed me to spend some time hovering by the front of the tent. It also allowed me to scan random minds, which was how I found Becky Dunham.

Becky was a twenty-four-year-old waitress who looked younger than her years, and she was convinced she managed to escape abduction because of that. The only reason I picked up on the young woman was because a group of people happened to be talking about a craft artisan handing out fliers regarding his missing daughter and it triggered something in Becky's mind. I was close enough to pick it up, which meant I was obsessed enough to draw her to my tent.

I used the same ploy I did with Troy, weaving a magical song to entice her before planting a suggestion in her head. By the time she walked into my tent, she was dazed ... and completely open to answering questions.

"Tell me what happened," I prodded.

"What do you mean? When?" Becky wasn't slow on the uptake, but she wasn't exactly one of the great thinkers of our time.

"You were almost abducted," I reminded her. "Tell me about it."

"Oh, that." Becky furrowed her brow. "I guess I don't know that I was almost abducted. I feel it ... in my bones."

"Tell me."

"It was almost six months ago. It was before we started hearing whispers about missing girls. Er, rather, it was before we started hearing whispers about a lot of missing girls. At that time only one of them had gone missing. Her name was Aubrey Partridge."

I filed the name away for further examination later. "What had you heard about her?"

"She was a good girl. That's what everyone kept saying. She was a good girl who never did anything wrong, yet she disappeared. Her car was found outside of the library, for crying out loud. I go to the library a lot because they have a coffee shop and it's a lot cheaper than Starbucks, so I heard the story almost before anyone else."

"Did she disappear from the library?"

"No one knows." Becky shrugged. "She was in the library the night before she disappeared working on a term paper or something. I'd seen her there before, but I'd never really talked to her.

"Anyway, according to the librarians, she said goodnight before leaving and seemed to be in a good mood," she continued. "She wasn't acting out of sorts or anything. She never made it to her car."

It was an intriguing story. "Did they find her purse?"

"Not that I know of."

"What about keys to the car?"

"I don't know."

I bit back my frustration. There was no way the woman could possibly know what the police did or didn't have. It was unfair to expect it. "Tell me why you think you were targeted."

"It was only a week after that. I was at the library for coffee and Aubrey was still the talk of the area," she continued. "When one girl goes missing, it's a big deal. When a bunch of them go missing, it seems people start ignoring it. I'm not sure why."

She had a point, but I didn't have time for a philosophical debate. "Did you see something?"

"I was already nervous because of Aubrey's disappearance, so I was hyper alert in the parking lot when I left," Becky replied. "I heard something behind me, so I sped up and had my keys ready so I could hop inside the car. I was afraid to look over my shoulder, but I imagined I saw something."

I poked further into her mind, wrinkling my forehead when I picked out an image. *That can't be right.* That's all I could think as I tugged tighter on the vision line. The shadow Becky saw that night had more than two arms – potentially eight if I counted correctly, which wasn't easy given the shadows – and whatever it was had to be seven feet tall. Surely someone would notice a seven-foot-tall creature with eight arms hanging around town.

"I was about to have a total meltdown when a woman appeared in front of me," Becky continued. "I swear, she came out of nowhere and I almost had a heart attack. Seriously … she was so quiet. I was relieved to see her, so I didn't really care where she came from."

"Did she say what she was doing in the parking lot?"

Becky shook her head. "She only asked me if something was wrong because she thought I looked upset. I was definitely upset, there's no getting around that, but I felt a little stupid once I'd calmed down. There was nothing chasing me. Obviously."

I wasn't so sure. "What did the woman look like?"

"Who?"

"The woman you found by your car," I prodded. "What did she look like?"

"Oh." Becky pursed her lips. "I don't really remember."

I searched through Becky's mind for an image but what came back was somehow distorted, the features twisted as if in one of Raven's funhouse mirrors. There was nothing there for me to use, which was frustrating ... but also interesting. "Was she young or old?"

"Um ... middle-aged."

"Is that like thirty in your mind? Forty?"

"In her late forties or so. She looked the same age as my mother."

"Brown hair or blond?"

"Brown. It was ... a bad color. It's not something anyone would pick while at the pharmacy."

That was an interesting observation. "What do you mean by that?"

"Her hair and eyes practically disappeared. There was nothing memorable about her."

"And the shadow you saw?" I asked. "Did it disappear when she showed up?"

"Yes. I'm thankful she saved me."

I didn't believe that was what happened, but I kept the theory to myself. "One more thing ... did anyone else show up in the parking lot before you left?"

"What do you mean?"

"I mean was the woman alone with you the entire time or did someone else arrive?"

"Oh, I understand what you're asking." Becky chewed her bottom lip as she considered the question. "Mr. Peck showed up. I only remember because he called out to me and told me not to walk to my car alone because of what happened to Aubrey. He lives three houses down from me and threatened to tell my parents if I didn't do the right thing.

"I still live with my parents," she added ruefully. "I'm hoping to save up to move out, which is what I was telling that lady when Mr. Peck arrived. She didn't believe me when I told her how old I was. She thought I was younger and wanted to see my identification to prove it."

"Yeah, that doesn't surprise me." I forced a tight-lipped smile. "Can you remember anything else about that night, Becky?"

"Just that I was happy to get home."

I couldn't blame her. She may never realize it, but she really did have a close call and probably narrowly escaped with her life. "Well, you're safe now. Mr. Peck was right, though. Don't go anywhere alone. Tell your friends. Tell everyone you know. Something dangerous is out there. You need to take care of yourself until the danger is over. Do you understand?"

Becky, her eyes still glazed, nodded. "I understand."

"Great. Now, let's talk about the best way to get you out of your parents' house. You're far too old to be living with them. I happen to have a few minutes, and your life will never be the same once I'm done."

21

TWENTY-ONE

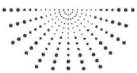

It wasn't quite dark when we shut down for the night. The sun was just starting its inevitable descent into the horizon, which meant we had time for dinner before embarking on our cave search. I somehow missed seeing Luke throughout the afternoon, so I had yet to tell him how he would be spending his evening. I didn't expect that conversation to go well.

Naida, Nixie and Raven were already working in the kitchen area when I arrived. It appeared Raven was keen to ruin Luke's night, so she was in the midst of explaining his upcoming duties while he drank lemonade at the picnic table and glared at her.

"Why do I have to be the one to do it?" Luke complained.

"Because you have a better nose," I answered, hoping that praise would force him to capitulate. "You're the best sniffer we have."

"Oh, well, there's something I want to boast about." Luke grimaced and I could practically see his mind working. He was trying to figure a way out of the search without looking like a douche. I decided to nip that impulse.

"Girls are missing, Luke," I reminded him. "They could still be alive. If you lead us to them, you'll be a hero."

Raven smirked. "And if you don't, you'll simply be the zero we already think you are."

I murdered Raven with a warning look before shuffling closer to the table. "It's important, Luke. You know we wouldn't ask if it wasn't absolutely necessary."

Luke remained unconvinced. "Why can't Seth do it? He's a tiger. They have good noses."

"Yes, but if a tiger is seen running around this area the cops will get involved," Seth pointed out. He was clearly enjoying Luke's discomfort and made no attempt to hide his smile. "We can pretend you're a dog."

The look Luke shot me was straight out of Petulant Quarterly. "Did you hear that? You can pretend I'm a dog."

"What do you want me to say, Luke?" My temper got the better of me. "We have to look and we need you to do it. If you don't want to be involved ... well, I guess I can't make you." That wasn't true. I could make him. But I would never use my powers on him, no matter the cost. It was an invasion I wasn't willing to spread around to those I loved. "I will be really disappointed, though."

"Oh, I hate it when you say things like that." Luke smacked his hand to his forehead. "You know I won't refuse. No one wants to be the jerk who says no to helping missing girls."

I squeezed his shoulder in appreciation. "I knew you'd come through."

"Yeah, yeah." Luke rolled his eyes. "I'm not shifting until we get up there. And if you try to put me on a leash I'll bite you."

"Fair enough." I moved to help with cooking preparations but Naida shooed me away. "You look tired. Sit down for a few minutes. I think you overexerted yourself by questioning that woman the way you did."

My eyebrows nearly flew off my forehead. "How did you know about that?"

"I saw you talking to her when she was by our booth. I thought there was something off about her, so I was watching, too. I was just about to approach her when I saw you do it."

"What did you think was off about her?" Raven asked.

"I should probably rephrase that," Naida cautioned. "I thought there was a pall hanging over her, something I couldn't quite identify. It was almost as if she had a shadow following her."

Well, that was intriguing. I related my talk with Becky, making sure to touch every corner of the tale. When I was done, everyone started talking at once.

"You saw a shadow with eight arms?" Naida asked.

"Do you think the woman was the shadow?" Nixie asked.

"Do you think the guy saved her or was it her age?" Raven asked.

I shrugged. I didn't have an answer to any of the questions. "I don't know. I think both Mr. Peck and her age probably played in her favor. I definitely think she was targeted. As for the woman, I can't get a clear picture of her in my head. I think that's purposeful."

"It's definitely purposeful," Raven agreed. "It's a witch trick. You do the same thing when you glamour yourself and make it appear as if you're someone else. You don't really change your looks. You don't have the power to do that. Instead you make other people think you've changed your looks. It sounds to me that this woman is doing the same."

We were back to witches. "What about the eight arms? I don't know any witches who have eight arms. Do you?"

"No, but I've heard about a few sirens that supposedly had eight arms," Nixie offered. "I've never seen one, but there's a legend that says a few sirens grew eight arms so they could be like an octopus and more easily catch their prey."

Hmm. "I don't know a lot about sirens. I thought they were bird-like. They sing a song and supposedly lure sailors. That legend could fit with the water, but eight arms don't suggest a bird."

"You're looking at it too literally," Raven countered. "Evolution doesn't happen only to humans. It happens to paranormals, too. Perhaps that's what we're dealing with here."

"If it is a siren, she's not luring sailors. She's luring young girls."

"Maybe she's a lesbian siren," Nixie suggested. "Sirens are

supposed to be ridiculously sexual. Maybe she's luring women because that's what she's into."

That didn't make me feel much better. "I guess it's possible."

"There's another possibility," Naida offered. "Greek myth talks about Centimanes, creatures that had hundreds of arms. They also had a bunch of heads, too, but that's not important to us. The stories were myths and the creatures most likely weren't real, but my mother once told me that there were magical creatures out there that stole arms from others to make themselves stronger."

I rolled my neck as I settled on the picnic table bench. "You think someone stole the story and is taking the arms of these women to make themselves stronger?" I felt sick to my stomach.

"No." Naida shook her head. "I think it's possible we're dealing with a witch who perverted the stories and thinks she can make herself stronger by stealing the life essence of others. That's why we don't have a lot of bodies. The others are alive. She's continually draining them to bolster herself."

It was an interesting theory. "What about the shadow?"

"It could be the woman casts a magical shadow. It wouldn't be the first time. The arms could be symbolic of how the woman feels, how she projects herself."

That was a lot better than thinking about fighting a creature with multiple arms. "That would also explain why we've only had three bodies. Something went wrong with those victims and she had to discard them. The others could very well be alive." I felt emotionally bolstered by the thought. "We could still save them."

"We could," Naida agreed, "but until we see what state they're in, I'm not comfortable getting anyone's hopes up. This is all conjecture."

"It's good conjecture. A witch would likely spend a lot of time researching power and how to attain it. If she were open-minded, she wouldn't only focus on pagan rites. She'd expand her repertoire to include mythology as well. I like where your mind is going."

"You only like it because you think it means we can save all those girls," Naida countered. "While I don't want to dampen your enthusiasm, I also don't want you to set your hopes too high. A byproduct of draining their life essences would involve atrophying their brains, essentially putting them into walking comas."

That didn't sound good. "We could heal them."

"Maybe. We won't know until we see them. Again, this is only a theory. We have no facts to back it up."

She was being rational, yet I didn't want to entertain the possibility that she was right. "I'm not giving up until I have no hope."

I rested my elbow on the table and rubbed my forehead, only dragging myself from my reverie when I heard approaching footsteps. I knew it was Kade before I lifted my head. He has a certain presence, and there are times I can feel his mind brush against mine from hundreds of feet away.

I smiled as I turned, excited to tell him what we'd been discussing. The words died on my lips when I saw the expression on his face. "What is it?"

Kade clenched his hands into fists at his sides as he met my gaze. "I have some bad news."

"Paige?"

"No. I have nothing on her."

"Then what?" Luke asked. "You're being a little dramatic. That's my job."

Kade never moved his eyes from my face. "My guy lost Melissa. She's missing."

And just like that, all of the oxygen escaped from my lungs and I had trouble breathing.

"Screw dinner," Raven announced, abandoning her preparations and wiping her hands on a towel. "We need to find that cave, and we need to find it now. Eating can wait."

WE DROVE TO THE SHORELINE after piling into three vehicles. Kade drove his truck, Luke and I crowding together in the passenger seat while Seth and Nellie sat in the back.

Kade felt helpless and guilty. Even if I weren't psychic I would've been able to pick up on that. There was very little I could do for him –

especially in front of an audience – but I gave his hand a reassuring squeeze as we piled out of the vehicles.

"It's not your fault."

Kade slid me a sidelong look. "There's no one else to blame."

"Maybe no one needs to be blamed. Melissa is an adult. She chose to take off on her own. If something happens to her … ." I trailed off, uncertain how to finish.

"If something happens to her you're going to blame yourself," Kade finished. "That's dumber than me blaming myself. I think she knew she was being followed. She went out of her way to slip away. She wasn't taken. He would've seen if that were the case."

"That's something at least. Hopefully she's merely out being stupid rather than victimized."

"I'm still sorry." Kade stroked his hand over the back of my head as he lowered his forehead to mine. "We'll find her. She could already be out here."

I didn't know if I should hope for that, so I merely pressed my lips together and smiled. "It's going to be okay. I have … faith."

Kade forced a smile. "Then I do, too." He gave me a quick kiss before turning his attention to a griping Luke. "What are you complaining about?"

"I hate shifting in front of people," Luke replied without hesitation. "It's undignified."

"Do I even want to know what that means?" Kade asked me.

I shook my head. "He'll survive. Shift now, Luke. We don't have time to mess around."

Luke cast a disdainful look in my direction as he stripped off his shirt and handed it to Nixie. "That's new and expensive. Take care of it."

Nixie nodded. "I've got it. I won't let anything happen to your precious clothes. Don't worry about it."

Luke's gaze snagged with mine, something unsaid passing between us. I'd seen him shift so many times I'd lost count, yet he remained shy in the moments before.

"Everyone turn around," I instructed, forcing a small smile for

Luke's benefit as he reached for the button on his jeans. "Give him some privacy."

"Like anyone wants to see that," Raven groused as she turned away from Luke's strip show. "Why do you think he's single?"

"Because he's picky," I shot back.

"I kind of want to see," Nixie admitted, "but I'll be good and keep my eyes to myself."

"Thank you."

Kade stood next to me, his shoulder brushing against mine as we linked fingers. "I'm kind of sad I don't get to see," he admitted. "I've always wanted to see him shift. I can't help it. I'm curious."

"It's interesting. It's also hard for him."

"Then we'll keep it easy." Kade jerked his head to the side at the sound of muscles and bone snapping. He somehow managed to keep himself from staring, although just barely. The transformation had begun. "Does it hurt?"

"He says it's not comfortable but not painful."

"That's good ... I guess."

It didn't take long, and when I felt Luke's cold snout press against my palm I smiled as I turned. I shot him a fond look as I ran my hand over his soft head. In his human form, Luke boasts blond hair. When he shifts, his coloring is more blondish-brown. He was a beautiful animal. I would expect nothing less from the fussy human version, of course.

"Here." Raven pulled a hoodie from a plastic bag and rubbed it in Luke's face. "Max got this from Paige's father. He gave it to me. See if this works to scent her."

"We should've brought something that belonged to Melissa," Kade suggested.

"We don't know that Melissa was taken," Naida pointed out. "In fact, it's highly unlikely that she was taken. She took off on her own because she figured out that she was being followed. I'm guessing she'll show up safe once her ego allows her."

"I hope so." Kade ran his hand over the top of his short-cropped hair. "So ... now what?"

"Now we let Luke search," I replied, watching as the huge wolf at my side lifted his nose and scented the air. "Stand back. He needs room. We need to stay back while he does his magic."

Kade did as instructed, sliding his arm around my waist to offer me solace and comfort while we waited. "So ... am I the only one who thought he would walk on two legs while in wolf form?"

I pursed my lips to keep from laughing. "Don't ever say anything like that to Luke. He hates it when people believe the stereotypes."

"Good to know."

We lapsed into silence. Kade was the first to break it.

"If it is a witch – one who can do the things you guys were talking about right before we left the circus – can you fight her?"

I shrugged. "I don't know. I won't be alone, though. That's why Naida and Raven are here. We can always pool our magic. I've never met a creature that could stand up to all three of us."

"And if that doesn't work, we've always got my ax," Nellie announced, brandishing his weapon of choice for good measure. Surprisingly, he'd dressed for the occasion, opting for jeans rather than a dress. That meant he expected a fight and wanted to be ready ... or perhaps simply that he didn't want to risk any of his pretty dresses. "You know how I feel about beheading witches."

I smirked at a memory. "Yes, I loved that one you took out in Maine. Her head continued spitting out curses even after it was severed from her body."

"She was a mean cuss," Nellie agreed. "We had to burn the head in a fire to shut her up."

"Good times."

Kade made an odd throat-clearing sound. "Sometimes you guys freak me out."

"Just wait until we find whoever is doing this," I offered. "We're going to be downright terrifying when that happens."

"I believe you."

TWENTY-TWO

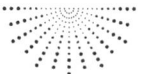

I knew Luke had found something before he shifted back into human form. He didn't bother hiding his nakedness when he rolled to his back feet and stood.

"Here!" He pointed toward a dark wall in the back of a rather distinct rock formation.

Kade, close at my heels, pulled up short. "Dude, where are your pants?"

Luke shot him a withering look. "Some of us don't need to cover our assets." As if to prove his point, he flexed his impressive arms. "Now, who wants to pet the dog and tell him he did a good job?"

I eyed my best friend for a long moment. "I don't even know what to say to that."

Luke smirked. "You don't have to say anything." He accepted his clothes from Nixie and immediately slid into his boxer shorts, which was frankly a relief for us all. "Paige has been here. Whether she was under duress or walked in herself, I can't say."

I turned serious as I focused on the wall. I couldn't find an opening, but that didn't mean it wasn't there, somehow hidden. "Okay. We need to fan out in this immediate area and see what we can find."

"It's dark," Nellie pointed out. "How are we supposed to see anything?"

"I've got it." Naida lifted her hand in the air and tossed a handful of pixie dust above our heads, muttering a word from her language – one I couldn't quite make out – and igniting the dust. It glowed like a million tiny fireflies and lighted the area immediately surrounding us. It was breathtaking ... and also a bit troublesome.

"What happens if anyone sees that?" I challenged.

"Then we'll have some explaining to do. We should work fast if we don't want to explain it."

Her answer was so simple it set my teeth on edge. "And if someone comes to investigate?"

"We'll use your handy-dandy mind powers to convince them they were never here. Do I have to think of everything?"

I blew out a sigh and risked a glance at Kade, only to find him smirking. "You're okay with that?"

"I wouldn't mind seeing you in action," he replied. "Naida is right about time being a factor. We need to find a way into ... whatever this is. There must be an opening."

"While you're looking for that, I'm going back into the water," Naida announced. "I want to double check that we're in the right area. I also want to get another look at the wards. I won't be gone long."

I balked. "What if we need you to get inside when we find an opening?"

"I won't be gone long," Naida repeated. "If something terrible happens, you're strong enough to call me. You've done it before."

"Fine." I wasn't happy, but I knew arguing with her was akin to beating my head against these very rocks. When Naida made up her mind to do something, she did it. "Hurry back."

"That's the plan."

WE SPLIT INTO GROUPS, Kade joining me and Luke in following Nellie toward the water line. I was curious why they headed in that direction, but Nellie merely grunted when I questioned him and made a rude gesture with his hand. I figured it was better to let him decide for himself.

That left Nixie and Raven to search with us. We split to either side of the rock formation. It made for slow going, but we didn't exactly have many options. The search took time and forced me to use my magic, glittery light flowing from my fingertips as I ran them over the rock face.

Kade sucked in a breath when he saw what I was doing, and even though I knew he tried to hide his surprise he was unable to stop himself from openly gaping.

"Problem?" I asked.

Kade shook his head. "No. I just ... I didn't know you could do that."

"I can do a lot of things. If you have questions, you're more than welcome to ask."

"Good to know."

I shifted my hands lower. "If you're afraid of me ... ."

"I'm not afraid of you," Kade said hurriedly. "Don't think that. It's more that I'm in awe of you."

"That's sweet, but you've seen me use magic before."

"I know. It's different this time, though."

"Why?"

"Because it's a quieter moment."

I flicked my eyes to Kade and furrowed my brow. "What do you mean?"

"I mean that it's a quieter moment," he repeated. "The other times I've seen you use your magic have been times of crisis. I never get a chance to watch because I'm too busy trying not to die. This is different."

I snorted. "I guess that makes sense. I never thought of it like that."

"What does it feel like?"

"The magic? Um ... I don't know. I don't even notice it any longer."

"Do your fingers burn?" Kade seemed legitimately curious.

"Come here," I prodded, gesturing for him to join me. "Stand behind me and put your hand over mine."

Kade did as instructed, not questioning whether he would be injured in the process. I waited until his hand rested over mine and then fired up the magic. Kade initially jerked back. I wasn't sure if the magic burned or he was merely surprised by the light.

His smile was on full display, though, and he moved his fingers back to mine right away. "It kind of tickles."

"It doesn't for me, but I'm so used to it I might simply push it out of my mind." I slowly moved my fingers to the east. "What else do you feel?"

"Honestly? I'm incredibly turned on."

"Well, I wish I could oblige you there." I really did. "But now doesn't seem like a good time."

"No, but can we do this again when we have time together, just the two of us?"

"I don't see why not."

"Fun." Kade pressed a kiss to my cheek. "Have you sensed anything?"

The question caused me to sober. "I've sensed a lot of things. We're definitely in the right place."

"Melissa?"

I shook my head. "No. I can't pick out individuals. But something terrible is inside this big bluff. Something very, very terrible."

"Then we need to find a way in." Kade pulled back his hand. "I don't want to get in your way. We'll play with your glowing hands later."

I didn't bother to hide my smirk. "Sounds like a plan."

"Oh, how cute," Raven drawled, catching us both off guard when she appeared directly behind Kade.

My smile dipped. "Are you spying on us?"

"No. I came to tell you we found something. I was a little worried for a minute that you guys were going to jump each other right here, so I decided to watch. What a disappointment."

I rolled my eyes as I dropped my hand and extinguished the magic. "What did you find?"

"You need to see it to believe it."

Kade and I exchanged a quick look before following Raven to the other side of the craggy rock formation. Nixie stood with her hands pressed to the stone exterior. The expression on her face was hard to read.

"What is it?" I asked, moving closer.

"Runes," Nixie replied. "I'm having trouble reading them. I was hoping you might be able to make them out."

"Okay." I glanced at Raven. "You couldn't make them out?"

"Two of them," she replied, all traces of mirth vanishing from her features. "Some of them are much more difficult. For example, this is the purification symbol. We've already seen that. It's inverted again."

"Which I understand is bad, right?" Kade prodded.

"It's not good. Whenever you have a symbol that's supposed to be used for good and it's upside down you can almost always be assured that you're dealing with abject evil. I'm having trouble making out this symbol."

I followed Raven's finger and leaned closer to study the faint lines. "Hmm."

"I think the only reason we can see the runes at all is because of the pixie dust," Nixie offered. "They weren't here when we first started searching. The longer the dust burns, the brighter they get."

"She's right," Raven said. "The runes were invisible at first and only showed when the dust was introduced. It seems the dust is fighting whatever magic we have going on over here. I was about to send Nixie down to Naida's clothes so she could grab more from her sister's pockets, but I wanted to hear your ideas first."

"I don't see how it could hurt," I replied after a beat. "Get the dust, Nixie."

She nodded and took off, seemingly excited to be able to contribute. That allowed me time to turn back to the runes. "I think this is four circles with x's in them, right?"

"That's what I believe, but I'm not certain," Raven replied. "If so, that makes it a strength symbol."

"Why is that important?" Kade asked.

"It's not important as much as interesting," I replied. "Whoever warded this cave wanted to make sure no one found their way inside. That means it might be tricky for us to try."

"You'll try, though, right?"

"We'll succeed," Raven answered. "We need to know how to approach it the right way. These runes are powerful."

"This one." I ran my finger over one of the runes that wasn't brightly illuminated. "It feels like an energy symbol." I dropped my fingers about six inches. "And this one feels like the health symbol, although it's also inverted."

"Really." Raven drew her eyebrows together and moved her fingers close to mine. She traced the symbol in question and then widened her eyes. "You're right."

"Don't sound so surprised."

Raven ignored my snark. "All of these symbols together mean something. We need to figure out how to separate the symbols before going inside. I think that's the only safe way to do this."

"Can you do that?" Kade shifted from one foot to the other, uncertain. "I mean … can you figure out a way inside that will keep you safe?"

"We can't guarantee anything, but we're always careful," I reassured him. "Feel this." I grabbed Raven's hand and moved it to the left. "Does that feel like the symbol for mother to you?"

Raven pursed her lips. "It does indeed. That's an odd symbol to include."

"Unless we've been looking at this the wrong way," I said. "Earlier we thought we might be dealing with a siren who happened to be a lesbian. What if we're not dealing with a siren, but rather a creature that fancies itself a mother?

"I mean, all the girls were roughly the same age," I continued. "My initial reaction was to think we were dealing with some sick pervert who was building himself a harem. Then we had the idea for the siren … or a very powerful witch. What if it is a witch, but one who thinks of herself as a mother – or at least a leader – of all the girls she's taken?"

"I get what you're saying and I'm intrigued by the notion," Raven said. "To what end, though?"

"I don't know. I wish I did." I moved my fingers back to the wall. "I can't sense an opening. Someone warded the heck out of this place, that much is obvious, but I can't find a door. Could it be possible that whoever is using this place only approaches through the water?"

"Perhaps if we're really dealing with a siren," Raven replied. "But that doesn't appear to be the case. In fact … ." She broke off, narrowing her eyes. "Make your fingers glow, Poet."

I didn't question why. I recognized the look on Raven's face and did as she asked, pushing my fingers closer to the wall and waiting for further instruction.

"There." Raven pointed. "That's the sign for Aquarius. And there." She pointed again. "That's the sign for Virgo. I'm willing to bet she has every astrological sign covered – probably more than once."

"Why is that important?" Kade asked. He was learning fast, but still at a disadvantage when it came to all things magical. "Why would astrological signs be important? I thought that was all hocus-pocus."

Raven and I chuckled.

"I'm sure people say that about us, too," I said. "Astrology is many things, but it's not hocus-pocus. It has its uses."

"It's not a strong field of study, but it's not complete bupkis," Raven added. "Look. There's the sign for Pisces."

"Gemini is over here," I added. "I think you're right. Each astrological sign is here."

"I still don't know why that's important," Kade pressed.

"Because our witch – and I do believe we're dealing with a witch, whether mutant or otherwise – bolstered her power base by getting someone from each astrological sign," Raven explained. "Whoever we're dealing with knows what she's doing."

"I'll definitely agree with that," Naida said, appearing from around the corner. Her hair dripped from her swim and her clothing clung to her body. That meant she'd been in a hurry.

"What is it?" I asked, instantly alert.

"I heard noises from the cave," Naida replied. "Crying. I tried to break in underwater again, but the wards are too strong for me to do it alone. Nixie was on the beach when I surfaced. She said you guys haven't found an opening."

"We haven't." My stomach twisted. "You heard crying?"

"Whether I really heard it or merely brushed up against their minds while I cast my net, I cannot say," Naida replied. "We can't wait any longer. We must go in."

"How do you expect us to go in?" Raven challenged. "We haven't found an opening."

"Then we shall make our own door." Naida was determined. "The time for indecision is over. We're going in."

Kade ran his tongue over his teeth as he regarded her. "Wow. I feel as if I just stepped into the middle of an old western. Are you going to challenge the crone to a gunfight at sunset?"

"I don't need a gun," Naida replied. "I do need help breaking the wards."

I figured that was the case. "What do you want us to do?"

"We'll have to weave a web of our own," Naida replied without hesitation. "We need to funnel as much power into the spell as possible. If I'm right, the magic will glow hot enough for us to smash the stone."

"How do you expect us to smash it?" Kade asked. "I didn't bring a sledgehammer."

Naida was blasé. "No, but we have a dwarf who carries an ax. Something tells me we'll be fine."

Something told me she was right ... and we were finally getting somewhere.

23
TWENTY-THREE

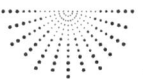

"We need to unravel the wards." Naida was singularly focused as Nixie stepped up to the plate. "That means attacking them one at a time. Go for the strength line first. Once we break that we can easily topple the others."

I had never seen Naida so determined. Whatever she heard inside was enough to propel her into action. It might not be smart action, or even mildly intelligent action, but she was going for it. I couldn't help being impressed.

I was also a little worried.

"Even if we manage to break the wards, there's still not an opening for us to enter through," I pointed out. "You said Nellie could use his ax, but I don't think that'll work. It's not big enough."

"Oh, it's plenty big," Nellie intoned, his grimace pronounced as he returned from his sojourn on the other side of the formation with Luke in tow.

I ignored him. "We'll need something bigger."

"You let me worry about that," Naida said grimly. "Break the ward first."

I pursed my lips, but fell into line, positioning myself with Raven and Nixie as Naida oversaw the work from behind. Kade and I exchanged a quick look – he clearly sensed that Naida's urgency had ratcheted up and didn't look any happier about it than I felt – and then forced a smile before taking a step back. Nellie and Luke stood next to him and waited for us to create an opening.

"Please tell me there's something inside that needs a good beheading," Nellie said, rubbing his hands together. "I haven't beheaded a witch in ages."

"You're truly frightening when you want to be." Kade made a clucking sound with his tongue as he shook his head. "I mean ... truly frightening."

Nellie was blasé. "I'm fine with that."

"Here we go," Nixie announced, furrowing her brow as she lifted her hands and muttered something I couldn't quite make out. The ward, an angry red line, lifted from the rock, and Raven and I attacked at the same time, shoving all our energy at the ward in an effort to break the string.

We were strong and expected it to crumble quickly.

That didn't happen.

"I was afraid of that," Naida muttered, shaking her head. "Either a coven put this up or the witch in question is more than just a witch."

Raven and I kept firm hold on the ward line. "What do you want us to do?"

"Hold it tight," Naida instructed.

Raven and I looked at each other, dubious, but did as she asked. The pixie was the most powerful of the four of us when it came to things like this, so we had no choice but to bow to her wishes.

"Whatever you're going to do, do it fast," Raven barked. "The ward is reverberating. I think that means it's using our power against us and is about to attack."

"Don't worry," Naida gritted out, focusing. "It won't get that far."

I opened my mouth to ask what she was going to do, but it was already too late. Naida lifted her hands, a cold blue magic racing out of her fingertips and colliding with the red ward. The reaction was instantaneous ... and loud. It sounded like a train collision, and when

Naida's power slammed into the ward the red magic held for what felt like the world's longest second and then shattered into a million pieces.

Kade instinctively covered my head from behind as the red magic glittered and fell around us. It was a sweet gesture, but completely unnecessary.

"This is freaking interesting," Raven muttered, catching some of the magic in her hand and watching as it turned to dust. "I need to collect some of this."

"Collect it." Naida was back to being proactive. "Poet, we need to take out one of the astrological wards. If we do that, the others will falter. That should be enough to allow me to punch through the wall."

"Okay." That seemed easy enough. "When you say you're going to punch through the wall, do you mean that literally?"

"Yes."

Hmm. That would be interesting to see. For now, though, I had other things to focus on. I pointed toward the left. "That Virgo rune is the weakest."

"Then let's attack that." Naida moved closer to me, tilting her head to the side as she regarded it. "Nixie, hit it with a dose of pixie dust. Poet, the second she does, we're attacking together. She's built a web and it's meant to hold as long as each strand remains. We can shred it if we take out one symbol."

I tried to concentrate. Naida sounded more certain than I felt. "Okay."

Nixie reached into the pouch secured to her belt and grabbed a handful of dust. "Get ready." She took a deep breath and then flung it at the rune. The moment it hit, the Virgo sign ignited into a green flame.

"Now!" Naida ordered.

I focused my energy, doing my best not to dwell on the fact that I felt drained. I pulsed out a purple beam, allowing Naida to catch it and shape it before she flung it at the ward. Initially I thought the magical burst would flare out and the ward would hold. Naida was in no mood to let that happen, though. She added a bit of her magic to the stew and when the symbol flared to life a second time it illuminated lines between the other astrological symbols. I could clearly see the lines breaking.

"It's working." I let out a relieved sigh. "You did it."

"We did it," Naida corrected. "Now it's my turn to do something." She cocked her head to the side and closed her eyes, her lips curving after a few seconds. "The wards are weak enough to get through now."

"Then let's get through them," Raven suggested. She looked tired, circles under her eyes. I wasn't the only one feeling drained thanks to the amount of magic we were expending. "I believe you said you could create a door."

"And that's what I'm going to do." Naida gestured for us to take a step back. "Give me some room to work here."

I gladly stepped away from her, pressing my back to Kade's chest when he moved behind me and slipped his arm around my waist.

"What is she going to do?" Kade asked, worry evident.

"You know how she can control the weather?"

Kade nodded.

"I believe you're going to get a chance to see a tornado up close and personal."

Kade widened his eyes but didn't protest. "Well, I can't say you guys aren't interesting." He tightened his grip on me and took a step back. "Do your thing, Naida."

Naida needed no further encouragement, screwing her face into a mask of concentration and ignoring the wind as it whipped about. She chanted under her breath, words I couldn't make out and knew I wouldn't understand even if I could, and as the winds built to a crescendo, Naida's eyes flashed with power.

"Go!"

Naida yelled instructions for the storm, forcing it forward. I tried to watch, but the blowing sand was too much as it pelted my face and eyes. All I could do was bury my face in Kade's chest and wait it out. It seemed to take a long time, and when I heard rock shifting I thought for sure the bluff might tumble into the ocean, but as the wind started to die and I finally risked opening my eyes, I found Naida standing in the same spot she'd inhabited moments before.

She looked triumphant.

"You are a terrifying piece of work," Raven announced, running her hands over her hair to smooth it. "That was freaking awesome."

Naida offered up a half-smile. "We have a door."

"We do," I agreed, leaning closer so I could peer inside. "It looks dark."

"It looks dirty," Luke corrected, wrinkling his nose. His hair stood up in thirty different directions and his new shirt looked as if it needed a long trip to the dry cleaners. "I'm not going in there."

"You don't have to go in there." I flashed him a smile. "I'll take it from here."

"Not without me you won't." Kade was adamant as he moved to my side. "We're doing this together."

"Oh, you're sweet when you want to be." I tapped his chin and smiled. Taking a moment to bask in what felt like a triumph before turning to the business at hand. "Okay, we need to go inside. Let's hope whatever we find isn't too terrible."

Naida's hand shot out and grabbed my wrist, her fingernails digging in as I widened my eyes.

"What's wrong with you?"

Naida opened her mouth, but no sound initially came out. It was as if she wanted to tell me something and had no idea how to do it. Instead, she opened her mind and allowed me to get a gander at what she sensed while beneath the water. It didn't take long for me to realize the truth of what we faced, and the realization was enough to make me sick to my stomach.

"Oh." I broke away from her and bent over, momentarily worried I'd vomit in front of everyone.

"What was that?" Kade was furious, his eyes flashing as they locked with Naida's. "What did you do to her?"

Naida's face flooded with sympathy. "Do you understand now?"

Unfortunately, I did. "Melissa."

Kade jolted. "What about her?"

"She's inside," I replied as I fought to come to grips with the vision. "She's inside and ... she's crying."

Kade's fury erupted. "Why didn't you say something before this?" he exploded. "Why not mention this while we were screwing around?"

"We weren't screwing around," Naida replied evenly. She wasn't afraid of Kade, and they both knew it. "I needed Poet to focus to get through the wards. If she knew Melissa was inside, that wouldn't have happened."

"I don't understand," Nellie interjected, all traces of mirth gone as he gripped his ax tighter. "Is Melissa dead?"

"I don't believe so," Naida replied. "I don't think she's herself. There is something else at play here. We won't know until we go inside."

"Then let's do it," Luke said, stepping forward. "Melissa needs us."

"I thought you weren't going into the cave," Raven challenged.

"Things change." Luke's eyes met mine. He was resigned and determined, and it was an impressive combination. "Let's get her."

THE CAVE WAS DARK at the start, but grew lighter the deeper we traveled. Someone installed lighting, which was eerie and odd, and the farther we explored inside the cave the more we realized it was a dwelling of sorts.

"Does anyone sense anything?" Nixie asked, her eyes keen as she scanned the walls. "By the way, these aren't electrical torches. They're real ones that have been spelled with endless flame."

"Oh, really?" Raven challenged dryly. "Are you telling me the witch behind this didn't get an electrician to trick out her cave? I'm shocked. Shocked, I tell you."

Nixie shot her a withering look. "That's not what I mean, jerkface. There's open flame in here. We provided the door, and the other entrance appears to be underwater. Shouldn't the oxygen in this cave run out if fire is burning?"

She had a point. "Hmm."

"Thank you." Nixie puffed out her chest as she turned a corner.

She was so proud of herself I didn't notice the shift in her demeanor until an image from her mind slammed into mine, causing me to lose my footing and stumble.

Kade caught me before I could hit the ground. "Are you okay? Did you twist your ankle?"

"I ... ." My mouth went dry. "I think Nixie found what we're looking for."

Kade made sure I was secure on my feet before pushing forward. He wasn't magical – or at least he didn't think he was magical – but he was head of security. In his mind that meant he should be the first through the door even though the rest of us had stronger weapons in our arsenals.

I didn't put up a fight because I knew it didn't matter. We were all about to walk into a horror movie, one I wasn't sure we could escape.

"Oh, my ... ." Nixie's mouth dropped open as we stepped into a larger room, this one lit with at least five lights.

There were alcoves carved into the stone, at least fifty of them. In each alcove stood a young woman. The missing girls, I'm sure, although they were altered. Each was dressed in an outfit straight out of a doll catalog – lacey skirts, ridiculous collared shirts, colored bloomers poking out from the bottom hems – and it looked as if someone had been playing dress-up with the women because they all had flowers in their hair and extreme makeup on their faces.

"Are they alive?" Kade rasped out, his eyes busy as they bounced among faces.

"They're alive, but they're in some sort of stasis or something," Raven replied, leaning in closer to a blond woman ... or, rather, human doll. "They're breathing, but their minds are on lockdown."

"Can you read their thoughts?" Naida asked, moving closer to a brunette doll with pigtails. "Is there anything there or have they been emptied out?"

That was a very good question. My heart pinged when I recognized Melissa in an alcove. I headed in her direction, instinctively reaching out to touch her. Kade grabbed my hand before I could.

"Are you sure that's a good idea?"

"I ... ." I wasn't sure of anything. "Shh." I closed my eyes and allowed myself to drift into Melissa's head. On a normal day I'd never attempt anything of the sort. This was far from a normal day.

Melissa's head was a mess. It was as if the interior designer from hell stopped by for a visit and segregated everything.

"She's disconnected," I supplied. "She's here, but ... she's confused. She can't see outside of herself."

"What does that mean?" Luke asked. He stood in front of a red-haired woman in pigtails and a checkered dress. The woman's makeup made her look as if she stepped straight off a horror movie set and into our nightmares. She was so pale she almost looked as if she might disappear, yet the flame-red hair was alive with ... mayhem. That was the only word I could think to describe it.

"I don't know," I replied after a beat. "She's not aware of what's happening. She's not in control of her faculties. In fact, she's drifting. She's here but not really here."

"Can you get her out of there?" Kade asked.

"I don't know. We might need the witch to do it."

"That means we have to find her," Naida said. "I'm not sure what we should do here. Moving them might not be in their best interests, and we can't sit here until the crone returns. This is ... new territory."

"I say we take them," Kade argued. "We can call back to the circus and get transport, use the trucks we pretend are for the animals. That way no one will see them, but they'll be safe from whoever did this."

"Unless they won't be," Naida argued. "Poet, what do you think?"

"I don't know." I focused on Melissa's face, my heart twisting. "I guess we should at least try to get them out of here. Leaving them makes me sick to my stomach."

"Okay. You're the boss."

"I ... ." Whatever I was about to say died on my lips as I widened my eyes. Melissa, who only seconds before stared off into glazed nothingness, focused her full attention on me. The thing inside her, the thing in charge, coursed through her with black thoughts and deeds, forcing Melissa's arm to shoot out and slash at my side. I saw the order whip through the wind moments before Melissa reacted.

What I didn't see was the knife in her hand. The blade was small, and Melissa moved fast. Much faster than she should've been capable of moving.

I grabbed at my side as I stumbled back, quickly losing my footing as blood gushed between my fingers.

"Poet!" Kade hurried in my direction.

I noticed the blond in front of Raven reach out in an attempt to grab Raven by the throat. Raven was ready for it, though, and wrapped her fingers around the woman's wrist.

"Well, this is fun," Raven groused.

"Poet!" Kade made to kneel next to me, but Melissa was on him before he got the chance. Kade's instincts took over. He slammed his fist into Melissa's face to keep her back, violence tempering his expression as his mind turned to survival rather than rescue.

"Don't hurt her!" I screamed, clutching my hands to my side to stem the flow of blood.

Kade's reflection expressed doubt, but he grabbed Mellissa by the shoulders and shoved her away from me, bending over and sliding an arm underneath my legs in a fluid motion as he hefted me into his arms.

"Out," Kade ordered, his voice allowing no argument.

"Are you sure?" Raven, who was doing her best to fight off the blond foaming at the mouth, looked as if she was ready to continue the battle. "We can take them!"

"We don't want to take them." I felt weak as I flicked my eyes to Melissa. She sat on the floor, Kade's shove enough to cause her to tumble, her gaze malevolent. "They're still people."

"Fine." Raven slammed her forehead into the girl's and watched with satisfaction as she reared back and stumbled. "But I'm not sure they're still people."

"We have to try." My head lolled against Kade's shoulder. "I think I might pass out."

"Don't you dare," Kade snapped, his temper getting the better of him. "I need you conscious!" He lowered his voice. "Please."

"I'm sorry." The darkness poked at the edges of my mind. "Listen to Naida. She'll get you out. I ... we'll have to come back for Melissa."

Kade knew trying to force me to stay awake was a wasted effort. "We'll definitely come back for her." He brushed a kiss against my forehead. "I promise. I'm getting you out of here right now. We'll come back when we have a better plan."

24
TWENTY-FOUR

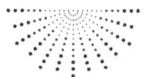

"**D**o something for her right now!"

Kade was not messing around once we hit the area outside the cave. The look he shot Raven was one of pure desperation. I barely clung to consciousness – in fact, I couldn't be sure that my subconscious wasn't watching the entire exchange from several feet above the spot where Kade held me – but I did my best to soothe him.

"It's okay."

"Shh." Kade pressed his lips to my forehead. "Do something, Raven!"

Raven moved to me, her fingers gentle as they prodded my side. "It's deep. We need to get her back to the circus."

"Then let's go," Kade barked, swiveling.

"What about them?" Nellie asked, glancing back at the cave. Melissa and the blond woman who attacked Raven stood on the other side of the opening Naida made, as if a barrier we couldn't see kept them trapped.

"We'll come back," Kade said. "We need help … and a new plan."

"We need Max," I murmured. "He'll know what to do."

"Then we'll get Max."

KADE PUT ME ON Luke's lap for the drive back to the circus. He didn't bother to make sure the others followed, instead tearing away from the cave and accelerating to well beyond the speed limit as he hit the pavement. He was a mess by the time we returned to the circus parking lot, slamming his truck into park and leaving the keys in the ignition as he raced to the other side and gathered me from Luke's arms.

"Get Max now!"

Luke didn't put up an argument and raced into the darkness.

I drifted in and out, the pain in my side enough to cause me to whimper when I felt a set of hands on me. I flicked my eyes to the side, forcing myself to focus, and found a grave-looking Naida and Raven poised to help.

"I think the blade was cursed," I muttered, unsure whether I was making sense. "It's hot."

"Hot?" Raven's eyebrows drew together. "We need that tonic you guys make, Nixie. Grab a lot of it … and more pixie dust."

Nixie didn't offer an argument before disappearing into the night.

Kade set me on the picnic table and ran his hand over my forehead, refusing to leave my side. He did his best to keep a tense smile on his face for my benefit, but I knew he was abysmally close to falling apart. "It'll be okay," he murmured.

"Of course it will." Raven wasn't the sympathetic sort. However, she hated to lose, and there was no way she'd allow that to happen. I had faith in her for that. "She'll be fine."

The group lapsed into silence as we waited for Nixie's return, the pain in my side growing with each labored breath.

"It's definitely poison," I gritted out, fiery lashes of torture shooting through me. "It's getting worse."

"Do something now!" Kade was at the point of no return. I wanted to offer him soothing words, promise everything would be okay and allow him to relax. I couldn't, because I wasn't sure that was true. Luckily for us, that's when Max appeared.

"Tell me exactly what happened," Max ordered, his hand moving to my forehead before he focused on the gaping wound at my side.

Luke opened his mouth to tell the tale, but Raven cut him off. "He needs the information quickly, Luke. Let me."

Raven told the story in measured tones. She didn't utilize any unnecessary words, covering everything in sixty seconds. When she was done, Max's face remained immovable.

"Well, that sounds terrifying." Max lowered his face to examine the wound. "She's right. It's poison."

"What kind of poison?" Kade asked, his voice cracking. "You have to do something for her!"

"We're doing something for her. I promise." Max shot Kade a kind look. "I know this is hard for you, but you need to let us do our jobs. We have no intention of letting anything bad happen to Poet. We love her, too."

"I don't," Raven volunteered. "She annoys me most of the time. But we still need her, so she's not going to die."

"Oh, well, that makes me feel so much better," Kade said dryly.

Max chuckled, taking some of the edge off the conversation. "I should be able to heal her once we remove the poison. We need the tonic to do that."

"Nixie is getting it," Naida supplied. "She'll be back any second."

"Good."

"You can heal people?" With nothing to do but fret, Kade latched onto a topic that interested him as he clutched my hand. "I didn't know you could do that."

"I'm a mage. It goes with the territory." Max licked his lips as he snagged my gaze. "We'll figure out a way to save Melissa just as soon as we get you back on your feet."

I gritted my teeth and nodded. I believed him. Max was powerful. Whatever we were up against was powerful, too, but I had to believe Max would outlast our new enemy. I was incapable of believing anything else.

"I've got it!" Nixie raced back to the table, pulling up short when she caught sight of Max. "Oh. I didn't know you were here. Can't you just heal her?"

Max kept his emotions in check. "As soon as we draw out the poison. The bottle, please." He extended his hand and Nixie dropped the tonic into his palm. "Hold still, Poet."

That wasn't a problem, because my muscles burned whenever I tried to move. I pressed my eyes shut as Max removed the stopper and upended the bottle, dumping the entire contents into the wound.

"Holy crap," Raven intoned, widening her eyes. "You used the whole bottle!"

"The poison spread fast."

"What does that mean?" Kade's knowledge of magical remedies lagged behind everyone else's. "Please tell me she'll be okay."

"She will." Luke rested his hand on Kade's shoulder in a show of solidarity, and even though the pain coursing through my veins was intensifying, the gesture warmed my heart. They were acting as a unit. Heck, they weren't even fighting.

"You guys look cute together," I forced out. "I sense a bromance in the making."

Luke made a face. "I'll have you know the second you're better I'm going back to making fun of him. This is a temporary truce."

"Whatever." I let loose with a strangled gasp when I felt the tonic course through me to intercept the poison.

"What's that?" Kade hunkered down. "Look at me. Poet, look at me!"

I obliged, although it was work.

"Don't leave me." Kade's eyes brimmed with tears. "Stay!"

"He's right," Luke said. "If you see a light, don't go into it."

I blinked rapidly, certain my blood was about to boil. "Oh, my ... ."

"Poet, focus on me," Max instructed, resting his hand on my forehead and positioning me so I had no choice but to look at him. "Look into my eyes. That's a girl. I want you to relax. I know it's hard, but try."

The burning sensation that threatened to overtake my body retreated a bit.

"Good girl." Max smiled. "The tonic is working. I can feel it. We're almost there. Just a bit longer."

"And then you'll heal her?" Kade asked.

"I will," Max confirmed without removing his gaze from my eyes. "I'll heal her and it will be like this never happened."

"I'll remember," Kade grumbled.

"Probably, but the most important thing is that Poet will be okay. We also know to be ready next time we face off against these ... living dolls."

I pursed my lips. "Dolls?"

"That's what they sound like to me."

"That's the first word that popped into my head," I admitted. "They were dressed like dolls. They acted like dolls being controlled by a force we didn't see. Their minds were still intact, buried deep."

"Then we'll find a way to unbury them." Max grinned as he lifted his hand, which was glowing blue. "Now it's time for the final step. Don't worry. This won't take long."

TRUE TO HIS WORD, Max had me back on my feet within minutes. I rolled to a standing position, doing my best to ignore Kade's mother hen impression as he shadowed me as I tested my limbs. When I was sure I was better, all traces of the poison gone from my system, I turned grim.

"We have to get Melissa."

Kade didn't immediately respond, instead dragging me in for a hug. He seemed relieved when he pressed his cheek against my forehead. "Your fever is gone."

"I'm still hot." I offered a soothing pat on the arm. "I'm okay. I'm sorry you were frightened."

"We'll talk about it later." Kade gave me a quick kiss before separating.

I had no idea what he planned to talk about, but I couldn't focus on that now. "Melissa was inside – so were the other girls – but they were dampened somehow."

"Did you get a chance to look at them closely?" Max asked, taking a seat at the table and smiling when Nixie handed him a mug of tea. "Were there other wounds?"

I searched my memory. "No. I didn't see anything on the girls in the cave. Not like what we saw on Katie's body when she was pulled from the water."

"What does that mean?" Luke asked, dragging a hand through his hair as he got comfortable. "Why would the dead girls be different? Is there a chance that we have more than one person responsible for this?"

"There's always a chance for just about anything," Max replied, his lips curving when he saw Kade absently massaging my shoulders. "Nothing is out of the realm of possibility. What we're dealing with here, though, sounds like a woman."

Raven balked. "You don't know that. Men are as sick as women."

"I won't argue with that, but the scene you described makes me think of a child dressing up dolls," Max argued. "You said all the girls were made up, right?"

"Gothic makeup in some instances," I supplied. "Lots of black eyeliner and colorful eyeshadows. White foundation making them paler than they should be, and bright blush and lipstick. It was an odd sight."

"And yet you also described outdated clothing," Max noted. "I can't remember the last time I saw anyone wearing bloomers."

"I can remember the last time someone wore chaps," Luke volunteered.

Raven scowled. "And I can remember the last time someone did a keg stand to fit in with his filthy wolf friends."

"Enough of that," Max ordered. "I don't care how hard you go after each other once this is over. We don't have time for it now. You said there were about fifty girls there, Poet. What happened to the other missing girls?"

I shrugged. "I don't know. I never believed all those girls were taken. Some of them had to be runaways."

"And more probably died than washed to shore," Luke added. "We probably will never know how many girls died and were dumped at sea."

"You're right, of course." Max rubbed the back of his neck, conflicted. "We only have about six hours before dawn. I suggest everyone get some sleep. I'll head to the cave once daylight hits to check out the situation. If I can solve it on my own, I will. If I can't, I'll return and we'll come up with a different plan."

His suggestion rankled. "You want us to leave Melissa out there all night?"

"Do you have another idea?"

"I ... ." As much as I hated to admit it, I didn't. "I don't like the idea of leaving her there. It doesn't seem right."

"And yet we can only do what we can do," Max said. "We'll meet again over breakfast and discuss our plans for the day. Until then, I expect everyone to get some rest." He leaned closer to me. "That goes double for you."

"I'll make sure she rests," Kade promised, earning a half smile from Max as the older man stood.

"I have no doubt that's true," Max said, widening his eyes when Kade threw a heartfelt hug around his father. "I ... well ... huh."

I pressed my lips together to keep from laughing at the disconcerted – and yet delighted – look on Max's face.

"Thank you for saving her," Kade said. "I ... just ... thank you."

"You're welcome." Max awkwardly patted his son's back. "I wouldn't have let anything happen to her. Take her to bed and force her to sleep. She needs rest for the day to come."

"I will."

Kade linked his fingers with mine before lightly tugging and directing me toward my trailer. I shared a rueful but amused look with Luke before turning my full attention to Kade.

"I really am sorry I frightened you," I offered. "I had no idea that was going to happen. I didn't realize there was a legitimate risk until it was too late. I hope you know that I would never purposely put myself in danger like that, so there's no need to be upset."

Kade said, "You always put yourself in danger to save others. That's what you do."

"I wouldn't phrase it like that."

"How would you phrase it?"

"Well ... I try to do what's best for people," I volunteered after a bit. "I try to be safe while I'm doing it. That's the best I can do."

"Do you hear me arguing with you about that?"

"No, but ... I could feel your fear. You did your best to hide it – and I did my best to shield my mind from being invasive – but I could still feel your fear. It was ... profound."

"Perhaps you inspire me."

"Or perhaps you think I'm a detriment to your mental wellbeing," I countered, my eyes serious as they locked with Kade's at the foot of the stairs that led to my trailer. "Are you thinking about taking a step back from all this? Before you answer, know that I won't blame you if that were the case."

Kade's expression was unreadable as he locked gazes with me. "Is that what you think?"

"I don't know. You said you wanted to talk and ... I'm afraid I don't want to hear what you have to say."

"Ah." Kade grinned, taking me by surprise. "I mean that we need to talk about safety procedures. There has to be a better way to approach things than the way we did today. That's all I wanted to talk about."

"Oh." I felt foolish. "So you don't want to take a step back?"

"No. We're getting a new trailer together, aren't we?"

"But ... you were so upset it hurt my heart," I argued. "I thought that meant you were keen to make sure that didn't happen again."

"If I could find a way to guarantee that you're never in danger I would do it. But that's not a possibility. I was attracted to you because of who you are. I don't suddenly want to change that."

"And who am I?"

Kade shrugged. "A hero. Now, come on. You need rest and I feel as if I'm asleep on my feet. I swear to you, we'll find a way to get Melissa back tomorrow. Until then, you need to recuperate."

"I feel normal. I'm great, in fact."

"Fine. I need to recuperate."

I followed him up the stairs. "You always manage to take me by surprise. I don't know how you do it, but you're a master."

"Thank you." Kade slipped his key into the lock and pressed a quick kiss to the corner of my mouth. "You manage to surprise me, too. If you could not get so close to dying next time you want to surprise me, though, that would be great."

"I'll keep that in mind."

"You do that."

25
TWENTY-FIVE

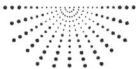

Kade was warm against my back when I woke and shifted my eyes to the window. It seemed earlier than it should be. My internal clock told me otherwise, and when I flicked my eyes to the clock on the nightstand I realized it was almost time for breakfast.

I hated the idea of waking Kade, his reassuring, even breath serving to lull me, but we had a busy day in front of us. I opened my mouth to cajole him to wakefulness, but he spoke before I could.

"Five more minutes."

I grinned. "How long have you been awake?"

"Not long. I think I was kind of awake a few minutes ago, but I didn't realize it was morning until you shifted to look out the window."

"It's overcast," I noted.

"It's Washington. I think rain is the norm in Washington." Kade rolled to his back and rubbed his forehead. Most of the time I took longer to wake than he did. He seemed reticent to get out of bed this morning, which meant he had something on his mind.

"Do you want to tell me what's bothering you?"

"How do you know something's bothering me?"

"When you answer a question with a question I know I'm right. Just a tip, by the way."

Kade chuckled. "Good to know." He lowered his hand and linked his fingers with mine. "I'm worried."

"I never would've figured that out myself," I said dryly. "Do you want to tell me what you're worried about?"

"Melissa."

The simple response was like an arrow to the heart. "We'll get her back." I meant it. "We'll get her back today."

"I hope so."

"We will."

"If we don't, I'll always know this was my fault." Kade wasn't one for melodrama, but I understood he felt a tremendous sense of guilt for what had happened. "I ordered my man to watch her and he lost her. She wouldn't be in danger if that didn't happen."

"You don't know that's true."

"But I do."

"But you don't." I was firm as I rolled to face him. "We have no idea if Melissa decided to run or if whoever took her cast a spell to more easily abduct her. Either way, your guy isn't to blame ... and you're certainly not at fault."

"It doesn't feel that way. I was hard on her over her attitude. I can't help but wonder if I pushed her too far. If she ran ... ."

"If she ran it's on her. We'll swoop in, save the day, and make her feel like an idiot. Then we'll coddle her for a few days and it will be right back to business as usual. You can't blame yourself. Melissa is powerful. She very likely confounded your guard so she could escape. She'll blame herself for that when we get her back."

"You sound sure we're going to get her back. I wish I could be as hopeful."

"Oh, we'll get her back." After a solid six hours of sleep I felt strong, more in control. "I pity whoever did this, because we're going to make her pay in ways you can't possibly imagine."

"And you're sure it's a woman?"

I shrugged. "That seems to fit the facts. It doesn't matter. If it's a man, we'll simply adjust our spell so it punches him in the nuts before we dispatch him."

Even though it was a serious moment, Kade barked out a laugh. "You have such a sunny way of looking at things sometimes."

"I do my very best."

KADE AND I WERE THE last to hit the breakfast area. I scanned faces looking for hints of new information.

"Where's Max?" I asked automatically.

"He's talking to the cops," Raven replied, pointing for emphasis.

I followed her finger and frowned. It was Detective Walker. "What is he doing here?"

"We don't know, but whatever it is I don't think it's good." Luke patted the open spot next to him. "How are you feeling this morning, Poet?"

"I feel good." I offered him a smile and a kiss on the cheek before taking the proffered seat. "How do you feel?"

"It's funny, but having to shift in front of people doesn't seem nearly as embarrassing when you realize young women are being turned into human dolls that can poison you."

"Good point." I sipped the coffee Nixie shoved in front of me. "How are you guys feeling after last night? I thought we might all have magic hangovers from the amount of power we expelled, but I feel okay."

"You got a boost of mage power," Raven pointed out. "You're one up on the rest of us."

"She almost died," Kade snapped.

"Sit down, sparky." Raven wrinkled her nose. "I was teasing her. We're fine. We'll be fully restocked by the time we need to move tonight."

"Tonight?" Kade tilted his head to the side, confused. "I thought we'd move together this morning. Why wait for tonight?"

"Because we have a show to perform," Luke replied. "We never miss our shows."

"But ...."

"It's not just that," I offered, my voice soft. "We don't want to embark on a magic fight during daylight hours. That's a lot of memories to modify, and if we miss one ...."

"You can modify memories?"

"To an extent. I can do it on an individual basis, but that's time consuming and draining. Nixie and Naida can do it with pixie dust, but that occasionally backfires. It's better if we can fight without anyone else seeing us."

"But we can't wait until dark," Kade pleaded.

"I don't see a way around it. I don't like the idea of leaving Melissa either, but we don't have a plan and Max needs to study the area. Who knows, he might figure out a way to end things on his own. It's happened before."

"He's that powerful?"

I nodded. "And then some. Most likely he won't be able to do it himself, though. It's a big job. When he gets back we'll come up with a plan and get everything in order before we descend on the cave. We'll need reinforcements."

"And a lot of tonic if they have more poisoned blades," Naida added. "I'm having Nixie whip up another batch this morning. It's better to have too much than too little."

"Good idea." I turned my eyes back to Max and watched as he trudged in our direction. He didn't necessarily look unhappy, but he was hardly giddy. Something was definitely wrong.

"What happened?" Luke asked as soon as Max was in earshot.

Max opted not to delay the inevitable. "There's been another death."

My heart rolled. "Melissa?"

Max shook his head. "Not one of the girls."

"Then who?" Raven asked.

"A man. He washed up in the surf this morning."

"A man?" That made absolutely no sense. "Why would she suddenly shift to going after men?"

"I don't know." Max held out his hands to signify helplessness. "It's a man we know."

"Who?"

"Barney Tolliver."

Well, that changed things. Significantly. "Maybe he got too close."

"Or maybe he knew who it was from the beginning and thought his daughter was safe," Max countered. "Either way, I'm heading to that cave. I need Nellie to show me where it is. The rest of you need to carry on as if it's a normal day. I'll be back in time for lunch and we'll discuss more then."

WORKING WHEN MY MIND WAS so busy wasn't easy. I knew I had to power through – which is what I did – but keeping my mind off Melissa was more difficult than I'd envisioned. That, coupled with Barney's death, had me struggling to make it through the few readings I had during the morning shift.

"You're never going to be the next Kanye West," I told the pale-faced boy sitting across from me. He was fifteen and thought he had a real shot at being a professional rapper.

"I don't want to be Kanye West," Dillan Baker sneered, making a face. "I want to be Eminem with a twist of Kanye. There's a difference."

Not from where I was sitting. "It's still not going to happen." I don't often try to crush dreams, but this kid was an entitled brat. "You don't have the talent. Try business school."

"Screw you!" Dillan hopped to his feet, his temper flaring. He had violence at the forefront of his mind – and, yes, it was against me – but he weighed a hundred and twenty pounds soaking wet and was hardly a threat.

"Sit down," I ordered.

"I want my money back," Dillan snapped. "You were supposed to give me a good fortune, not a bad one. If I wanted to hear crap like that I'd spend more time with my father."

"Sit down," I repeated, allowing a hint of chilly menace to creep into my voice. "I'm not kidding."

Perhaps the kid was smarter than he looked because he grudgingly reclaimed his seat. "I want a refund." He was petulant and morose, a dangerous combination.

I pointed to the "no refunds" sign on the wall and pinned him with a hard look. "Now, you listen to me. You're not going to be the next Eminem. You're not even going to be the next roadie for Eminem. You don't have musical talent. You can't rhyme. In fact, you're rhythmically challenged."

Dillan made an exaggerated face. "I can learn to dance. I can pay someone else to play the music. I can find someone to write the songs."

"So you're saying you basically want to be famous for nothing," I mused.

"Is that so wrong?"

It was annoying more than anything else. "If you want to be famous, here's the way to do it." I outlined a plan that would allow Dillan to be the next Kardashian – he would have less talent, of course, if that were even possible – and when I was done, he was furious.

"I don't want to start a reality show for wannabe rappers," he snapped. "People will laugh at us."

"Yes, but you will be famous for exactly fifteen minutes."

"I'm done listening to you." Dillan was back on his feet. "You're a terrible person. I hope you know that." He stomped out of my tent, whatever attitude he could muster on full display.

Kade appeared in his wake, and the smile on his face reflected amusement. "And how has your morning been?"

"Pretty much as you'd expect." I stood and grabbed the "be back soon" sign from the back of the tent flap and moved it to the front. "I want to stop by Nixie and Naida's booth before lunch. I want to make sure they have enough tonic when it's time to move."

"Okay." Kade didn't offer an argument, instead linking his fingers with mine and leading the way to the pixies' tent. "The circus is dead today. I think the weather is keeping people away."

"That would normally upset me, but I'm kind of happy about it. We'll be able to get people out of here on time and then move on the cave right after we close the gates."

"What about the money we'll be losing out on?"

I shrugged. "There are more important things than money."

"There definitely are."

NAIDA AND NIXIE WERE arguing when we approached. It was hardly out of the ordinary, but they sounded intense.

"We need more than that," Naida announced, hands on hips, as she stared at the box of tonic Nixie held. "We need enough for everyone to have two bottles."

"How many people do you think are going out there?" Nixie asked. "I've got fifteen bottles. We only had seven people out there last night. When you add Max, that's eight people. We should be fine."

"We need at least fifteen more bottles," Naida pressed, refusing to back down. "I'm not kidding. We'll have more bodies with us, and now that the attacker knows her poisoned blades work she'll go all out."

"How can you possibly know that?" Nixie challenged.

"I know all and see all."

"Oh, you're making that up." Nixie pinched her face into a disgusted expression as she darted her eyes to me. "Will you tell her she's overreacting?"

I wasn't so sure that was the truth. "I agree with Naida. We need more. I'm pretty sure we'll have to take Seth at the very least ... and probably Dolph. Do you want someone to die because we didn't have enough tonic?"

Nixie was sheepish. "Of course not. It's just ... we know what to expect now. We won't be caught off guard."

"They still outnumber us," Kade pointed out. "There are fifty of those girls who are controllable. There are only about ten of us. Do the math."

Nixie pressed her lips together, giving the impression that she was indeed doing the math. Finally she heaved a sigh. "Fine. But I think this is overkill."

"We'll have it for next time if we don't use it," Naida said, shuffling to the edge of the booth and catching my gaze. "How do you feel? We're going to need you at full strength for the fight tonight. If you feel you need a nap I'm sure you could get away with it. This place is dead."

"It is dead," I agreed, snagging one of the voodoo dolls from the nearby shelf. It was a former insurance salesman who purposely sold his clients bogus policies that paid him before killing them. Nixie shrank him down in Georgia almost eight months ago. "Are their souls really trapped in these husks?"

Kade let loose with an involuntary shudder when he realized what I held. "Do you have to play with those things? They give me the heebie-jeebies."

Naida ignored his whining. "They are. It's a byproduct of the dust Nixie uses. The souls are trapped until the husks are destroyed."

"And then the souls are freed," I mused. "Do you believe in reincarnation?"

"We don't face death in our realm like you do here. I've never really thought about it, but I would have to say no if pressed."

"So you think when your soul passes on that's it."

"Pretty much."

"Then explain ghosts." I had no idea why I was in a combative mood, but something niggled the back of my mind and I was desperate to work it out.

"Ghosts are trapped souls," Naida replied simply. "They don't know enough to pass over. They remain here until they're somehow directed to the other side. Sometimes that doesn't happen. It's not an ideal outcome, but it's not always avoidable."

I ran my tongue over my teeth. "Do you think there's a way to make sure souls stay local?"

Naida knit her eyebrows. "What do you mean?"

"A spell. Do you think there's a spell that relegates souls to a certain corner or something, and allows something else to control the bodies while the souls are kept separate?"

Naida caught on to what I was asking. "I don't know. Why?"

"What if we can craft a counter-spell to release those souls? I mean, in theory that would mean they could take over their bodies again, right?"

"As long as their bodies weren't decayed or long gone, that's definitely possible. Is that what you want to do for Melissa?"

"It's a thought."

"It is," Naida agreed. "Freeing all those souls at once is going to take power."

"It's going to take a nexus of power, something our enemy has at the cave and we have here." I mused, returning the doll to the shelf. "What if we can get our enemy to come to us?"

Naida leaned forward, intrigued. "What do you have in mind?"

"I'm not sure. It's a hypothesis more than anything else, but I want to work on it."

"We should check with Max first," Kade supplied. "He might have already solved the problem."

"It's possible but unlikely," Naida said.

"We can still check." I squeezed Kade's hand. "If he didn't fix things, I think we should bring the fight here. We have the advantage here."

"That's easier said than done," Naida said. "Still ... I agree. If we can swing it, that's definitely the way to go. No one can beat us here."

"I'm hoping that our enemy is cocky enough to believe the exact opposite."

TWENTY-SIX

I read a few more fortunes – basically busy work – and then shut my tent down early. The sky was ominous and threatening, and it kept visitors away. From a business standpoint, that wasn't good. From a personal standpoint, it made things better.

I decided to go for a walk along the boardwalk, if only to see if I could pick a few stray thoughts from random minds. I expected to go alone, but Kade caught up with me and silently matched my pace as I swung myself toward the crafts fair.

"I'm okay on my own," I offered, my voice gentle. "I'm not going to suddenly fall down and have a relapse."

"I didn't say you were." Kade kept his gaze on the crowd. "Maybe I simply want to take a walk. Have you ever considered that?"

"I don't want you to worry."

"It's too late for that."

It was far too late for both of us on that front. "Did you see her face?" I had to force out the words, Melissa's pale countenance from the night before haunting me. "If I couldn't see into her mind, I wouldn't have known she was there. She was like an empty shell."

Kade slipped his fingers between mine and grasped my hand. "I saw. I'm still not sure I believe it."

"Well, believe it. We have a fight on our hands."

"It's been that way since I joined." Kade flashed a smile that didn't make it all the way to his eyes. "This is no different. We'll win."

I wanted to believe him, yet something dark niggled at the back of my mind. "I handle things better when I'm the one in danger," I admitted. "I don't like worrying about other people."

"You were in plenty of danger last night. I could practically feel the life spilling out of you."

"That's not exactly what I meant." I slowed my pace. "I meant that I don't often think before I rush into danger because I'd rather sacrifice myself than someone else. But now Melissa is in real danger and I don't think I'm handling it very well."

Kade grimaced. "I don't know what you want me to say," he said finally. "If you expect me to be happy that you're fine sacrificing yourself for others … ."

"No, I don't expect you to be okay with that." I took pity on him, his palpable misery slamming into my chest. "I get it from your point of view now. That's what I'm saying. I understand that my being an idiot has a profound effect on you, just like Melissa being an idiot hurts me."

"Does that mean you'll stop being an idiot?"

"Probably not. I'm going to be really sorry when I succumb to idiocy, though."

Kade cracked a smile as he leaned closer and gave me a quick kiss. "I guess that's progress."

We resumed our walk, taking a moment to watch the scurrying artisans cover their booths with tarps. I flicked my eyes to the beach, an involuntary shudder running through me when I caught sight of the building storm clouds.

"I think it's about to get ugly."

"I was just thinking that myself," Kade admitted. "How soon?"

"I don't … ." I didn't get a chance to finish because a hint of movement caught my attention.

At first I thought the girl standing next to Barney's booth was someone who merely resembled Paige. The way the muted light hit the young woman's hair and highlighted the intermixing red gave me pause.

As if sensing my presence, she turned and met my gaze, causing me to gasp. Kade thought something was wrong and instantly went on alert.

"What? Are you okay? Do you need me to carry you?"

That last question was something that would've normally set me off, but given the circumstances, given the expression on Paige's face, I barely heard him. "I'm fine ... but she's not going to be for much longer."

"Who?" Kade furrowed his brow as he followed my gaze. "Holy ... what is she doing here? I thought she was missing."

"I think we've been mistaken on a few things." I squared my shoulders as I strode toward Paige. I opted for a brisk pace in case she decided to run, but she didn't look as if that was a consideration.

"Hello, Poet," Paige sang out. "I'm afraid you've picked a bad day for shopping, but if you want to come back tomorrow I'm sure you'll find something that will strike your fancy." Paige acted as if nothing out of the ordinary was happening.

"Where have you been?" Kade barked, his temper flaring. "People have been looking for you."

"I've been around." Paige's tone was light, airy. She was playing a game. I knew it. She knew it. Only Kade seemed to be lagging. "I've been around for a very long time, in fact. You'd be surprised how long."

Kade made a face. "How great for you. You know your father is dead, right?"

"I heard." Paige didn't seem upset. "Terrible news, isn't it? The police stopped by this morning. They seem to think he got drunk and mouthed off to the wrong person on the beach last night. I have no idea what he was doing down there."

I had an idea ... and it wasn't a pretty thought. "What are you?"

Kade was more caught off guard by the question than Paige. "What do you mean?"

I ignored his question. "You're not a simple witch."

"And you're not too quick on the uptake," Paige countered. "Did you really think I was a witch?"

"You have abilities that suggest you're a witch. I should've seen that from the beginning. You heard the lullaby, after all."

Kade realized fairly quickly that Paige was done pretending and wisely took a step back. He didn't move so far away that he couldn't jump in should she attack, but he let me handle the talking.

"Is that what you call it?" Paige pursed her lips. "Back in my day we called it a Wailing Whisper and made it strong enough to drown out everything in its path. Your attempt was weak."

"It was meant to be unobtrusive."

"It was still weak."

I narrowed my eyes. "What was Barney to you?"

"My, you're full of questions, aren't you?" Paige made a tsking sound with her tongue. "I guess you're used to people answering your questions because you enjoy invading minds – just like you're trying to do now – but that won't work with me."

Under normal circumstances I would've been embarrassed to be caught poking in someone's mind. These were not normal circumstances. "What are you?"

"What are you?" Paige fired back. "I've been searching Melissa's memories for an explanation for what you can do and why you all group together, but she doesn't know nearly as much as she thinks she does."

Paige's words made my blood run cold. "You befriended her to get close to us."

"Oh, well, that's egocentric." Paige's eyes lit with mirth, the clear blue jarring something in my memory, although I couldn't remember exactly what. "Not everything has to do with you, Poet. Melissa is powerful in her own right. I was drawn to the power, not you."

Kade slid me a look and I knew his silent streak wouldn't continue. I wanted to admonish him to keep his mouth shut, but I couldn't. Not only was it rude, but he had a right to ask questions. Given the fact that Melissa was under his care, there was absolutely no way he would back down now.

"You've had your fun with Melissa," Kade said. "You need to let her go."

Paige's turn was slow and deliberate, the look she graced Kade with menacing and smoldering. "And why would I do that?"

"Because we won't leave without her."

"Are you suggesting I should fear you?"

"I'm suggesting you won't survive this if you don't cut your losses and run," Kade clarified. "You have to know that you're not stronger than us."

Paige snorted, genuinely amused. "You are ridiculously handsome. I see why Poet is with you. You're not very bright, though, are you?" She didn't give Kade a chance to respond. "You're powerful, although you have absolutely no idea about the magic that's coiled inside you. What is that?"

She leaned forward and sniffed the air. "I don't believe I've ever come across anything like that," she continued. "Forget what I am. What are you?"

Kade balked. "I'm a man."

"You're definitely a fine specimen of a man," Paige agreed. "You're something more, though." She slid her eyes to me. "What is he? I'll share my secret if you grace me with his."

There was no way that would happen, mostly because tipping Paige to Kade's lineage would also give her hints to Max's power. I couldn't remember Paige ever crossing paths with Max – which was a good thing, because he was our most powerful weapon.

"We're not here to share secrets," I supplied, rapidly changing course. "We're here to come to a meeting of the minds. You're clearly not willing to share your secrets – and don't worry, I've already figured out Barney wasn't your father, so that's hardly a secret. We're not willing to share our secrets either."

"You have no secrets," Paige shot back. "Everything Melissa knows, I know. That's the way my particular gift works. That's the way I want it to work."

Something about the way she phrased the statement caused a few things to slip into place in my busy brain. "Is that it? Did you pick girls who boasted specific skill sets? That Aubrey Partridge girl. Everyone said she was smart and unobtrusive. If you know everything she did, that means you're as smart as she was."

"Don't try to figure me out," Paige admonished. "Your tiny brain isn't capable of comprehending what you're dealing with."

"You talk big, yet you're afraid," I argued. "You're afraid because we broke your wards and made it inside the cave. I can see the fear. It practically rolls off you in waves."

Paige made a derisive sound in the back of her throat. "You don't have any idea who you're dealing with."

"I don't know that it matters. You think you know us because you have access to Melissa's mind. The thing is, she didn't know everything about us. She was new. We purposely kept her in the dark about a great many things."

That wasn't a lie. While I inherently trusted Melissa, I hardly shared most of Mystic Caravan's secrets with her. I figured she would learn those for herself when the time was right ... and since she'd been with us only a few weeks that time had yet to come.

"While you may think you have the advantage because Melissa knew things, I can guarantee she didn't know nearly enough to help you overcome the magic storm we're going to be sending your way," I said, offering up a sneer of my own. "If I were you, I'd start running now."

"You're not me." Paige wasn't frightened, yet something about my words shook her. She wasn't as steady as she was only moments before. "This is my habitat. This is my space. This is my realm. You can't beat me when you don't even know what you're fighting."

"I wouldn't be so sure of that." I moved to touch her, perhaps jolt her with my magic, but I didn't get a chance because Paige slapped up an invisible energy field to stop me, forcing my fingers to glance to the side.

"Don't even think about it." Paige skirted the edge of the booth and increased the distance between us. "I know you're used to winning. That's what your magical menagerie does, right? You win. That's not going to happen this time."

"You don't believe that." I allowed a smug smile to play at the corner of my lips. She was about to run. Here, without aid, she was exposed. She didn't want this to turn into a fight, which is why she allowed me to see her when witnesses were afoot. She wanted to verbally spar and boast, but the physical and spiritual fights were yet to come. "You know we can beat you. Your ego won't allow you to run and survive. You feel the need to take us on.

"I've seen creatures like you before," I continued. "It's always your ego that brings you down. So … sit back and relax. We'll bring the fight to you soon enough. If you insist on winning, that means you're willing to risk losing … and that's exactly what's going to happen."

Paige barked out a laugh, the sound high-pitched and eerie. It came straight from a nightmare and invaded my reality, causing me to tilt my head to the side as I regarded her.

"You're the one who will fall," Paige said, her words accompanied by a terrific bolt of lightning. "You've never lost, so you think you're invincible. You're about to find out otherwise."

"Yes, you're about to find out otherwise," a voice cackled, causing me to jerk my head to the left. There, one of Bates' dolls – the original one that caused my skin to crawl – sat with bright eyes, staring at me. The doll moved of its own volition, extending a finger and pointing at me. "We're coming for you."

The doll laughed maniacally.

"We're coming, and there's no way you'll defeat us," she said.

"What the … ?" Kade appeared at my side, pressing his body against mine as the first drops of rain hit. "Did that doll just talk?"

I nodded as I stared at the doll, a multitude of things converging in my mind. I flicked my eyes to where Paige had stood only seconds before, but it was empty. I gave the area a brief scan, but she was gone. I wasn't surprised. She'd used the doll as a diversion. She'd also given me an idea, and that wouldn't end well for her.

"We have to get back," I said, jolting as a rumble of thunder shook the ground. "We don't have much time, and we have things to get in place before Paige moves on us."

Kade arched a surprised eyebrow. "Moves on us?"

"Yup. She's coming … and soon. We need to be ready."

27
TWENTY-SEVEN

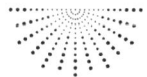

I went into research mode when we got back to the circus. The gates were closed in anticipation of the upcoming storm and it was absolutely deserted, everyone taking cover inside.

I headed straight for my trailer, Kade close at my heels. He waited until we were inside to start asking questions.

"What just happened?"

It was a simple question, without any easy answers.

"Paige is doing this."

"Yeah, I figured that out myself. Why, though?"

"She gains power and knowledge from the girls. She also gets something else, although I'm waffling on what that is. At first I thought she was sick and wanted to play dress-up – that was before I realized she was the culprit and not a victim, and thought someone else was behind this – but now I think it's something more than that."

"What?"

"She wants her own army."

"An army of young women? Why?"

"I'm not sure," I admitted. "There could be a multitude of reasons. Women control sex, which is a biggie. They're also more open to possibilities, which probably allowed Paige to get a foothold inside her victims' heads."

"I don't understand any of this." Kade sat next to me on the couch and watched as I booted my laptop. "Why would a girl like Paige – a young girl with her whole life ahead of her – enslave other girls to do her bidding? And you mentioned sex. Do you think she's using the mindless things she created for sexual purposes?"

He wasn't getting it. I licked my lips and took in a calming breath. Explaining this wouldn't be easy. Him accepting it would be another struggle entirely.

"Okay, here's the thing: She's not a young girl," I started. "She's something more than that. She's older ... and fouler."

"But what?"

"I don't know. I think she started as a witch. The symbols ... the magic I've seen on display ... it all stems from that branch of the pagan tree."

"How old do you think she is?"

"At least a century. It would take her that long to build up enough power to do what she's doing."

"But how could she live that long?" Kade pressed. "The way you described it before, witches are merely humans with magical abilities ... like you. Does that mean you'll live forever and look young and hot the entire time?"

I pursed my lips to keep from laughing. It was clear the notion both worried and intrigued him. "No. I have a normal lifespan ... at least by your standards."

"That's good, right? That means we'll grow old together."

It warmed my heart that he thought about our relationship in those terms, but we didn't have time to dwell on that now. "That's our norm," I clarified. "Nixie and Naida, for example, are from different planes. Their lifespan is much longer than ours. They seem young to you. I see it when you look at them."

"Nixie seems young," Kade clarified. "Naida seems somehow older, yet they're supposed to be twins."

"They are twins, and they've been alive for more than a hundred years. That's barely a breath in their dimension. They'll be here long after we're gone ... and they'll still look the same."

Kade rubbed the back of his neck. "That doesn't seem fair."

"Life isn't fair."

"I know." He rested his hand on my knee. "Go back to Paige. I don't think I understand what's going on here. How is she old yet looks young?"

"I'm guessing part of it is what she's doing to the girls she chooses for her ... army." I explained. "She's stealing more than their freedom and knowledge. She's also stealing their youth. I also believe she's forcing them to perhaps act as prostitutes in some shape or form."

Kade was understandably horrified. "How is she doing that?"

"They're empty vessels when she has them locked in that cave. She can animate them. You saw that with Melissa and the one who turned on Raven. Paige can make them do things – say things – and that means she can force them to complete tasks."

"I really want to kill her."

"Join the club."

"I don't understand about the prostitution thing," Kade said. "Is she doing it for money? Is all of this about money?"

"She's doing it for power. She needs money, too. If she sends one of her creations to seduce a man, I'm guessing sex and payment isn't the only thing she's looking for. She also probably wants secrets ... and bank account information ... and insight into other things. This is all theory, but I believe her approach is multi-pronged. Ultimately, it doesn't matter what she's trying to do. It only matters that we can stop her."

"You said that she'll come to us. How do you know that?"

"Because she believes she'll catch us off guard," I replied, opting for the simplest answer. "She thinks she'll be able to take us by surprise when she attacks. We need to make sure we're ready."

"And when will she attack?"

As if on cue, lightning split the sky through the window, accompanied by a terrifying shriek of thunder.

"Soon," I said, moving my fingers to the keyboard. "We don't have much time. I need you to message everyone in our group – Nixie, Naida, Luke, Raven, Dolph, Seth, Nellie and especially Max – and tell them to gather in the big tent in thirty minutes."

"Do you think she'll move that fast?" Kade was flabbergasted. "How could she mobilize her ... human dolls ... that fast? It seems impossible."

"She's strong and determined. She knows we outnumber her, although the girls make it doubly difficult for us. If we kill them, we can't save them. If we don't, that won't stop them from trying to kill us."

Kade understood what I was saying. "We'll save as many as we can."

"We will."

"We'll save Melissa."

I was less sure of that. I had no doubt that Paige would use Melissa as a very special weapon against me. "We'll do our best. Call them. Make sure they have the supplies we need."

"I'm on it." Kade got to his feet. "What are you going to do?"

"I'm going to see if I can track down background information on Paige," I replied. "I don't know if it will help, but it certainly can't hurt."

"How will you do that? You said she was older than she looked."

"And yet she clearly had some sort of tie to Barney ... and if I'm not mistaken, Bates, too. She controlled Bates' doll, and I got the feeling that it wasn't the first time. If I'm lucky, I'll be able to figure out those ties before the fight."

"And that helps us how?"

I shrugged. "I don't know. Knowledge is power, though."

"Okay." Kade leaned over and kissed my forehead. "Get to it. We don't have a lot of time."

KADE LEFT ME TO finish my research, braving the storm to make sure everything was battened down outside and promising to meet me in the tent as soon as he was finished. I was worried Paige would mobilize faster than I envisioned, but there was very little I could do about that, so I trusted him to protect himself and he believed I would do the same.

Finding information on Paige wasn't easy, but I knew a thing or two about reading family trees. Paige's ego wouldn't allow for her to completely eradicate information from websites like Legacy.com, so I had a working idea of the family dynamics by the time I let myself into the main tent.

I shook my head, spraying water on Luke as I passed. He made a face but didn't complain. He understood things were about to get serious. One look at the assembled faces told me they all understood that.

"I know who Paige is," I announced.

"Kade has been filling us in," Max supplied. He looked grave. "I can't believe it's been Paige all along."

"I don't get it," Luke interjected. "She's been on the circus grounds. Shouldn't she have alerted the dreamcatcher?"

"I've been thinking about that," I said, rubbing my hands over my cargo pants and flicking my eyes to the tent flap to make sure we remained alone. "She was only on the circus grounds the first night. Then she and Melissa moved outside the dreamcatcher line before we erected it."

"Are you sure?" Raven's eyes were keen. "I've never known the dreamcatcher to fail like this, but if it did, we need to know."

"I'm sure. I've been racking my brain for images of Paige on the circus grounds and the only time I can come up with is that first night. Otherwise she's been very careful not to slip over the dreamcatcher. She must have recognized it for what it was."

"The night she heard us whispering the lullaby," Raven noted. "You said you thought she heard us."

"She seemed surprised we called it that. She referred to it as a Wailing Whisper."

Max furrowed his brow. "That's a very old term. I mean … like a hundred-and-fifty-years old."

"I think she's at least a hundred-and-thirty-years old," I supplied. "I also think she was Barney's great-grandmother, not his daughter."

A series of hushed whispers flitted through the tent. Naida was the first to speak.

"How did you figure that out?"

"Because Paige Tolliver is on Barney's family tree as a great-grandmother and his daughter," I replied. "He put his entire lineage out there on Legacy.com. You would almost think he was proud of it."

"I don't understand," Kade said. "How could Paige be his great-grandmother?"

"Because she's been doing this a long time. This isn't the first harem of sorts she's built. I tracked the cities Barney moved through – we're talking Salem, New Orleans, Austin and now Seattle – and all of them were plagued by stories of missing girls."

"They're all supernatural hotbeds, too," Raven noted. "They're easy locations to hide paranormal activities."

"They are," I agreed. "In each city, human remains were found in bodies of water after Barney and Paige left. I also found a few photos – we're talking images from fifteen, thirty and fifty years ago – and in each one Paige looks the same."

"So Barney knew who she was." Max stroked his chin. "He fell in with his great-grandmother, realized she had power, and then turned into her father when he was old enough to pass without drawing questions. That allowed him to play the game, too."

"Why would he do that?" Luke asked. "He'd have to be a sociopath to participate."

"He probably was, but I'm guessing Paige promised him a present or two if he helped her," I said. "She's been alive for a long time, and she's still young. Barney probably wanted that, too, and that's the carrot she dangled."

"But he's dead," Dolph pointed out. "Why would she kill him if they were working together?"

"Maybe she thought he was a liability," Raven suggested. "I watched her that first night. She rolled her eyes whenever he told a story. Also, Poet is right. She didn't cross the dreamcatcher the second night. She and Melissa were on the other side of it, whispering and giggling. I have a clear vision from that evening. Paige never crossed. After that, we only saw her away from here. She never risked exposing herself."

"I have no idea why she killed Barney," I said. "He might have wanted to run. He might have been afraid. I do know that their story of constantly traveling is something of a lie. They do travel to fairs and whatnot, but only in this immediate area of late. I found a listing for a house ... and it's not far from the cave."

"Well, that's convenient." Nellie made a face. "Are we going up there to take her out?"

"No, because she's on her way here."

Nellie cocked an eyebrow. "How do you know that?"

"She practically told me. Of course, I was baiting her at the time. I told her we would go after her tonight, and she was so smug she couldn't stop herself from tipping her hand."

"That means she'll want to attack us first," Max said. "Poet is right; she's on her way."

"She'll set off the dreamcatcher as soon as she crosses the boundaries," Nixie said. "We'll know when she's here."

"Probably. Do we know if the possessed girls will set off the dreamcatcher?" This was the part of the equation that troubled me most. "They're not technically evil."

"If Paige is sending them here, they're going to do evil," Nixie said.

"They're empty shells. They only do what Paige wants them to do. They might not set off the dreamcatcher until they're ordered to kill, if they set it off at all."

Nixie straightened her shoulders. "Then they could already be here."

"They certainly could." I nodded. "Paige is strong. She's a witch with enhanced abilities. She knows everything Melissa knows about us. She thinks it's everything, but we know it's not."

"No, Melissa had no idea about a lot of things," Raven said. "Especially Max. We kept his abilities fairly well hidden. She knows he's magical, but she asked me if he was a magician about two weeks ago. I only laughed and didn't answer."

"Max is definitely our secret weapon, but we have a huge issue to deal with." My palms were sweaty and I continuously rubbed them against my pants. "We have to decide what we're going to do with the girls."

Kade balked. "What do you mean? We're going to protect them. We're going to take out Paige and then find a way to fix them."

"When we saw them in the cave they were docile until Paige ordered them to strike," I said, choosing my words carefully. "Paige only ordered two of them to strike. They have poisoned blades. I'm not sure we'll be able to save them all."

Even though Kade refused to accept my words, Max understood what I was saying.

"We need to fashion traps," Max said after a beat. "If we can trap them, it doesn't matter how much damage they're ordered to do. It also means we won't have to destroy them to save ourselves."

"Wait a second." Kade was beside himself. "Are you really considering killing them?"

"I'm not sure we'll have a choice in the thick of things." Max kept his tone soft and even. "We want to save all of them, but … it might not be possible."

"Well, then we'll have to think of another way." Kade was determined as he folded his arms across his chest. "If we lose one of them it's too many."

"You have a good heart and you're brave and true," Max told his son. "You're also foolhardy on things like this. We can't save the day if we're dead."

Kade opened his mouth to argue, but Max cut him off with a firm head shake.

"Think about it, son," Max prodded. "Poet is one of our strongest fighters and she was almost killed by a poison blade. Our enemy is fifty strong, which means we're already fighting five-to-one odds. Are you willing to give up Poet to save the other girls?"

Kade's face drained of color. "There has to be something. They're innocent."

"They are, and I have a plan. I hope to save most of them. That doesn't mean we can save all of them. I'm sorry."

"Don't be sorry." Kade squared his shoulders. "I understand what you're saying. You're right, I won't sacrifice Poet."

"What about me?" Luke asked, batting his eyelashes as he leaned closer to Kade. His joke was ill-timed, yet it elicited a few chuckles.

"I won't sacrifice you either," Kade replied, taking me by surprise when he planted a mock kiss on Luke's forehead.

Luke sobered as he straightened. "Oh, I'm starting to like you. I didn't think it would happen … but, well, there it is."

"We're all starting to like him," Nellie said. "What's the plan for capturing them?"

"Nixie, I believe you have a box of crystals in your tent," Max noted. "I need them. If I charm them and then we put three together …."

"We can build devil's traps," Raven finished. "That's a really good idea."

"I've been known to have them a time or two," Max said dryly. "Get the crystals, girls. Poet is right. We don't have much time. Once the crystals are charmed, we'll split them up and go in groups of two. No one fights alone."

"The key is to find Paige," I reminded everyone. "She can die. I have no qualms about killing her. Once she's gone, I think the girls will naturally break from the spell she has them under."

"And if they don't?" Raven asked.

I held my hands palms out. "We'll have to deal with it then. For now, Paige is our main concern. I don't look for her to cross the dreamcatcher right away. She'll send the girls first."

"I agree." Max was grave. "Once she realizes we're trapping her dolls, she'll have no choice but to cross the dreamcatcher. That's when we'll make our move."

"We'll have to bait her across," I said. "She seems the type to fall for the bait. That's good for us."

"That's our biggest advantage," Max agreed. "Okay, everyone knows what they're doing. We'll get the charms and go from there. This fight is going to be big, but I have no doubt we'll prevail."

Luke cast Max a sidelong look. "I expected a better war speech."

Max patted Luke's shoulder. "I'll work on it and get back to you."

28
TWENTY-EIGHT

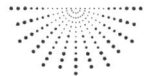

"I dosed these extra strong." Max was businesslike as he doled out the charmed crystals. "We can't do the normal thing of planting three to trap an enemy. That was the original plan, but I've thought about it, and it opens us to attack. We have too many enemies and not enough bodies."

"So what do we do?" Raven asked, her eyebrows knit as she studied the white crystal in her hand. "Do we throw them at them?"

"No, because I don't trust your aim." Despite the serious nature of the situation, Max's eyes twinkled. "You have to touch one stone to a girl. It should freeze her, but only for an hour."

My eyebrows winged up as I slid my stones in a pouch and affixed it to a belt loop. "An hour? Do you think that's enough time?"

"It'll have to be. It's the best I could do."

I licked my lips and nodded as I regarded him. It wasn't often that I went into battle with Max. Usually he preferred sitting back and letting us fight our enemies, only swooping in to save the day at the last minute. I realized after a moment of contemplation that was probably exactly what he was doing.

"Are you saving the day?"

Max was amused. "What do you mean?"

"I was just thinking that you generally don't show up until we need saving. I'm most likely captured or unconscious at this point. Is this what it's like when you ride in on a stallion to save us?"

Max chuckled. "I love the way your mind works. Have I ever told you that?"

I shook my head. "No, but ... if I don't get a chance to thank you later I want to make sure you know how grateful I am that you're helping Kade and me move in together. I didn't know if you would agree to buy another trailer, thought he was foolish for asking, but you came through."

Max's expression turned serious. "Are you saying your goodbyes?"

"Of course not."

"Then don't thank me." Max was grave. "You'll be okay, Poet. I won't let anything happen to you. More importantly, Kade won't let anything happen to you."

That was exactly the opening I'd been waiting for. "I think he should go with you."

Max's eyes lit with something I couldn't quite identify. "Excuse me?"

I kept my voice low. "I think he should go with you," I repeated, flicking a glance to Kade as he collected crystals from Nixie. "You'll be able to keep him safe no matter what."

"And you think you won't?"

"I'm going to be her primary target," I clarified. "I'm the one she's dealt with the most. I'm not trying to be egotistical or anything ... it's just that she's seen me and thinks I'm in charge. That will ultimately be good for us because she won't see Raven, Naida, Nixie and you as genuine threats."

"If I'm reading you correctly, you believe that Paige will move on you first." Max chose his words carefully. "You think that she believes taking you out will strengthen her position."

"I think it's personal with me, even more personal than I realize," I said. "She'll come after me hard."

"And you want me to separate Kade from you and keep him with me because of that?"

"I want him safe."

Max met my steady gaze with a weighted one of his own. "We both want him safe. That doesn't mean I'm separating him from you."

"But ... ."

"No." Max shook his head, firm. "He would rather die than lose you."

"That's exactly what I'm afraid of."

"He won't die either." Max patted my shoulder. "You're off your game because Melissa was taken from us. You didn't see it coming and you blame yourself. I know you, Poet. You're a master at taking guilt on those diminutive shoulders. It's not necessary. None of us could've seen this coming."

I wasn't sure I believed that. "I should've seen it coming. I'm a fortune teller."

"And Paige realized that from the start and distanced herself in such a way that it was impossible for you to read her. She knew what she was doing and played us. There's no going back and fixing that now. We can only look forward."

"And what do you see looking forward?"

"A battle ... and her end."

"I wish I had your faith."

"You do. You're merely keyed up." Max swallowed hard before turning his full attention to the rest of our group. "Stay in teams. Watch your backs." Lightning flashed ominously through the tent flap. "She'll use the storm. Don't let her. She thinks she's smarter than us, stronger than us. We know that's not true."

"It's definitely not true," Raven said, her eyes turning yellow and reptilian as she lifted her nose to the air.

"What was that?" Kade was flabbergasted as he moved to my side.

"You haven't seen the true breadth of her power."

"I guess not, but ... that's creepy."

I smiled, the weight on my shoulders lifting, if only marginally. "You haven't seen anything yet."

KADE AND I TOOK THE area at the front of the circus grounds. We had to split into groups of two, and even though Max didn't take Kade with him I was relieved to find Luke at his side as they disappeared into the storm. Max would never let anything happen to Luke. That was one less thing to worry about.

"What are you thinking?" Kade asked, dragging a hand through his soaked hair.

"That I don't like being so spread out. It makes us more vulnerable."

"And here I thought you were lamenting the fact that Max didn't take me with him."

I froze at the words. "What?" The question came out a bit squeaky.

"I know what you were talking to Max about." Kade was calm, his tone free of recrimination.

"But how? He didn't have time to tell you."

"I knew before you cornered him that you would try to protect me. I worried he might agree for obvious reasons, so I talked to him before that became an issue."

I was dumbfounded. "You knew I would try to protect you?"

Kade ran his finger over my damp cheek. "I knew that my biggest urge was to protect you. It only made sense that would be your biggest urge, too. You had to know I wouldn't allow that to happen."

"I did know that. That doesn't mean I wasn't still hopeful."

"Yeah? Well, now we're going to be hopeful together. This is a group fight. You're my partner. Don't even think about trying to leave me behind so you can be a hero. I won't take that well."

It was a serious moment, yet I couldn't stop myself from smiling. "We'll do it together."

"We definitely will." Kade tilted his head to the side when the eerie sound of laughter filled his ears. It was high-pitched and in stereo, so to speak. It was also eerie enough to make the hair on my arms stand on end. "Good grief. Is that what you heard in your dreams?"

I nodded, my stomach twisting. "It is. They're here."

"Do you see Paige?" Kade scanned the outskirts of the circus grounds. Even though it wasn't dark yet, the deluge of rain and heavy storm clouds gave the illusion that night was already upon us.

"No. She won't show herself right away. We have to fight the underlings first. She wants to see how we perform."

"Then we'd best get on that."

I nodded and pointed to a spot between my tent and Nellie's booth. "That's as good a place as any. We can only be approached on two sides."

"Sounds like a plan to me."

THE WAITING GAME IS my least favorite. I much prefer long stretches of Monopoly, Clue, Scrabble and even Risk when the mood strikes, boredom prevails or the weather is bad. Waiting is torture.

Today was no different.

The first hint of movement came in the form of shuffling feet. I dug in the pouch on my hip and grabbed a crystal, keeping my eyes focused on the opening to my right, while Kade fixated on the left. It was by tacit agreement that we decided to split our focus. We couldn't afford blind spots, which meant I had to trust Kade to handle magical crystals even though he'd never touched one before.

I could only hope that as the son of a mage Kade's instincts would be sharper than most. Otherwise I worried he would be at risk ... and that thought threatened to overwhelm me.

The sound of footsteps drew my attention to the aisle on the other side of the opening and I crept forward, a crystal clutched in my hand. I briefly closed my eyes, allowing my spatial awareness to kick in, and then lunged forward and slapped a crystal against the front of a pink dress.

The girl, a bright-eyed blond with over-plumped lips, made a face as she tried to move forward. The crystal kept her rooted to her spot, fusing to her dress and offering a reassuring purple glow. The girl struggled to move – probably listening to a command in her head only she could hear – but she was unable to break the trap.

"It's working," I announced, relieved.

"I know." Kade looked smug when I spared him a glance. He'd trapped his own human doll and she looked positively murderous as she glared at him.

"Look at the knife in her hand." I inclined my chin for emphasis. "Do you know what that is?"

"It looks wicked sharp," Kade replied. "Does it matter what kind of knife it is?"

"This one has a similar knife. It's an athame. There are runes carved into the handle. I think the handle is ivory."

"Why is that important?"

"It means they're old."

"And, again, why is that important?"

"Because I think Paige is relying on old world magical rules," I replied. "That means she believes certain things that might not be true. It also might explain why the girl at the library saw the shadow with multiple arms. That's how Paige sees herself, with the power of many at her fingertips. If she's bound by old world magical rules, we might be able to use that ... if I can just figure out how."

Kade was intrigued. "Like what, for example?"

"A woman living by old rules might not realize new possibilities ... like traveling between planes."

"Ah." Realization dawned on Kade's face. "You don't think she understands exactly what Naida and Nixie are capable of."

"Exactly." I bobbed my head. "She probably knows what a lamia is. Raven is of this world. Nixie and Naida are something else."

"Do you think we can use that?"

I shrugged, uncertain. "I don't know. It's interesting to think about, though. In fact ... ." I didn't finish my sentence, instead whirling and pinning with a crystal the girl who thought she was sneaking up behind me before she could lash out with a wicked-looking knife. The girl widened her eyes when she realized what happened, causing me to tilt my head to the side. This one stopped fighting quicker than the other two.

"They're learning," I noted, doing my best to wrap my head around the situation. "They're absorbing knowledge from one another. This one stopped fighting quicker. That means she realizes it's fruitless and doesn't want to expend unnecessary energy."

"Which means Paige realizes it's fruitless," Kade surmised. "That's three down. Only forty-seven or so to go, right?" He flashed a winning smile, one I was obliged to return.

"Probably fewer. I'm guessing that Paige spread her minions and approached the grounds from a variety of directions. I'm sure the other teams have taken out some of the girls. That doesn't mean we don't have a lot more to tackle before the end of the day."

"Where next?"

That was a good question. "I don't know. I ... ."

The sound of cackling caused me to shift my eyes to the right and I almost fell over when I saw a small hand gripping the tent flap and peering around it. The face meeting mine was straight out of a nightmare. Heck, it was straight out of my nightmare.

"What are you looking at?" Kade was determined as he strode through the opening and joined me on the other side, his eyes going wide when he recognized the doll from Bates' booth. "Son of a ... !" He swore under his breath, his vehemence washing over me in a furious wave. "I guess you were right about those dolls being possessed."

I swallowed hard, refusing to break eye contact with the doll. "I really wish I'd been right about something else."

Kade gave my hand a reassuring squeeze. "This is like your worst nightmare, isn't it?"

"You have no idea."

Kade slid his arm around my waist and gave me a tug, moving me away from the doll's evil glare. "How many of those do you think she has?"

"Too many."

"Do you think they have poisonous blades, too?"

I shrugged, helplessness washing over me. "I have no idea, but I think I might pass out or something. Human dolls are one thing. It's bad, but I can find the courage to look past them. These things are so much worse."

Kade didn't look convinced. "Those things are fabric and wood."

"So?"

"So you can do this."

My mouth dropped open as Kade dropped his arm and swiveled, lifting his foot and slamming it down on the doll. In the split second before he smashed the creature's face into the dirt she looked as surprised as I felt. Then her face met the mud. Kade was enthusiastic as he ground her into the dirt, flashing me a triumphant look as he moved his foot.

"See. That wasn't so bad."

Strangely enough, I felt bolstered by his easy takedown of the doll. Then she stirred, lifting her small head in my direction and fixing a set of murderous eyes on me. Her fabric face was soaked and stained. One of her button eyes looked as if it might fall off, but she was back on her tiny feet and her muddy face promised mayhem.

"You were saying?"

"Oh, geez." Kade grabbed my arm and gave me a tug. "I thought it was going to be easy."

"That will teach you to underestimate dolls. They're evil."

"I've seen the light. Now … run!"

THE GROUND GREW SLIPPERY fast, dirt turning to mud and the overabundance of rain adding an inch or two of standing water to the mix over some portions of the pathways. Kade was in front of me, his eyes trained to the left. I took the right, slapping a crystal against an approaching girl before she could round the corner next to one of the game booths.

"Have you seen anyone else?" Kade asked, his chest heaving as he stopped to catch his breath. "What about Max or Raven?"

I shook my head as I wiped the accumulating water from my forehead. "They're around. Don't worry about that. I would know if something happened."

"To all of them?"

"I … ." I broke off, considering. Finally, I nodded. "I would know.

Luke is with Max. He's talking up a storm because that's what he does when he's nervous. Max is tuning him out, but he's not agitated. Well, at least not yet. They've tagged some of the girls. Raven and Seth, too."

"What about Naida and Nixie?"

"They're making good headway. So are Dolph and Nellie. Nellie is small enough that he can slip under things. He's slapping crystals against ankles as they run by." I smiled at the image flitting through my head. "They're okay. Everyone is okay."

"And everyone else, the midway folk and clowns, are still in their trailers?"

"They know something is going on, but they're not sure what. This isn't the first time something like this has happened. They're fine letting us sort things out on our own and staying out of the melee.

"Paige isn't focused on them," I continued. "She wants ... us."

"You mean she wants you." Kade's expression darkened. "Why is she focused on you?"

"I don't know."

"I don't believe that."

I balked. "I'm not lying."

"Oh, don't do that again." Kade wagged a finger in my face as he stepped closer. "I'm not calling you a liar. I think you don't want to say what you believe for some reason. We don't have time for that. Tell me."

"I ... ." I honestly didn't know what to say.

Kade stared for a long moment. "Paige thinks you're the strongest one here, doesn't she?"

Even though the pelting rain was cold, my cheeks burned. "I think so. I don't know why she would believe that, though."

"I do." Kade adopted a reasonable tone. "To Melissa, you're the hero. You plucked her from a life she hated and gave her a shot at accomplishing everything she's ever wanted. She's seen you in action a few times, and you're always strong in battle.

"Melissa hasn't seen Max in action all that much and she's been shielded from some of the things Naida and Raven can do," he continued. "In Melissa's mind you're the star ... and that means Paige thinks she only needs to take you out to win."

I opened my mouth to argue. Instead I merely shrugged. "I don't believe that. I don't want you thinking that I somehow fancy myself above everyone else."

Kade cracked a smile. "Do you think that's what I'm worried about?"

"I don't know. What are you worried about?"

"Exactly what means Paige will use to get to you," Kade replied without hesitation. "She's turned the focus to you, which means ... ."

As if on cue, the dreamcatcher picked that moment to alert, a whooping pulse of magic moving through me as the sky illuminated with a multitude of magical sparks.

"What's that?" Kade asked, looking upward.

"Paige crossed the boundary. She's here."

Kade turned grim. "Good. That means we can end this. Which way?"

I wasn't entirely sure ... and then the answer hit me hard. "My tent. She'll go to my tent."

"Then I guess we'll meet her there."

TWENTY-NINE

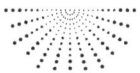

We tagged three more invaders on the way back to my tent. I could feel Paige's presence inside the moment we closed the distance, causing my anxiety to ratchet up a notch. Even though I knew it was fruitless, I made a heartfelt suggestion all the same.

"Perhaps you should find Max and tell him where we are."

Kade didn't as much as blink. "No."

"We could use his help."

"If you can sense him, he can sense you." Kade was firm. "He'll come on his own."

I knew that to be true. I also knew that if Paige really wanted to hurt me she'd go after Kade. I was desperate to protect him.

"But...."

"Shut up," Kade ordered, his eyes flashing. "Together. For good or bad, we're together. I don't want to hear another word about it."

I nodded, resigned. "Be careful."

"That goes double for you."

Paige sat in my chair as we entered, a bright smile on her face. Even though she didn't move, I caught a glimpse of Melissa standing in the corner. Paige was the immediate threat, so I focused on her.

"I was wondering if you would bother to join me." Paige leaned back in my chair and gestured to one of the seats across from her. "Have a seat."

It was a power play, and a weak one at that. "I'm good."

Paige's smile didn't slip. "I don't believe you heard me. Have a seat."

"I heard you. And I'm good."

Paige narrowed her eyes. It wasn't until the exact moment that she sent out the command – it was nothing more than a whisper on the wind that caused my blood to run cold – that I realized her intentions.

Melissa moved from the corner and, without hesitation, slammed her head into the pole at the center of the tent.

I couldn't contain my gasp when she did it a second time, blankly ignoring the blood running down the side of her face as she readied herself for a third round.

"Stop it!" Kade ordered, taking a step toward Melissa. The intention to stop her by whatever means necessary was written all over his face.

I reached out and grabbed his arm, refusing to let him move closer to Melissa or Paige should the latter decide attacking seemed fun. "I'll sit."

Kade cast me a sidelong look. "Are you sure that's a good idea?"

I didn't answer, instead keeping a firm grip on his arm as I led him toward the chairs. He shot me one more dubious look before sitting. I did the same. Paige smiled maniacally as she mentally ordered Melissa to return to the corner. I could hear the conversation, and there was nothing but acquiescence on Melissa's end. Paige was completely in charge.

"That's better, isn't it?" Paige was back to projecting an air of faux innocence and light. "Now we can get comfortable for our conversation."

"What is it you want, Paige? I mean … what do you think you're going to get out of all of this?"

"Well, at first I thought I was going to learn a bit about magical circus folk and perhaps expand my powers," Paige replied. "Now I'm simply hoping to add a doll or two to my collection."

She was so matter-of-fact it set my teeth on edge. "I see. And who did you think would willingly turn themselves over to be your playthings?"

"Willingly? No one. Raven and you will make nice additions to my collection. You're the most powerful ones. I think you'd fit in nicely."

"That's not going to happen," Kade seethed, leaning forward. "If you think I'm going to let you touch her ... ."

Paige flicked a dismissive look to Kade. "I don't believe you're going to have a say in the matter. You're powerful, and yet ... you don't use your powers. You don't even know how to tap into them. I'm not sure what to make of that."

Kade practically vibrated with rage beneath my fingertips as I rested them on his forearm. "I'm not powerful."

"Do you believe that or merely want it to be true?" Paige stared hard into Kade's eyes, involuntarily shuddering. "I look forward to finding out."

"And how do you figure you're going to do that?"

"Once Poet is one of my dolls, you won't have a choice," Paige replied smoothly. "Once she's under my command, you'll bend your knee and join me or I'll kill her. You won't have any choice."

Paige's smile was evil as she steepled her fingers in front of her. "Something tells me you'll do whatever it takes to keep Poet alive. You think you're her hero and will protect her with your life. I'm counting on that ... and I'm looking forward to spending time with you so we can explore your powers together."

Paige shifted her eyes back to me, perhaps sensing that I was getting ready to strike. "Of course, you won't mind if I turn the time I spend with Kade into something romantic, will you? Of course you won't. You won't have enough brain power to mind anything."

"I'll never give you what you want," Kade argued. "It simply won't happen."

"We shall see." Paige licked her lips. Now that I could look upon her with knowledge, she seemed much older than the young girl I originally pegged her for. "Something tells me Poet is going to give me what I want ... mostly because she knows I'll kill Melissa if she doesn't."

I knew that would be her play. Unfortunately for Paige, I learned a long time ago that giving in to blackmail was a fool's errand. "If you kill Melissa, I will be profoundly sad," I admitted. "I'll blame myself and feel guilt for a very long time. But I won't sacrifice myself to save her. At least not the way you want me to. I don't have it in me."

Paige pursed her lips. "I think you're wrong."

"And I think you've underestimated me." A mental flash from Max – *I'm coming, hold the line* – allowed me to feel bolder, and I squared my shoulders and sat straighter on my chair. "You've handled this battle poorly, Paige. In fact, if we were playing Risk you already would've lost."

"Is that so?" Paige let loose with a hollow chuckle. "How do you figure that?"

"You think because you know what Melissa knew that you're somehow ahead of the game. The thing is, Melissa didn't know all that much about us. Sure, she learned something new every day. That doesn't mean she knew our darkest secrets."

"Really?" Paige feigned interest. "Is this when you're going to tell me what he is?" She inclined her head toward Kade. "He doesn't even know what he is. He certainly doesn't know the power he possesses. Are you trying to say he's going to kill me?"

I shrugged, noncommittal. "I'm sure he would like to kill you with his bare hands."

"You've got that right," Kade growled.

"He probably won't get a shot," I added. "You'll be gone long before he can put a hand on you."

"And why do you say that?"

"Because your dolls, as you like to call them, are falling outside. They're being trapped at a rapid clip right now because my friends are converging on this tent. They're almost here, and when they arrive you're going to learn a hard lesson about what is and is not proper behavior."

Paige snorted. "I've been around much longer than you. I know a thing or two about threats, and that was an empty one."

"No, it wasn't." Now it was my turn to be matter-of-fact. "You've been alive – and vital – for almost a hundred and fifty years. That's impressive. I am curious how you convinced Barney to pretend to be your father when you were really his great-grandmother."

Even though she did her best to cover, I could tell Paige was shaken.

"And how did you figure that out?" Paige queried.

"Barney was big on filling out his family tree online. It wasn't difficult."

"Yes, well … ."

I cut her off before she could take control of the conversation a second time. "You found the key to everlasting youth, but you did it at the price of the dolls you created. You stole their life essences and extended your life while draining their power and strength."

"That's hardly rocket science." Paige made a big show of studying her cuticles. "Do you want a cookie for figuring out the obvious?"

I shook my head. "It was easier before. You could take a lot of girls in a small area and no one ever managed to put together a pattern because you weren't leaving behind bodies. But as technology grew, you found you had to move more often."

"What a riveting story." Paige rolled her eyes. "Let's go back to talking about you serving me."

I ignored her tone. "Austin. New Orleans. Salem. Now here. You picked supernatural nexuses so you could operate freely and then you went about your hunting. The thing is, you've taken a lot of girls in this area in six months. The information I got regarding your activities in the other locations seems to indicate that you weren't working nearly as fast when you visited. I think I know why."

"You seem to think you know a lot about a great many things, yet you're ignorant," Paige fired back. "You don't know anything."

"I know it all." I wasn't boasting. I'd figured it out and my fingers itched to unleash my building power. It wasn't quite time yet. "I know that you're failing. Even though you're strong and thought you'd live forever, your magic is starting to diminish."

Paige shot me a haughty look. "You wish that were true."

"It is true," I countered. "That's why you took so many girls while you were here. I mean, you took way more girls than was safe. That was by necessity. It wasn't a whim. You were hoping that if you drained more of them faster it would reverse the signs you were seeing. But the aging process only increased.

"You're desperate for a new influx of power to stave off the inevitable," I continued. "That's why you were so intrigued to meet Melissa. She has magic, and you found by enslaving her that it made you feel a little better. You think adding Raven and me to that mix will make things perfect again."

The eerie smile slipped from Paige's face. "You don't know what you're talking about."

"Oh, but I do." I let loose a grating smile of my own. "You killed Barney because he was on you to gift him the same way you gifted yourself. You've been stringing him along for years, but he'd finally had enough. You knew that he was no longer of use, so you killed him."

"You have a marvelous imagination," Paige drawled. "You really should write books rather than tell fortunes."

"I'll keep that in mind." I stretched my long legs out in front of me as I leaned back in the chair. "You didn't worry about killing Barney because you had another friend to help you. In fact, that friend dumped Barney's body in the water because you were in hiding at the time."

Paige's eyes turned dark. "Excuse me?"

"I'm talking about Bates. He was your other partner. He traveled with you to festivals. You didn't have to promise him eternal life to join you either. You only needed to let him play with your dolls."

I felt sick to my stomach. I knew something was off about Bates, but I had no idea it was this bad.

"I see. And how do you know that?" For the first time, Paige looked uneasy. It was obvious she realized she'd overplayed her hand and was no longer in charge. She thought she might still be able to escape, but she was feeling me out to see exactly what I knew.

It was time to drop the hammer.

"I know that because my friends have captured Bates," I supplied, grinning. "He got knocked down by a dwarf in a dress and then locked in the tiger cage by our strongman – who is definitely not happy, by the way. He was poisoned by one of your dolls, but he's already on the mend thanks to our pixies."

"Pixies?" Paige cocked a haughty eyebrow. "Melissa used that word, too. It makes me laugh."

"That's because Melissa didn't understand what it truly meant, so you're incapable of wrapping your mind around it." I readied myself to move, hoping Kade would jump into the action when he realized what I was about to do. "Your dolls are down and out. The human ones are trapped until we can free them. The cloth ones are ... thankfully ... being burned in a fire bin."

Paige made a face. "Burned?"

"That's right. Our resident dwarf doesn't like dolls any more than I do."

Paige tilted her head to the side, and I could feel her desperately sending out mental search beacons. She had no idea how bad off she was, which made me chuckle.

"You've been cut off from them for some time," I supplied. "Raven put a dampening field over the tent and reflected your thoughts back to you so it would seem things were carrying on outside as they were before."

Paige's face drained of color. "I don't believe you."

"Sadly, you do. That's why you're so terrified. You realize you overplayed your hand."

Paige shakily got to her feet. "I am still in control here."

"That's important to you, isn't it? Being in control, I mean. You desperately want to be in control, but now that you're not things are about to fall apart."

"You have no idea what you're talking about," Paige gritted out. "I can still kill Melissa."

"You probably can," I conceded, my heart twisting. "But I'm going to do my very best to stop it."

"And how will you do that?"

"With a little help from her friends," Naida announced, striding through the tent opening and fixing Paige with a look straight out of a horror movie. Her aquamarine hair was wild, her eyes filled with fire, and she boasted a gash on her cheek that looked angry and painful. "I've had enough of your mouth."

Paige swallowed hard, the truth finally overwhelming her. "What are you?"

"She's a pixie." I smiled as I got to my feet. "And we're going to show you a few of the horrors you've graced your dolls with." I didn't look at Kade as I moved across the tent, instead joining my magic with Naida's as we descended on a quaking Paige.

The crone knew the game was over, yet she tried to scamper away all the same. "What are you doing? I'll kill Melissa if you don't let me go. I'll do it right now."

"I don't think so," Kade countered, grabbing Melissa around the waist and pinning the hand that held the dangerous knife above her head. "Hurry up, Poet. I'm not sure how long I can hold her."

I flashed him a grateful look. "Turn away. You don't want to see this."

"You're wrong. I'm not afraid of what you're about to do ... and I want to see it. I promise it won't change anything."

I couldn't give thought to the promise because it was time to end Paige. She'd earned it, and the danger wouldn't be completely past until we'd removed her from the life to which she so desperately clung. I moved to the right, Naida to the left, and we pressed our hands to her head at the same time. We started in English.

"I am the bringer of death," we intoned. "Pass over. Pass on. Let go."

Raven joined us from outside, her voice smoothly intermixing with ours as we continued in English another two times.

Then we switched to Latin and the chanting intensified.

"*Mortem ferens venio. Transite. Discede. Concede.*"

Over and over, we repeated the words. Even when Paige started screaming, our busy fingers drawing the light out of her and letting it loose into the night air, we didn't stop chanting. Our united powers continued to build, growing to a point of overwhelming completion when Nixie joined the fray.

At some point Kade stopped struggling with Melissa, going from holding her back to propping her up.

The chanting built to a crescendo, and with one final cry the last bit of Paige's light dimmed and the husk she left behind crumpled to the floor.

We were one.

We had won.

We were done.

30
THIRTY

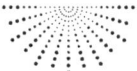

Cleanup wasn't easy.

In addition to Paige's body we had almost sixty lost girls to deliver to worried parents and loved ones, and a weeping and remorseful Charles Bates to deal with. Faced with Paige's death and no hope of escape, he spun a yarn that was so ridiculous I could do nothing but laugh … and fight the urge to rip his head from his shoulders.

"And you think we should let you go after knowing what you were getting out of this little arrangement?" I challenged.

Bates adopted a look of absolute contrition. "I didn't mean to do anything wrong. I was afraid of Paige."

I saw glimpses of what he did while the girls could do nothing but take it, so I didn't buy that for a second. "Shut your mouth!" I turned to Max, running a restless hand through my unruly hair as I studied the bonfire Nellie tended. The rain died soon after Paige did, which was a welcome turn because we had evidence to burn. "We can't just set him free."

"No, we can't," Max agreed, his distaste for Bates coming out to play. "Let Nixie do what she likes to do."

"What does that mean?" Bates' face turned ashen. "What does Nixie like to do?"

"Nothing you will enjoy," Max replied, making a clucking sound with his tongue. "Hold him until Nixie gets back, Dolph. She's tending to Seth, who was grazed by a blade. She'll be back shortly. She'll know exactly what to do with Mr. Bates."

"What is she going to do?" Bates was on the verge of panicking. If he knew what was really coming, he'd risk his life to escape. Instead he remained where he was, pathetic and sobbing. "I want to go home."

"I'm sure the girls felt the same way." Max directed me to a spot away from the fire, smirking when he saw Nellie approach with a squirming doll in his hand. "Is that the last of them?"

"The last I can find," Nellie replied, tossing the squawking doll into the fire and grinning when it screeched and attempted to claw its way out. "They're vicious little things. Once Seth is back on his feet, I'm taking him for another tour. They seem to be attracted to him for some reason."

"It's probably because he looks like a model," Raven offered, standing in front of one of the confused girls and holding up several fingers. "How many fingers do you see?"

"I want to go home," the girl sniffed, tears streaming down her face. Like the others, she woke in a state of confusion. Several were bad enough that they needed to be transported to a hospital. Luke and Naida were handling that, mostly because memories needed to be modified and the dropoff had to be done in absolute secrecy.

"You're going home soon," Raven promised. She wasn't exactly sympathetic, but she wasn't mean. "It will be soon. Then you'll be able to put all of this behind you."

I caught her gaze. "Someone should tell Desdemona before she hears it on the news."

Raven was grim. "I was thinking the same thing. I'll do it. I'll ... say goodbye for all of us." She looked satisfied at the prospect. "I agree that she should find out from us rather than the news."

I smiled. "Good. I think that's good."

I followed Max, who didn't stop until he was sure we were out of earshot.

"You did well." Max graced me with a heartfelt smile. "You kept her busy so we could get in position. I figured you would understand the plan if I sent the right images."

"You were right." I moved my eyes to the front of Melissa's trailer. She sat on the front step, dazed and let Nixie treat her head wound. "Do you think we should modify her memory?"

Max was surprised by the question. "Do you?"

"Part of me wants to shield her from this."

"And if you were subverted by evil, would you want to be shielded?"

"I ... ." In truth, I had no idea how to answer. "She'll struggle with this. It will weigh her down."

"It will," Max agreed, his gaze lingering on Melissa. "She's a strong girl. She will come out the other side. I don't think stripping her memory will do her any good."

"Why?"

"We learn from our mistakes," Max replied without hesitation. "She is not innocent in this. She was taken in by Paige. Yes, she was a victim, but I'll bet she saw warning signs in Paige's behavior and didn't follow her head when it came time to address them. She won't do that again."

"This was an awful hard punishment for doing something we all did as teenagers."

"It was," Max agreed. "Luckily she was not one of the girls Paige experimented on."

Experimented? I lifted my eyes. "The dead girls. Paige tried something different with them?"

"She did," Max confirmed. "She tried enchanting rope to make them magical marionettes of sorts, thinking that she could tie the other end of the rope to her and bolster her power through artificial means, a new process she'd yet to master. That's the way Bates explained it anyway."

That explained why the wounds reminded me of what happened

under the bridge so long ago. "We still don't have all the missing girls," I pointed out.

"No, but we will probably never know what happened to those other girls." Max flashed a sympathetic smile. "I'm sure Paige killed some and dumped them in the ocean. Not all the bodies would've washed to shore. That is a tragedy, but there's nothing we can do about it.

"You need to look at this as what it truly is, Poet," he continued. "It's a victory. Because of you ... because of what we can do when we're together ... we're sending quite a few girls home. That wouldn't have happened without our intervention."

"I get that, but I can't help thinking about the parents who will hear about these girls coming home tomorrow. They'll become hopeful and think their daughters are coming home ... but it's not going to happen for all of them."

"Not for all," Max agreed. "For many, though, it will. You can't let this weigh you down. You did your very best. You won. That's the most important thing."

I knew he was right. Being morose wasn't going to help anyone. Still, I couldn't quite force myself to be happy. "I'll be glad when we leave here," I said after a beat. "It was a nice experiment, but I haven't slept well since we hit."

Max turned his eyes to the fire, where Nellie poked a burning doll with a stick. "Something tells me you'll sleep better tonight. The doll nightmares won't return. That was your subconscious trying to tip you off to what was happening."

"I hope you're right." I rolled my neck. "I should probably check on Melissa and then get back to work. The weather is supposed to be nice tomorrow, which means big crowds."

"Ah, yes. The show must go on." Max patted my shoulder. "Put Melissa to bed. Have Nixie give her a sleeping draught. Make her stay there until we leave this place. She'll be better for it in the long haul."

"Okay. That sounds good." It honestly did, and this time the smile I mustered was legitimate. "So, when does our new trailer arrive?"

Max chuckled, genuinely amused. "It will be delivered the day we arrive at our next location."

"Really?" That was fast. "How did you manage that?"

"I haven't been able to give my son much, so when he actually made a request did you really think I wouldn't exert a little effort to give him what he wanted?"

I shook my head. "He thanked you, right?"

"He did. He's warming up to me."

"Well, you bought him a hugely expensive trailer so he could live with his girlfriend. Who wouldn't warm up after that? You're like ... the best dad ever."

"You are funny." Max flicked my ear. "I'm looking forward to seeing this trailer. The saleswoman I talked to over the phone couldn't stop gushing. It's supposed to be totally rad."

I snorted. "Well, I guess we all have something to look forward to."

"We do indeed." Max nodded. "Onward and upward, Poet. It's always best to look forward. You can't change the past, but you can better understand the future."

"I'll keep that in mind."

"You do that. And ... oh." Max stilled before he walked too far away. "Luke plans to dress like a doll and scare you in the middle of the night. You might want to talk him out of that if you want a good night's sleep."

I bit the inside of my cheek to keep from swearing. "I'll make him cry if he tries. In fact ... I think it's time to break out the keg stand video."

Max's grin was so wide it almost swallowed his entire face. "That sounds like a plan to me. Make sure you send me a copy."

"You'll be on top of the list." I squared my shoulders as I turned back to the fairgrounds. "Luke!"

"He's not back from the hospital yet," Nellie barked. "He can't hear you."

"Oh, he can hear me ... and he'd better start running now."

Made in the USA
Monee, IL
23 August 2020